DARK DECEPTION

AMANDA JAMES

First Published in 2019 by Bloodhound Books

www.bloodhoundbooks.com

Print ISBN : 978-1-912986-80-4

ALSO BY AMANDA JAMES

The Feud

Another Mother

The Calico Cat

The Cornish Retribution

Deep Water

To my daughter Tanya, the phoenix.
With much love.

1

FIVE YEARS AGO

Billy Simpson can't remember how long he's been tied to the chair. It feels like a week, but he's guessing by the changing patterns of light filtering through the broken pane of the grimy window, it's probably only a few days. He appears to be in a disused workshop – there's a lingering smell of oil and a discarded car door leaning against the wall. His captors come now and then and beat him some more, force water down his throat, but they haven't fed him.

A growl from his stomach reminds him of how hungry he is, and he strains against the ties round his chest and wrists. A waste of time. He doesn't want to end up on the floor again either. The first day he'd toppled the chair over and had to lay on his side on the concrete floor for hours. Cold and wet from his own urine. The humiliation hurts nearly as much as his wounds. He's a grown man reduced to pissing in his pants. The stink of him turns his stomach.

The constant drip, drip, drip of water on the concrete floor leaked from somewhere above in the rusty girders is driving him crazy. He's not sure how much he can take. Billy's heart hopes they'll release him. Yes, obviously he'll be sacked, and warned if he did anything like this again, he'd be dead. But he'd be free.

His head is more realistic. Billy's seen the men's faces. They are two of the five or six thugs his boss keeps, and Billy's noticed them around. They're bodyguards when the boss is out and about, and apparently deal with problems arising from the seedier side of the business. So why would these men reveal themselves to him if they were thinking of release? Surely they'd worry that Billy would tip off the police somehow, once he'd got far away from them and the clutches of the boss. Did this mean Billy would die here? They'd kill him? He'd heard rumours...

Billy looks at a shaft of sunlight angling in through the broken pane and longs to be free. Tears run down his face, soak into the gag stuffed into his mouth secured with tape, and he thinks of people walking past in the spring sunshine, oblivious to his plight. His girlfriend Lucy must be out of her mind with worry by now, but he knows he'll never be found. These men are clever, sly. Billy can take no more. Next time the thugs arrive he'll come clean. So far, he's denied the accusations levelled at him, but if he confesses, they might be lenient. Playing dumb has got him precisely nowhere. Besides, what choice does he have?

The sound of a bolt sliding open and keys jingling stop his pondering, and every inch of his body tenses. A bare bulb flickers into life overhead. Fear blooms in his chest and he tries to calm himself – regulate his breathing. Because of the gag, when he panics, he has a struggle to get air in. Square Head, as Billy thinks of him, draws up a chair, scraping the wooden legs over the hard floor, and sits astride it. Squashed Nose hovers near the door – seems nervous and fiddles with something inside his coat.

'How's Billy today?' Square Head asks, flashing a shark grin. 'Not looking so great.' He turns his bottom lip down in mock sympathy. 'You stink like a urinal.' He tips his head toward the side wall. 'There's a hosepipe back there somewhere. Shall I wash you down?' The shark grin again. Billy shakes his head. 'You ready to confess...? Silly me, you can't answer, can you?'

Billy flinches and groans as the gag is ripped from his mouth. It feels as if his mouth has changed shape and he can hardly close it because it's been stretched open for so long. Square Head is waiting for an answer, Billy realises. 'If I confess, will you go easy on me?' Because of his numb mouth, his voice sounds as if he's borrowed it from a drunk.

Square Head's eyes light up. 'Oh, we will... but first we want your admission of fleecing the gaffer, and who was in on it with you. Because there had to *be* someone, Billy. We know that much.'

Billy thinks for a while. It's one thing admitting his own guilt, but dropping Gary in it too...

'Changed your mind?' Square Head balls the gag up and moves towards Billy.

'No. No... okay.' His voice is a croak and he tries to lick his dry lips, but there's no spit. Square Head pulls a drinking bottle out of his bag and squirts water down Billy's throat. Luckily, he's so thirsty he manages to swallow it instead of choking as he has before.

'Right, start talking, or I'll snip off those elegant fingers you have.' Square Head puts the bottle back in his bag and pulls out some cruel-looking bladed pliers. He opens and closes the blades, watching Billy's face intently.

Billy's stomach turns and he blurts, 'Yes, I took a bit of cash when I collected the takings from *Tropicana Nights*, but I didn't fleece Paul. I just needed a bit extra, as I'm planning on getting married this–'

'Nobody cares about that. And it's not Paul, it's Mr Donaldson. You stole from him, Billy, and he won't allow it. He won't allow betrayal from his staff.' Square Head's eyes narrow and he puts the pliers back in his bag. 'Who else was in on it?'

Billy sighs. 'Gary Meadows... he doctored the accounts so P... Mr Donaldson wouldn't notice the missing cash.'

Square Head folds his arms. 'For a cut?' Billy nods. 'Hmm. We thought as much. He's been under surveillance for some time. Accountants are always letting themselves down. All that money they deal with every day does something to their heads. Seems they think they're cleverer than everyone else too, just because they can do sums.'

'Will you do the same to him as what you've done to me?' Billy feels terrible, but he has to get out of this place.

'Oh yes. We'll pick him up after we've killed you.' Square Head stands, picks up his bag and brushes down his coat.

Billy's bowels turn to water. 'What! You said you would go easy on me if I confessed!'

'And we are. Before we killed you today, I intended to remove all your fingers with that little gadget I showed you just now... toes as well.' A wink. 'And perhaps any other appendage I might have found.' Square Head shrugs and walks over to where Squashed Nose is still standing by the door. 'Spoilt my fun really, you confessing. But I always keep my word.' He turns and gives Billy a little smile. 'See you then, Billy. Safe journey.' Then he opens the door and walks through it.

Billy wants to scream but he's frozen. Fear's encased his vital organs in ice. Squashed Nose walks towards him and pulls a gun out of his coat. He still looks nervous, but Billy can see he's determined to go ahead. His eyes are wide. Fixed. Billy finds his voice. 'No... NO! PLEASE! You don't have to do this!'

Squashed Nose says, 'Sorry but I do. If I don't, I'll end up like you.' The man raises the gun, presses the cold metal barrel against Billy's right temple and whispers, 'Nothing personal.' He pulls the trigger.

2

PRESENT DAY

The retiring sun sets the sky on fire and burnishes hints of copper along the Atlantic waves. I watch the tide creep up along the still-warm sand of Constantine Bay, like a salty blanket – its sleepy rollers whisper a lullaby. Down the beach near my house, a few lovers walk hand in hand, the sunset turns them into dark silhouettes and lengthens their shadows. On the wind comes an excited shriek of a woman. A man picks her up and runs to the water's edge, threatens to throw her in. I smile and watch him spin her round, set her back on the sand, their silhouettes becoming one as they draw close.

Before I go up the steps to my house, I brush the sand from my feet and take one last deep breath of salt air. The weather so far has been chilly for June but today has been one of the hottest this year. All windows will need to be open tonight, or I'll never sleep. My heart lifts as I think of tomorrow. Leo will be home after three long nights in London. Even though this is the norm, I still can't get used to it, even after five years. I mustn't complain though. Without my husband's job in the capital, we wouldn't be living here in a fantastic house on a Cornish beach, would we?

No. And I'd still be teaching in the local primary school instead of following my dream.

I look up at the house before I climb the wooden steps to the front door. Originally a couple of fisherman's cottages, we knocked them through, added a balcony and refurbished the inside both structurally, where needed, and aesthetically. The fire-red sky behind me is reflected in the floor-to-ceiling arched windows fronting the living room, and as I open the door, I count my blessings and give a nod to my good fortune. It wouldn't do to be blasé. Many would give their right arm to live here in this house... or their left, come to that.

In the kitchen, I decide a simple supper of salmon and salad will be enhanced by a few new potatoes and a light dressing. As I reach in the fridge for a lemon, I think some more about my dream and people's reaction to it. My ex-colleague and friend Jenna had tried hard to keep a sneer out of her voice the other day when we'd met for lunch. When I'd told her about how my shop would be up and running for business next week, she said something about a tiny kiosk-sized hut squashed in between holiday flats on the beach road could hardly be called a shop. Furthermore, was there really a market for art and crafts made from recycled detritus found on beaches? She wouldn't imagine so. I'd been fuming and told her she needed to work on her imagination. There had been a lot of interest shown in my driftwood and bottle-top picture frames online actually. She changed the subject.

At the table, I set down my plate and pour a glass of crisp Sauvignon Blanc. If I'm honest, Jenna's reaction to my change of career isn't uncommon. My parents cheered me on, and Leo of course. But others don't really get it. Do I care? What's wrong with wanting to turn waste into works of art and share the message of recycling and caring for the planet? Why do people always only care about how much money you make? Okay, I'm lucky. Leo, over the past five years, has made more money than we could ever have dreamed of when we met eight years ago. But even if he hadn't, I'd still want to do this. My gran always said following your dreams is the most important thing in the world. Because if you don't have dreams, what is there?

The salmon is delicious, but I've cooked too many potatoes... enough for Leo. Never mind. Tomorrow night I'll make his favourite – fillet steak and my 'fancy rice' as he calls it. All I do is add garlic, ginger and a few stir-fry veg to it. He's easy to please though. Takeaways and food on the run is starting to tell on him – I've noticed he's a sizeable paunch developing. But healthy and simple food over the weekend and the early part of next week will help.

Out on the balcony, glass in hand, I watch the stars switch themselves on across the vast navy sky. A backdrop to the sleepy ocean. The gulls have fallen silent and the long beach is empty of walkers. Sometimes, at this time of day, if I really concentrate, I can believe there's just me floating in a perfect universe of sand, sea and sky. I never tire of watching the ever-changing scene and realise how very lucky I am to live here. It's a far cry from the council house in Camborne where I grew up. My parents worked hard to keep me and my brother Ed clothed, fed and happy. But we never had anything to spare. Luxuries were beyond our reach.

A sudden chill tickles my bare back, and I realise the beginning of June might be a little early for halterneck tops outside, at nine in the evening. I raise my glass to the stars and finish the wine. Time to go inside and get warm. Though celestial beings might be pretty, the real star of our show is Mr Paul Donaldson. Since the business magnate employed my husband as his personal financial advisor, we've never looked back. Such a lovely man too. Charming, caring – down to earth. I remember him telling me that he worked his way up and out of the east end of London. Now he's made his fortune, he likes to pay it forward. Pity there's not more men like him around.

Leo rubs his eyes and shoves his wheeled chair back from the computer, scooting himself across the polished oak floorboards of his penthouse flat. Enough for one night. Tomorrow at this time he'll have had dinner with Kerensa and be tucked up on the sofa with her under their old "snuggle" blanket. He smiles. They've had that blanket for nearly as long as they've been together. Almost nine years, just after he qualified as an accountant. Where's the time gone? To Leo it only seems a few years since he first saw Kerensa across a bar in Padstow. Long red curls and lively green eyes – almost catlike, and that slow sexy smile that still sets his heart racing.

Standing to a stretch, the mirror behind the desk confirms the passage of time. He's thirty-four but looks every bit of that and more. His chestnut hair, once luxurious, is thinning from his temples, and fine lines around his hazel eyes appear deeper every day. Sideways on, he lifts his shirt and pats his protruding belly. When did that happen? When he ordered the last few dozen pizzas and curries perhaps. Not long now. Soon he'll have enough squirrelled away to never have to work again. Time to start that family they've always talked about too. Just one more big deal should do it. A cloud breezes in just then, hovers above his sunny ideal of the future – threatens rain. He hasn't forgotten the rumours that went around when he got his present post five years ago.

Leo pours a whisky and sits down in his favourite red leather armchair, flicks off the table lamp, and gazes out of his wraparound apartment windows at the illuminated London city skyline, his mind rehashing old memories. The hovering cloud breaks, unleashing a downpour and Leo wonders what the hell he's got himself into. When he became Paul Donaldson's accountant and financial advisor, the hushed names of Gary Meadows, Leo's predecessor, and Billy Simpson, a guy who collected the takings from Donaldson's various businesses around the city, were often on the lips of several employees about the office. When Leo had walked in on such conversations, the talk had quickly turned to other things.

Curious, Leo had done a bit of digging and had eventually found out from one of the secretaries, that these two men had gone missing a few weeks previously, but the police had turned up no clue. The word around the office was either that they had done a runner with some takings, or that Mr Donaldson had made them disappear for double-crossing him. Or more accurately, the driver-cum-bodyguard, Frank Delaney had made them disappear. Leo had seen him around. Big, muscly, with a high square forehead – a bit like Lurch from the Addams Family. At first Leo thought they were joking, because Mr Donaldson, though an astute businessman, had always seemed fair, kind and polite. But no. The rumour persisted, until it became known that anyone discussing it would be sacked. The rumours fell silent.

After a while, Leo had almost forgotten about it until Donaldson had called him into the office and in a roundabout way mentioned that he wasn't averse to a little initiative on his accountant's part, if Leo took his meaning. Leo wasn't entirely sure that he did, so Donaldson had said he wasn't overjoyed that he had to pay so much tax and rewarded those who could help in any way. Nothing more was said, and while a little surprised, Leo hadn't been shocked. After all, a businessman of Donaldson's stature didn't get where he was by following the rules.

The whisky glass reflects the lights of the building across, and as Leo tips the glass back and forth, the amber contents swirl, like his thoughts. Not for the first time he wishes he'd stopped with a gentle doctoring of the books. But ever ambitious, once he'd become privy to some stocks and shares information through a friend of a friend, he'd sounded the boss out on a new scheme. Donaldson had leapt at it, and forever afterwards, insider dealing had become an extremely lucrative sideline for them both. More so for Donaldson, obviously, though Leo had been pleased to receive some hefty crumbs from his table in reward.

Leo downs the last of the whisky and tries to submerge the names of Gary Meadows and Billy Simpson to the dark recesses of his mind. They don't remain submerged though... just keep bobbing back up like corks in a bucket. Leo shoves his hands through his thinning hair and closes his eyes against the bright lights. Why couldn't he have been content with what he had? Over the first four years he'd amassed a tidy sum from his not-so-honest dealings. There was nearly 800,000 pounds squirrelled away in an offshore account. But he got greedy. This last year alone, he'd made twice that again... and today he's siphoned another 300,000. So going on for 3,000,000. If Donaldson found out how he'd done it... well. It didn't bear thinking about.

The more he'd got to know Donaldson, the more he'd believed the rumours about him making those two men disappear five years ago. On the surface, he came across as avuncular and jovial, but scratch the surface and it wasn't pretty. Leo had witnessed his boss's meltdowns with some poor unsuspecting employee from time to time. Once, it was over something so trivial, it had been almost laughable. Donaldson had remarked to Leo afterwards that it wasn't the issue at hand that infuriated him but the principal. Furthermore, he couldn't abide liars and wouldn't stand for betrayal of any type. Leo had worried this little speech was aimed at him, but it couldn't have been. He was still standing, wasn't he?

Noticing it's past midnight, Leo hauls himself out of the chair and makes for the bathroom. He has to be at the airport early tomorrow for his flight to Newquay. How he longs to be in Kerensa's arms and how distraught she'd be if she knew what he was up to. It would be the end of their marriage, that is certain. His wife is the most honest and law-abiding person he knows. Lying to her makes him cringe and feel desperately ashamed, but it has to be done. He spits toothpaste into the sink and catches a guilty side-glimpse in his eyes in the bathroom mirror.

Not long now, it will all be over, and I'll be home for good, he tells his reflection.

His reflection doesn't look convinced. If Donaldson susses that Leo has grown tired of crumbs and has been slicing himself big slabs of cake, it will be over all right. But not in a good way.

3

'Leo Pethick!' I say to the figure on my doorstep obscured by roses, champagne, chocolate and balloons. A giggle in my throat, I grab him by the shoulder. 'Come inside out of the cold and bring that lot with you.'

'But how did you guess it was me?' He laughs and follows me through to the kitchen.

I turn and take the yellow roses from him and a petal or two scatter themselves along the worktop. 'How many other men am I expecting today?'

'Hopefully none.' Leo puts down the rest of the gifts, pulls me into a bear hug and showers me with kisses.

I stop him, hold him at arm's length. 'Hang on.' I do my best frowny face. 'How come I'm being lavished with gifts? What are you guilty about?'

Leo frowns back. 'How very dare you!' He puts the back of his hand against his forehead in a dramatic show of pathos. 'Can't a man tell his wife how much she means to him without being suspected of ill-doings?'

I laugh and play-punch him in the chest. 'Okay, I'll let you off. You hungry?' I run water into a vase and stick the champagne in the fridge.

In an American accent he says, 'Hungry for lurv.' Then he comes up behind me, encircles my waist and kisses my neck.

'Down boy – after lunch. I have fresh pasties in the oven, and there might even be cake too.'

'From Sally's?' Leo lets me go and sets off on a cake hunt.

'Oh, I see. One sniff of Sally's cake and you lose interest in me?'

'I'm only human, honey.' Leo finds the box, lifts the lid and pretends to devour the chocolate cake in one.

I take the box away and push him toward the kitchen table. 'All good things come to those who wait.'

A sexy smile plays over his lips and he gives me the look I find hard to resist. 'I'll hold you to that.'

We eat our lunch and talk about his work, my shop opening next week and all matters big and small. It feels like we've been apart forever, not just a few days. I'll never get used to him working in London. I miss him so much. I take a sip of champagne. Champagne and pasties do go together – who'd have thought it? I smile at my husband demolishing his cake and shake my head. It's crazy how much we miss each other, given the time we've been a couple. Friends of mine who have been with their partners only a few years often say their other half drives them mad. They say I'm lucky having all that "me time". And what they wouldn't give to have my life. Me time? I don't need it. Happiness is being with Leo. Always has been, always will be. God knows what I'd do if I ever lost him.

He catches my eye as he dabs chocolate cake crumbs from his mouth. 'What's up, love?'

I swallow an unexpected lump of emotion. 'Nothing. Just thinking how happy we are, and how lucky I am to have you.'

A cloud passes over his hazel eyes and he looks away. 'I'm the lucky one. I don't deserve you.'

Apprehension fills my chest. He looks serious. Sad. 'What's wrong?' I stretch my hand across the table, place it on his.

A few blinks clear the cloud and he smiles. 'Nothing really. I'm just aware that I'm away a lot – leaving you to your own devices. I don't know how you put up with it.' His hand squeezes mine and he becomes animated. 'But I've been thinking. I might be able to work from home in the next few months. I've been doing incredibly well financially over the last few years, as you know, and I've managed to squirrel quite a bit away. Wouldn't that be great – never having to be parted again?'

I knew he'd done well, but not well enough to leave his job. Mind you, he does all the banking stuff. I just draw it out as and when I need it. I don't even look at the statement very often. The last time I think it said we had 30,000 saved. Nice. But is that enough? I smile and squeeze his hand back. 'It would be fantastic never to be parted again... but when you say work from home. Do you mean for yourself, or still for Mr Donaldson?'

'For myself. I could go part time too, or even have a break for a few years.'

I look into his excited eyes and wonder if he's taken leave of his senses. I don't want to pour cold water on his plans, but he needs to get real. 'But, Leo... I don't think that thirty thousand-odd will be enough for you to do all that. My business won't bring much in. I'm mainly doing it because it's my dream. *And* I have been able to do that because of your job.' I stop. It sounds like I'm making it all about me. But it is a worry. I packed my teaching job in on the strength of it, after all.

'Thirty thousand-odd?' He furrows his brow. Then he tips his head back and laughs. 'No. Not in that account. I have another that I've been saving in.' Leo shifts his gaze, pokes some crumbs round his plate. 'And let's just say there's significantly more than thirty grand in it.'

I feel uncomfortable with his body language, his evasive manner. Leo's never been secretive about money, so why doesn't he just tell me? 'How much more?'

He still won't look at me. Gets up, sides the dishes. 'I'll tell you when it's a done deal and everything is up together.' He turns and throws his arms wide. 'It'll be a wonderful surprise!'

I don't like this glassy-eyed over-excited Leo. It's not like him. He's hiding something, I can feel it. 'Okay. Suit yourself... I just hope you know what you're doing.'

'Of course I do.' He comes over, pulls me out of my chair and hugs me to his chest. 'Nothing for you to worry about, Kerensa. I would never pack my job in if I thought we couldn't manage. Another few weeks and it'll be all organised.'

The soothing, patronising tone of his voice puts my back up further. I expect him to say, don't you worry your pretty little head, or something. A thought occurs and I look up into his eyes. 'You said you'd have a break for a few years. Wouldn't you be bored?'

He smiles. 'Not if I was a house husband and daddy.'

My heart soars. I've been trying to convince him for the past few years to start a family, but he kept saying the time wasn't right. Seems it is now. Leo calling the shots as usual. Any irritation at his controlling nature is short-lived, as I picture a gorgeous little baby in my arms, and I whoop with joy. 'You wouldn't be bored then, that's for sure! Imagine, Leo. Our own little baby.' My eyes brim with happy tears.

'Yes, I can.' Leo grins and leads me toward the bedroom. 'We've got to make one first though. And there's no time like the present!'

. . .

That day we stayed in bed all afternoon and into the early evening. Now, four weeks later, my period is three days late. This is unusual for me, as I'm usually as regular as the proverbial. I try to push all thoughts of babies from my mind and concentrate on the sea-glass and driftwood wall art I'm working on. Nevertheless, a few minutes later I find my thoughts are drifting too.

From the workbench in *Sea Treasures*, my little shop, I look out of the window at passers-by on their way to the beach at Constantine Bay. I've been doing more window-gazing than working this morning, if I'm honest. *Sea Treasures* has done really well in the two weeks it's been open and will build up more, as the summer high season is about to peak. A woman commissioned me to make a wall hanging out of the materials she saw in my tray when she came in. How exciting. The trouble is, now I'm late, I can't settle to anything.

Tea often helps, I find. So I wander into the tiny offshoot kitchen, make a brew and grab a shortbread biscuit too. Now, back to work.

Five minutes later, I'm drifting again. This is because in the bathroom cupboard at home, the pregnancy tester waits. I picture it rattling about in there – doing a little dance and taunting me. A sure sign I'm getting over-anxious. I daren't do the test yet because I want it so much. If it proves false, I don't think I could cope. Of course I could, I'd have to. But I want to wait until Leo is home.

He's supposed to be telling Mr Donaldson he's quitting today and then working a week's notice. He'll be back later for the weekend though first. He told me Donaldson doesn't always insist on the month. If someone wants to leave, he wants them gone. Odd that he isn't the nice guy I thought he was. Leo told me a few home truths about how ruthless he was with some staff. A shame. I had really looked up to him. Maybe I should do the test and, if it's positive, tell Leo over the phone.

No. I want to see the look in his eye. I'll wait until he comes home.

Leo's stomach is rumbling, churning, and his heart is thundering. He sounds like a walking tornado. Good job he's got his jaw clenched or his teeth would be chattering too. Leo relaxes his grip on the handle of his office door and takes a deep breath. Before he walks through it, down the stairs and along the corridor to Donaldson's room, he needs to be in full control of his faculties. The resignation speech he's rehearsed is waiting on his tongue and it's believable, natural and sound. There's no need to get himself into a hideous, anxious mess. *But that's the thing, isn't it?* a little voice asks in his head. It's all a big fat lie. All. Of. It.

The rehearsed speech says he's very grateful for the start Mr Donaldson has given him over these five years. Leo will be forever in his debt for this invaluable experience. But the thing is, he's missing his wife. Cornwall is his home and they are hoping to start a family very soon. Once they have children, working in London won't be an option, so he's hoping to set up his own accountancy advice business. Leo releases a slow breath and imagines Donaldson nodding and smiling. Shaking his hand. That's better. And actually, it's not all a lie, is it? It's true that he misses his wife and wants to start a family. Before he can bottle it, he grabs the handle and opens the door.

After a few paces he stops. At the top of the stairs he leans his back against the wall and closes his eyes. The bit of confidence he found before he left his own office is seeping away and he's shaking. If Donaldson sees through him somehow, he'll be a goner. The little voice is back to prod him. The real reason he's leaving is because he's been pocketing huge wads of the profits from the insider deals and there's no way he can pretend to himself otherwise. He's stashed it in a secret offshore account, and covered his tracks fastidiously, so nothing looks untoward on the books. Donaldson never really keeps track of the investment in shares, sales and how they do, so it's been easy to say to his boss that the gamble didn't pay as well as the information Leo acquired had led him to believe. Donaldson has more money than sense. There's no way Leo's under suspicion. He opens his eyes. *Come on, Leo. Get it done. It'll all be fine.*

Just before he reaches Donaldson's office, he hears the low rumble of men talking. Men talking who don't want to be overheard. He creeps up to the office door which is ajar and holds his breath as he recognises Matt Kane's voice. Donaldson's nephew started working here about six months back. A right creep and slimy character. Leo caught Matt snooping round his office on more than one occasion. He was apparently looking for a stapler the first time and a laptop lead the next. There's no way he's clever enough to latch onto what Leo's up to though... is there? Leo wipes sweat from his top lip. Inches closer to the gap in the door.

'You have to be absolutely sure of this, Matt. Because if you're not, nephew or no, you'll pay,' Donaldson says.

'I am. I wouldn't be here with half a story. The last few deals Leo told you weren't that good were actually excellent. You should have made at least half as much again as you did on that kind of investment.'

Fuck! Leo covers his mouth and tries to make his breath shallow. Difficult, given the fact that his heart is trying to smash through his chest.

'What about the takeover of Barnfield's Furniture Land? Leo said that was particularly disappointing given the word on the grapevine.'

'Another lie. He's been ripping you off, Uncle Paul. And I've got a feeling that I've only scratched the tip of a very big iceberg.'

Outside the room, Leo swallows hard. He wants to get out of there, but he needs to hear the rest. If he just runs it will look like he's guilty. He should stay and face it out. Leaving will have to wait until all this blows over. Matt's a nasty little snake who's fresh out of uni. He's no match for Leo. Even as he tells himself this, he's beginning to have second thoughts. Donaldson's talking again, his voice quieter than before, and Leo has to strain to hear him.

'Right. Thanks, Matt. I want you to call Frank Delaney, tell him what you told me and tell him to deal with it. Make the problem disappear. He'll know what you mean. If he needs confirmation, just say – like Billy and Gary.'

No. No, NO! The rumours were all true then. His predecessor and the collection guy were *actually* made to disappear... *killed.* It's as if Leo's in some nightmare, but it's all terrifyingly real. He knows he's no choice now. He turns, and as quietly as possible, hurries down the corridor, stopping only to grab his laptop and bag from the office and then he races to the car park. He hasn't used his company car for ages, but he can't risk the airport as normal. Donaldson might send his thugs there.

Behind the wheel, he guns the engine and screeches onto the road. What's he going to do? Where's he going to go? What about Kerensa? An image of her lovely face comes to him. Her big green eyes wide with shock. A question on her lips. Oh God, why did he do this? Why has he been so greedy? He's no real idea where he's going, apart from away from London. His mind is in turmoil – it's a wonder he can function, let alone drive.

An hour later he pulls off the motorway and into some services. Leo looks at his hands, the white-knuckled grip on the wheel, and he releases a breath, forces himself to let go, and folds his hands in his lap. Calm. He needs calm.

After a few minutes of deep breathing, he has a plan. Ring Will. Will would know what to do, always did. He was the one who provided calm and reason. Even when they first met at the age of seven, Leo had looked up to Will, gone to him if he'd been in trouble. He always knew what to do. He'd been such fun company too – all the girls had fancied him, but Leo didn't mind. Will was just the kind of boy who everyone loved. Inseparable all through juniors and in high school, Leo had been in bits when Will emigrated to Australia with his family after their GCSEs. They'd kept in touch for a while by email, but they'd both gone off to university and they'd lost contact a little. But only last week he'd got a message to say he was back in the UK for good.

Mobile in hand, Leo scrolls down his contact list. His finger hovers over Will's number... Has it been too long to land this on him out of the blue? Perhaps, but nobody knows Will, or where he lives. None of Leo's friends anyway, or even Kerensa. He's the perfect choice... his only choice.

'You have reached the number of William Gray, please leave a message after the tone...'

Shit! That's all he needs. Now what? Leo hangs up without leaving a message. It occurs to him that his phone might be traceable too. Unlikely, but he would put nothing past Donaldson. He'll stop at the nearest town and buy another... Then the phone rings in his hand, startling him. It's Will, thank God! 'Will, it's Leo...'

Will laughs that old noisy gleeful laugh he always had, and immediately Leo feels a tiny bit of tension ebb away. He says, 'I know that, I just rang your number back, you daft bastard.'

Leo pushes his hand through his hair and watches a group of teenagers horsing about outside the services. One's leapfrogging over the others. 'Oh yeah. Sorry, my mind's all over the place.'

'You okay, Leo? Your voice sounds a bit strange.'

The teenagers are running from one of the gang, who's shaking a can of Coke and threatening to pull the ring tab. Leo feels like he's the can of Coke. They charge off through the car park, threading through the cars until they're out of sight. It doesn't seem that long ago that he and Will were their age. Leo releases a long breath. 'No. No, I'm not okay at all, Will. You're the only person who can help me… if anyone can.'

'Hey mate.' Will's voice is serious now, lost its jokey edge. 'Of course. Anything I can do, you know that. Just ask.'

Leo swallows. 'Can I come and stay with you? It would only be for a while. I've got myself into a huge fucking shit-pile, and I can't see myself climbing out anytime soon.'

'Yeah of course. Have you and Kerensa split up?'

Leo gives a hollow laugh. 'If only it were that simple. No. And she knows n-nothing about this.' His voice breaks and he shoves his knuckles to his mouth, stifles a sob.

'Shit, mate. Sounds like hell.' Will sighs down the phone. 'Okay, I'll text you the address. I only moved in a few days back. It's a big five-bed place in Truro – so loads of room.'

'Cornwall? I thought you were in Exeter?'

'That was only rented while I got sorted back in the UK. My new post is in Truro.'

'Must be good to afford a five-bed just like that.'

'It is. But then I have worked bloody hard for it. Look, Leo, I have to run. But when will I expect you?'

Leo glances at the dashboard clock. 'Should take a good five hours… not exactly sure where I am. So about seven this evening?'

'Perfect. I'll make dinner. Text you the address. See you later.'

Leo feels better already. If he stays with Will, he'll only be half an hour from Kerensa... even though he won't be able to see her for a while, at least he'll feel near to her. After grabbing a coffee and a sandwich, he gets back onto the motorway, just as the heavens open. Leo looks at the dark clouds on the horizon and hopes they'll be gone tomorrow.

4

I end the call to Leo's office and throw the phone hard against the sofa cushions. Nobody knows where he is. The secretary went to ask Mr Donaldson, and he said he'd not seen him since before lunch. I'm going out of my mind. It's not like him to just disappear. I pick up the phone again and count the times I've called Leo's number... seven. I've left as many messages too. Where the hell is he? It's nearly five o'clock and he told me he'd let me know when he was leaving London. He always does. Always. A sick feeling rolls in my belly and I have to sit on the arm of the chair. Has something happened to him? A road accident perhaps, and he's lying somewhere in a crumpled car or taxi? Should I start ringing the hospitals in London? I decide to phone Mum. She'll know what to do.

'Calm down, Enza sweetheart. There'll be a perfectly simple explanation.' Mum sounds as if she's trying to convince herself as well as me. 'What time does he usually phone?'

'About one-ish. His flight normally leaves at ten past three. So where is he?'

'Have you checked the flights? There might have been a delay of some sort.'

She's right and I feel stupid for not doing it. 'No. Not yet... I was so worried that he didn't phone at the normal time.'

'There might be something wrong with his phone. He might have lost it.'

'So why didn't he use a public phone?'

'I don't know, love. Perhaps he was trying to find his phone and was in a rush?'

Thank God I phoned Mum. Her logical thinking is helping to calm me down. 'Yes. That makes sense. I'll phone the airline now. Thanks, Mum. I'll let you know.'

Ten minutes later my panic levels are through the roof again. The flight was on time and it has landed at Newquay airport. There's sweat on my top lip and I have to steady myself as the room spins. My stomach churns. Nausea rises and I rush to the loo and vomit.

Shaking, I get to my feet and splash my face with cold water, swill my mouth out and look at my reflection in the bathroom cabinet mirror. My eyes look feverish. Two emeralds in a snow-blanket face. Hope I'm not coming down with something on top of all this... then I remember that I might be pregnant and can't wait any longer. I heave a sigh and tell myself Leo will be okay. He will be fine. He'll walk through the door any minute with some story about a phone, and I'll be able to tell him I'm pregnant. Please, God. Let me be pregnant.

My reflection swings away as I open the cupboard and pull out the tester. My fingers are trembling so much I can hardly open the packet, but then it's there in my hand. The little plastic stick that has the answer to my question. Sitting on the loo, I pee on the stick and then wait.

. . .

Three minutes feel like hours, but then there it is. The result. Pregnant. Three weeks plus. Tears of joy pour down my face and I send a thank you to Him upstairs. Laughing, I hug myself, rock back and forth on the loo until it strikes me how daft I must look. Seconds later, joy turns to anxiety. Leo. I want Leo. I want to tell Leo he's going to be a dad.

In the kitchen I fill the kettle and flick it on. If he doesn't contact me in the next half hour, I'll ring the police and ask their advice. Sunshine breaks through the clouds and drives spikes of gold into the ocean. Beautiful. I stroke my flat stomach and picture how it will look in a few months. Will we have a boy or a girl? A boy, I think. It's just a feeling I have. A faint beep from the living room has me rushing to the sofa. It's the sound my phone makes when I get a message. Leo! My heart soars. *Thank God!*

My darling, Kerensa, this will come as a shock, but I won't be home for a while. Don't worry, I'm safe. Donaldson isn't who you think he is. I told you he was a bastard to some of his staff. But that's only half of it. I discovered recently that he is ruthless, and will stop at nothing to get his way. I won't go into detail, except to say I'm no longer safe at work. You can't contact me on my normal number now either, but I will be in touch as soon as I can. I will text you again soon to stop you worrying. I love you so much. Don't contact the police as there's nothing they can do. Besides, it might make things worse for me. If Donaldson phones, tell him what I said about him and that I'm in hiding. He'll probably tell you a load of lies – don't believe any of it. I can't speak on the phone to you as I'm too upset, and I know you will be. I need to keep a clear head. Hopefully all this will blow over soon xxx

Immediately I try to call back, but just get number unobtainable. What the hell's going on? I read and reread the message over and over, but it's as if I'm reading a foreign language. It doesn't make sense. Won't go into my numb brain. What on earth has Donaldson done to frighten my husband so much that he daren't come home? Has to go into hiding. My husband isn't easily frightened. I've a good mind to phone the bastard and ask... but something stops me. This is serious. If I mess it up for Leo and he gets hurt, I'll never forgive myself.

I wonder about telling Mum, my cousin Anna, or my good friend Sally who runs the cake and coffee shop just down from mine. But instinct tells me to keep it secret. Reading between the lines of the message again – *Besides, it might make things worse for me* – stands out. If my husband is in danger and news gets out about it to the police, and they investigate Donaldson, poke about into his affairs, God knows what he might do if he catches up with poor Leo.

I curl up on the sofa and sob. I can't help it. What should be one of the best days of our lives has turned into the worst. Here I am, just found out I'm carrying our first child and my husband is oblivious. There's no way I can contact him either, and I don't know how long he'll be away. What a nightmare! Leo did say he'd be in touch though, and that's what I must cling onto. I close my eyes and picture his face, imagine kissing his lips. Poor baby. How I want to hold him and make it all go away.

An hour later I wake cold and groggy, must have conked out on the sofa. There's a distant tune playing somewhere and then I realise it's the ringtone on my phone. I find it under the sofa, must have kicked it off in my sleep. There's no caller ID.

'Hello?'

'Kerensa Pethick?'

I think it's Donaldson but can't be sure. I swallow hard, try to calm myself. 'Yes?'

'It's Paul Donaldson here. Nice to speak with you again... You phoned earlier today asking after Leo. Has he returned home yet?'

'No. No, he has not, and it's thanks to you.' My voice is sharp, icy. I'm not scared of him.

'I beg your pardon?'

'You heard.'

All pretence of pleasantness leaves his tone. 'I did, young woman, and I would like an explanation.'

'I got a text from my husband to say he's in hiding because he fears what you'll do to him. I have no idea where he is, or how long he'll be gone. His phone's no longer obtainable, and he says not to contact the police either. Is that enough of an explanation?'

'Mind your tone, Kerensa.' The menace in his voice reaches into my heart and squeezes. I cover my mouth to stop a cry escaping. 'I have no idea what he thinks *I* will do to *him*. What he *has* done to *me* is a different point entirely.'

'Leo? Leo hasn't done anything.' Even as I say this, a voice in my head starts to whisper doubts.

'I think you'll find he has. He's been managing my, let's say, less-above-board business ventures the last few years–'

'No. Leo would never–'

'Shut the fuck up and listen.'

I'm so shocked I can't speak.

'Leo would, and Leo has. He's also been helping himself to a large share of the profits. My nephew found out and told me, just today. I'm very disappointed in your husband. Very disappointed indeed. So, when he contacts you again, you can tell him I know all about his sneaky ways. But then, he obviously knows that I know. Hence his disappearing act. I'd love to know how he found out – but no matter.'

'But...' I begin, then falter. I have no idea what to say, or to think.

'Exactly. Not much to say, is there?' Donaldson sighs. 'Oh. Except this... He'll not be safe anywhere. Nobody betrays me like that and lives to tell the tale. Nobody steals from me and gets away with it. Ever.'

'But Leo has never done anything like that. He's always been law abiding and...' Again, words fail me.

'Always a first time, m'dear. And despite your indignant act, as far as I know, you might be in on it all with him. Tell hubby that if he doesn't give himself up, one of my men will pop down there to have a nice chat with you. He'll enjoy that – from what I remember you're quite the beauty. Cornwall is gorgeous too at this time of year, isn't it?'

A cold finger of fear traces the length of my spine and I tremble. My god. A thug will come here and do fuck knows what... My baby. I can't have anyone harm my baby. 'I've told you I can't get in touch with him!' My voice sounds desperate, whiny, and I hate it.

'Yes. You said. Not sure I believe you though.'

'It's true!'

'Hmm. We'll see. Goodbye, Kerensa.'

I sit there looking at my phone, incredulous.

An inner voice drives me into action. *Get out. Get out. Pack some things and get out. Now!*

5

A week later I'm sitting on a bench on Plymouth Hoe. I'm looking across the choppy blue Plymouth Sound at Drake's Island – watching boats big and small sailing this way and that. I can't remember exactly the last time I visited... think I must have been about ten. I do remember being fascinated by the statue of Sir Francis Drake, a little to my left behind my bench. He's gazing at the same view as me. It hardly seemed possible that he set off from the little island in front of me to circumnavigate the globe all those years ago. It's not easy nowadays, but back in the sixteenth century he had no state-of-the-art navigation, or powerful engines to speed his voyage. The early explorers were incredibly brave. They must have realised there was a chance they'd die at sea, or never return to their homeland. I wish I had even a scrap of his courage to help me get through this crazy time.

My days have been mostly taken up with looking over my shoulder and pretending that I'm Helen Ford, a writer researching a book about Plymouth's maritime past. Marge, the landlady of The Seahorse B&B, asks lots of questions; more than she should, but I'm always ready. I bought a book about the history of Plymouth from the local bookshop and have been cramming as if I've been about to take an exam. Marge asks questions about my personal life too, which I field by changing the subject and being non-committal. I've told Marge I'm separated from my husband, true, and that I'm not sure if we'll get back together – hopefully not true. I have paid for my accommodation in cash, in case Donaldson can somehow trace my credit card. I've drawn it out from various cashpoints around the county. Can't be too careful.

A huge sea tanker glides slowly into view across the horizon as if it weighs no more than a feather. I'm reminded of a jumbo jet coming in to land. They always look like they are about to stop, hanging in the air, their enormous bulk incredulously suspended. They don't stop, of course, just gracefully touch down and juggernaut to a standstill. My woes feel as heavy as that tanker out there, or a jumbo. At the moment I feel the weight of them will crush me. Steamroller me flat. Leave me for dead. It's as if I'm wading through a surreal dream and can't wake up. A little voice of doom keeps whispering in my ear that things will get worse. Something bad is going to happen soon. What it is, it won't say. But my gut believes it. My gut knows it will be devastating.

Mum has gut feelings like this. When I lived at home, we intuitively knew when something was wrong with each other – our moods and suchlike. Or if we went through a bad patch, we knew when things were going to be okay again. Sometimes we got our hunches wrong, but more often than not we didn't. Dad said it was like living with a couple of witches. He always laughed at us, but we ignored him. Mum said he felt a bit out of it when we got together, plotting and talking about our gut feelings. Dad is solid, dependable, not given to flights of fancy.

The tanker is just a dot on the horizon now. I wonder how many people are on board and where it's going. Its movement is direct, purposeful. The ship knows its destination... Unlike me. I finger my mobile in my pocket – I want to ring Mum, ask her what to do. Just hearing her voice would help. But I can't, can I? No. As far as she knows, Leo and I are having some quiet time away in the Lake District. My cousin Anna thinks we are too. She's looking after my shop, and will tell anyone who comes looking for me that I'm away in the Lakes. She doesn't know where. This should fox Donaldson's thugs, if indeed he sends any. The threats on the phone last week might all have been for show. The voice of doom laughs at this. To shut it up, I get up from the bench and make my way to the ice cream van at the end of the walkway.

I hold my swirly ice cream up to Smeaton's Tower, stripy red and white against the blue sky. I shut one eye, and from this distance and angle, the flake in the top almost matches the height of the structure. A blob of ice cream lands on my wrist, so I twist the cone in my hand and lick round the edge. Just then my mobile jingles in my back pocket and I pull it out.

Caller unknown. Is it Donaldson? My heart thumps in my chest. It could be Leo. I had a text two days ago telling me not to worry, but he will have changed his phone again. He said he would on the text. Apprehension immobilises me. I feel slightly nauseous. The ice cream suddenly tastes cheesy. I swallow, wipe my mouth on the back of my sleeve. *No use staring at the damn thing – answer it.*

'Hello?'

'Is that Kerensa?'

Not Donaldson or Leo then. 'Who wants to know?'

'My name is William Gray. I... I'm calling about Leo.' He's got an Australian twang in his voice.

'Who? I've never heard of you.'

'I'm one of his oldest friends... His best friend. He's been staying with me.'

A distant memory of Leo saying his best friend emigrated surfaces, but given the circumstances, I need to be sure before I start talking to a complete stranger about my husband. 'You could be anyone. If you're who you say you are, what's his mum's name?'

'Okay, I can see why you're cautious. I'm not one of Donaldson's thugs though... Her name is Janice and his dad's name is Derek.'

No hesitation there... I think of one more question to be sure. 'And he has a birthmark. Where?'

'Left shoulder. Looks like a footprint but with just the big toe.'

I'm satisfied. 'Okay, William. What's the problem? Is Leo okay?'

'I need to see you ... Can we meet?'

My gut is giving me that sinking feeling. And the ice cream is flowing over the lip of the cone and onto my fingers in thick, sticky rivulets. 'Why? What's happened to Leo?'

'Trust me, Kerensa. I need to see you – talk to you face to face.'

His voice sounds like it's trying to be brave but it's failing. 'William, you're scaring me.' I wipe my fingers on the grass and look around for a bin.

'Are you at home?'

'No. I left because I didn't feel safe. Donaldson threatened me. I'm in Plymouth, staying at a B&B.'

'Okay. I can be with you in an hour and a half. Tell me where.'

'Can't you just tell me over the bloody phone?'

'I'd rather not.'

For fuck's sake. 'Fine. I'll be on the Hoe. On a bench near the statue of Drake.'

'Right. See you then.'

Nearly two hours later, I'm going out of my mind. After I ended the call, I chucked the ice cream in a bin and walked round the town and back. I couldn't say where I went. Wandered through the shops, head down, not wanting to look at anyone. On the occasion I did catch a male eye, it appeared as if they were glaring, or suspicious. Did they know about Donaldson and Leo? Were they trying to track me down? Then I pulled myself together. William had rattled me with all the cloak and dagger stuff. I'd meet him shortly and probably find out it's just a message from Leo telling me what to do next. My voice of doom started up, so I squashed it like a bug under a stone.

Now on the Hoe, the bug's made a miraculous recovery and has heaved the stone aside. Why isn't William here? He said an hour and a half. I check my phone. It's two hours and five minutes since he phoned. And if it was just a message about what to do next, he'd tell me on the phone, wouldn't he? Unless he was worried about his call being traced or something. In the distance there's a tall man wearing a light-blue T-shirt and black jeans hurrying along towards the path.

As he draws closer, I can see he has blond wavy hair which he's shoving out of his navy-blue eyes. His expression is pensive, anxious even, but he's striking nonetheless. He stops, shades his eyes with his hand, turns in a circle and looks at his watch. Is this William? There's a family group partially obscuring me, so I move away from them and raise my hand tentatively. He waves back, hurries over.

'Kerensa?' He sticks out his hand, gives a little smile.

'Hi, William.' I shake his hand. It's hot, sweaty. I drop my hand and surreptitiously blot my palm on my jeans.

'Call me Will.' Then the smile is gone. He folds his arms. 'Can we go to your B&B... somewhere more private?'

Alarm bells ring at this. There's no way I'm taking him back to my room. He could try anything, for all I know. 'Not sure I want to do that. I think you're genuine, but...'

Will's face flushes and he shoves his hand through his hair. 'Oh God, I'm a stranger to you. I didn't think how that must sound.' He blows out through his mouth. 'The thing is, Kerensa...' His eyes flit to mine and then away. 'I have some very upsetting news... and out here with people walking past might not be such a great place to tell you.' He looks back, holds my gaze. His eyes are full of compassion and his bottom lip trembles.

Despite the heat of the day, a chill runs through my whole body. I can stand it no longer. 'Just tell me, Will. Now.'

Will takes one of my hands, but I snatch it back. Fold my arms, swallow down a ball of apprehension. He sighs. 'Kerensa... I... I'm sorry to tell you that...' He blinks a few times. 'That Leo died yesterday in a climbing accident.'

6

Will's mouth is moving and there are words coming out, but I can't hear them. My brain's put a barrier up. All I can hear inside my head are the same few sentences over and over again. *This is not true.*

This is not true.

Leo's alive.

He is. Don't listen.

Don't listen.

DON'T!

I stand, clamp the palms of my hands against my ears, and set off at a run down the hill. I nearly go flying because my legs feel like I've borrowed them from someone else, so take my hands down, shove them in my pockets – slow my speed to a brisk walk. I hear the thump of feet on the tarmac behind me and then a large hand grabs my arm. Stops me.

'Kerensa. This is why I said we needed to go somewhere private. You're distraught, in terrible shock.' Will's eyes are brimming with unshed tears and he blinks them away.

'It's not true. Can't be.' I shake my arm free and walk on. I don't know where I'm going. My feet turn and lead me back the way I've come.

The hand on my arm again. 'Please, Kerensa. Let's sit down on the bench over there, hmm?'

I ignore him and speed up. Sir Francis Drake's statue is growing closer. I hurry across to it, climb across the chain barrier and place my hand on the plinth. It's cool and flat. I press my forehead against it and close my eyes. *Leo's dead. Dead. No. No.* I take deep breaths in and out but it does no good. I feel an ocean of tears swelling in my chest.

Will's voice whispers in my ear. 'Come on, Kerensa. Let's sit on the bench over there.'

'No.' I open my eyes, look up at him. 'Did you know that Sir Francis Drake circumnavigated the globe? It took him three years – 1577-1580 – in a ship called the Golden Hind. Can you imagine that? All those years ago...?' My voice is loud, but my words are suddenly cut off by a sob. Will shakes his head, puts his hand on my shoulder, but I slap it away. Then the ocean breaches its flood barriers and I crumple at the foot of the statue.

I feel Will slide his hands under my armpits and he more or less carries me to a bench. Little groups of people have stopped talking and walking and are staring at us open-mouthed. I don't care. I don't care about anything anymore. A torrent of grief renders me limp, incapable of anything apart from tears. Will's arm is around me and he pulls me into him. I'm too weak to pull away and I lean against his chest, wetting it through with tears and snot.

A few minutes later I sit up straight, reach into my bag for tissues. Will watches silently as I blow my nose, wipe my face.

'How did it happen?' I ask. My voice sounds flat, hollow, like my heart.

'Like I say we, well – Leo was out climbing.'

'Climbing? Where?'

'Not far from St Agnes. We'd gone for the day because he insisted he wanted to do the stuff we'd done when we were kids. Because of all the madness going on with Donaldson, Leo had been very down, as you know. I agreed, though I hadn't much enthusiasm for it.'

I close my eyes, put my head in my hands. None of this seems real. Through the fog of my thoughts, something Will said doesn't make sense either. 'But if you *both* were out climbing, why did you say it was just Leo?'

'Because he left without me. I was in the shop getting a few supplies, and when I came out, he'd gone. I rang him but there was no reply. Then I waited, thinking he might have gone to find a toilet or something. He didn't come back so then I set off along the route we'd planned.'

I shake my head. Why the hell would Leo have done that? He must have been seriously disturbed. 'That was so reckless. He hadn't been climbing for years.'

'Yes, I know. We were only going up a few crags – nothing major, but even so it's not advisable to climb alone really...'

We sit in silence. I have a thousand questions but none of them really matter. My husband is dead. Dead. And I will never see his face again. I burst out crying. I'm helpless and start wailing, howling. Will finds more tissues, suggests we go to a café. Get a cup of tea. I agree only because I can't think of what else to do and people are staring at me. I feel exposed – vulnerable. I don't know what to do with myself. I do know that I don't want to be alone in my B&B room.

. . .

I cup my hands round the mug and look out through the steamy café window. It's raining outside, and stuffy and warm inside. I'm beginning to feel suffocated. Trapped. Will's talking, but I'm not really paying attention. He's told me that he found Leo at the bottom of the crags. His climbing rope looked like it hadn't been strong enough to bear his weight. Will's a doctor in a private practice. He'd done all the necessaries and ordered a private ambulance. He said he'll sort out all the funeral stuff too, if I want. I watch a woman walk past, pushing a buggy with a little boy inside. He's sticking his tongue out to catch raindrops and I have to look away. I find Will's gaze on my face. He looks like he's expecting me to say something.

'Sorry. What?'

'I was just saying I'll come with you to tell your mum and dad, if you like. Leo's parents will have to be told also.'

I picture my parents' faces, his too. God. I can't cope with it. Can't cope with any of it. I have the urge to cry again but no tears form. Maybe the well is dry. 'I don't know what I want... apart from my husband.'

Will sighs and looks into his cup. 'I'm so sorry, Kerensa. I wish I could bring him back.'

'He was going to be a father and never knew,' I say in a small voice and take a gulp of tea as the well fills up.

The colour drains from Will's face and he shakes his head in bewilderment. 'Oh my god, you're pregnant.'

'Yes. Leo would have been so thrilled. He was going to quit his job and work part-time. He wanted to be a stay-at-home dad. But then I suppose he told you all this.'

He nods. 'Yes. That's what he'd hoped.'

Unexpected fury rushes through me and my suspicions about Leo are unleashed. 'Except it wasn't all his hard work that would have allowed him to do this, was it? This sodding nest egg he's got hidden somewhere is nicked from his boss, isn't it?'

Will can't look at me. He looks out of the window, strokes his hand down his chin. 'I don't know.'

'You *must* know!' A few heads swivel in my direction so I glare at them.

Will lowers his voice. 'Okay, yes, I think he did take money that wasn't his from work.'

I knew it! How could Leo have been so stupid? And then some of the questions I couldn't voice earlier tumble out. 'When did he get so greedy? Why did he put us all in danger? Why did he go off climbing alone, make me a widow? Make my child fatherless!'

The café falls silent this time, and everyone looks at me. Will blushes and says we should go to his car. I couldn't care less where we go and allow myself to be led outside into the rain. My feet carry me forward as if on autopilot and Will guides me along the streets to a car park.

Once I'm in the passenger seat, I close my eyes. I want to sleep so I don't have to think anymore. When I wake maybe all this will have been a nightmare.

As I'm drifting, Will says, 'I don't know why he went off on his own... but I have my suspicions. I think he was in it all too deep and couldn't cope.' Will sighs and looks at me. 'I'll come clean. He had been organising insider dealing for Donaldson, but then saying to him that the investment on the stock market wasn't as lucrative as Leo had been led to believe.'

'But it was?'

'Yes. And Leo had been taking the extras from the deals. He thought he'd covered his tracks, but Donaldson's nephew – new to the firm, somehow discovered what Leo had been up to.'

I shake my head. My Leo. I'd never have thought he'd do anything like that. 'You say he was in too deep and couldn't cope?'

'Yes. He wasn't thinking straight that day. I told him he

should be in hiding, not climbing, even though it was unlikely that Donaldson would be searching for him in the hills. Leo wouldn't listen to me. It was as if he was on a mission. I could be wrong, though. But if questions are asked, I'll make sure they think it was an accident, pure and simple. That way you'll get the life insurance. You...' He swallows. 'You and the baby will want for nothing.'

Is he saying what I think he's saying? 'You think Leo killed himself?'

Will releases a slow breath. 'I don't know for certain, but it's possible. He wasn't himself to say the least.'

Oh my god. All thoughts of sleep are gone now. And what life insurance? 'How come you know more than I do about my husband's finances?'

'He talked to me about it a few days before the accident. He said he'd life insurance. Told me which company too. He also said he'd an offshore account but was evasive about how much was in it.' Will looks across the car park. 'That's when he admitted it was ill-gotten gains from his work, told me all about it. He said he'd tell me how to access it in case something happened to him. At the time, I thought he meant if Donaldson's men caught up with him... now I'm not so sure. But then if he'd planned to take his life, he'd have given the information to access the hidden account, wouldn't he? I suppose we'll never know. His head was all over the place.'

I listen to this but can't believe it. I want to be home. I want to be away from Will, from Plymouth, from this whole terrible situation. 'Can you drive me back to my B&B so I can check out and get my car?'

Will looks horror-struck. 'Kerensa. You can't drive. You're too upset. Leave your car and I'll arrange for someone to collect it. I'll drive you–'

'Drive me to my B&B or I'll walk.'

He opens his mouth to respond but my no-nonsense tone and manner has him shutting it again and driving off under my direction.

He pulls to a stop in the street outside my digs and I open the car door to leave but find his hand on my arm. 'Kerensa. Please reconsider. You're in no fit state to drive yourself.'

'It's an hour and a half – I think I can manage. Thanks for offering and coming to tell me about... about...' I can't finish the sentence and push the door wider, kick it hard with my foot when the wind pushes it back.

'You have my number. Please don't hesitate to call me, I'll tell Leo's parents if you want. I'll organise the funeral, like I said. Anything at all I–'

'Thanks, Will,' I say over my shoulder as I scramble out and stand up. 'I'll call you tomorrow. I need to sleep on it – try to make some sense out of...' I sigh and slam the door. Then run up the steps to the guest house before he can say anything else.

7

Fourteen days feel like as many years. I've spent most of that time living in my bedroom, staring at the ceiling. Mum and Dad have been practically living with me, especially Mum, now she's retired from the library. Dad's popped back into his garage a few days here and there, just to make sure my brother Ed is managing to run the business without him. I wish my parents would leave me alone. They mean well, but all the fussing and the wearing of pinched, concerned faces is making me want to scream. Nothing will help. Leo is dead. I won't ever see him again. Ever.

I look at the ceiling once more and decide enough is enough, time to have a shower. Try to get back into the land of the living. As Mum keeps saying, I have to think of the baby. I can hear her voice in my head as I haul myself up. *Come on, sweetheart. I know times are dark, but at least we have the little one to prepare for – a beautiful reminder of Leo to keep us going.* Yada yada, blah, blah. Simmering anger, never far away, flares up in my chest. I'm not sure I want a reminder of him. Because what was my husband *actually* fucking thinking when he set off that day to climb alone? Was he intending to never come back or was it an accident? And why did he get so greedy? Why did he decide to risk everything?

Then I remember that he wouldn't have been thinking properly at all on that day, would he? As Will said, his head was all over the place because he was worried so much about what Donaldson's thugs were going to do. I sink back down on the edge of the bed and put my head in my hands. But then if Leo had played everything by the book, hadn't agreed to do dodgy deals for his boss and then later try to shaft him, he wouldn't have had to worry, would he? I'm so sick of these circular arguments. So sick of being trapped in a hellhole where nothing makes sense anymore. A hellhole where everything is dark, desperate. A hellhole with slippery sides made of old memories, lost love and aching hearts. I can't climb out into the light. Do I even want to?

In the shower I promise myself that I won't get back into bed until this evening. I have to climb out of the hole, for the baby's sake. I'll go in the kitchen, have lunch with Mum and try to at least talk about the next steps. Baby steps in more ways than one. Will has been fantastic. He's done all the funeral arrangements and spoken to Leo's parents. He went down to St Ives to tell them face to face. I spoke to his mum Janice on the phone for a few minutes the other day, but neither of us could stop sobbing long enough to have a proper conversation. Will's also contacted the insurance company over the life cover. I couldn't care less about that, but Mum says we have to be practical, especially now as there'll be another mouth to feed soon.

Anna has kept the shop open for me and says I've sold loads over this main tourist period. Again, I'm finding it hard to give a toss. But then that's to be expected, isn't it? People say that a lot to me these days. But how do they know what is to be expected? Are they privy to some important information I know nothing about, because I don't know what is to be expected. I don't know how to feel, how to act, what to say, what to think, what to expect at all. The funeral is in a few days and I don't know what to expect from that either. I do know I don't want to go. Can't see the point really. Apparently, it's to give me closure. Closure is what's needed, they tell me. It is expected. So that will be nice, won't it?

It's one of the hottest days of the year, but it's cold in the crematorium. I'm cold through and through, even though Mum has her arm round me and Dad is sitting close by on my other side. So far, I have avoided speaking to most people. Just smiled and listened to them saying how sorry they are for my loss. It's as if I'm in a play I've not rehearsed. I've lost my lines too, so there's no hope of a curtain call. I hugged Leo's parents as I came through the door and we three stood sobbing in a huddle for a while. I'm wondering where this closure is.

There's a tap on my shoulder and I turn to see Will's sad face and wistful smile.

'How are you, Kerensa?'

How am I? For God's sake. How does he *think* I am? 'Oh, you know. As you'd expect.' I smile and turn back as the celebrant walks to the front and Blink-182's *All the Small Things* starts to play. Will told me on the phone the other day it was Leo's favourite song when they'd been in their last years at school. He'd asked if I could think of some music I'd like played, and all I could come up with was *Just the Way You Are* by Bruno Mars. It seemed to be on the radio all the time after we met. Leo used to sing it to me often.

Memories of that time make themselves pointy and stab.

STAB.

Stab through my heart until I'm gasping for air and bent double in my seat.

'Oh, love. Do you want to go out? There's no shame in it if you do,' Mum coos in my ear and strokes my back.

Taking a deep breath, I shake my head and I sit up straight, just in time to see the coffin being carried past. It's plain lightwood bearing a wreath of red roses. There will be individual roses to place on top later too. I bite my lip and stare at the end of the aisle where a big photo of Leo looks back at me from a plinth. He's on the beach laughing. The sun's going down and he's full of life. I took the photo. He was laughing at something I'd said. The fact that I'll never hear him laugh again twists my gut and I focus on my hands folded in my lap. Stretch my fingers and think how ridiculous the pale pink nail varnish looks on my short square nails. I painted them last night because I'd bitten them, and they looked scruffy. Who cares? Nobody will be looking at them, will they?

Nausea rolls in my stomach and a dull ache and a flutter of panic follow in its wake. I want to get up and run. I can't stand much more of it. Why doesn't the celebrant just start? Turn the music off and say what he has to say then we can all leave.

As if he's heard my silent plea, this is exactly what happens. His words wash over me. Will and Janice have given him Leo's story and I try to shut out the more poignant bits or I will run out of here. I won't be able to stop myself. Will does a reading, and swinging my hair forward, I put my fingers in my ears and wiggle them about. I remove them every now and then to see if he's finished because I can't look up.

Eventually there's silence and Bruno Mars starts up. I know this is the signal for me to lay the first rose, but I can't move. It's as if I'm glued to the seat. The dull ache is increasing, and a tremor runs the length of me.

Between them, Mum and Dad somehow manage to get me

to my feet and I walk the few steps to the coffin and look at the photo of Leo again. I select a rose, but my hand's shaking so much, the head of the flower knocks against the wood. 'My Leo,' I say. Then stop as a sob blocks my words. 'My darling, Leo... I will love you forever and... a-always.' I drop the rose and collapse sobbing into Dad's arms. He supports me up the aisle and outside into the blinding sunshine. We sit on a bench next to the carpet of flowers from friends and family, and when I've regained some semblance of composure, Dad reads some of the cards to me.

People file past to tell me how sorry they are again, and Dad reminds them the wake is in the hotel up the road and we'd see them there. I don't want to go, but Mum says my presence will be "expected", and we won't stay long. Dad goes off to talk to Leo's parents and I wipe my eyes and take some calming breaths. A man comes and stands in front of me and I look up but can't see him too well as the sunshine is in my eyes. When he speaks I know immediately who it is.

'Kerensa, please accept my deepest condolences.' Donaldson extends a hand, but I look at it in disgust.

'How dare you come here!'

He lowers his tall frame next to me on the bench like a huge spider, all knees and elbows. His grey hair's thinned considerably since last we met, and he's sporting a comb-over. His dark eyes look more shark-like than I remember, and his expensive suit and cologne can't disguise the cheap thug he really is. 'I suggest you keep your voice down, people will stare.'

'I don't care. I can't believe you would come here after everything you've done.' My voice sounds unsure, weak.

Donaldson makes a noise in his throat that passes for laughter and he smiles good-naturedly. But his voice is anything but pleasant. There's ice in it and it chills my blood. 'I think you'll find I did nothing, except try to find out what your thief of a husband did with my money.'

'He's dead. Isn't that enough?'

'Not really.' Donaldson's voice is barely a whisper. 'I'm glad he's paid for his betrayal, but I'd like my money back. Where is it?'

'I have no idea. Now leave me alone.' I make as if to get up, but he slips his arm through mine, clamps me to his side. His expression is sorrowful, as if he's comforting me for the benefit of onlookers.

'You expect me to believe that?' he says.

His nearness is making my skin crawl. Through gritted teeth I say, 'I don't care what you believe, it's the truth. I searched his little wooden box where he keeps his important documents – there's nothing. Tell the police – they might track it down. Oh wait, you can't can you? No. Because you got it illegally, didn't you?' This time my voice sounds stronger and I shake him off, stand up and look around for a friendly face.

Donaldson gets up and turn me back. 'Don't push it, madam. I'd have sent my boys round earlier, but I do have a heart. We draw the line at threatening pregnant women.' He twists his mouth to one side. 'Or... we did.'

That shocks me. I'm hardly showing yet, so how does he know? 'Who told you about my baby?' I say, pulling my jacket tight across my tummy.

'Same person that told me Leo was dead. That nice William chap phoned a few days after it happened.' Donaldson smiles. 'Most endearing really. Tried to warn me off. He said I should do the decent thing and leave it.' Donaldson stops smiling. 'And I will, once you tell me where the money is.'

'I don't know!' I yell in his face. He pulls his neck back and I see fury in his eyes, but I have a whole load of that too, and out it comes. 'I knew nothing about all this until Will told me Leo was dead. I have a baby who will never know his father, no husband, and quite frankly, I couldn't care a fuck about your filthy money. If you find it, you're welcome to it!'

Dad hurries over followed by Will and Mum. They're all talking at once, asking what's wrong. Before I can speak, Donaldson makes a swift exit across the lawn to a waiting limousine. And then the dull ache that's been nagging in my belly for the last while becomes more intense. Cramping. I double over – exhale through the pain.

Mum puts her arm around me. 'Enza? Enza, love. What's wrong?'

'I-I don't know...' I have my suspicions, but I can't allow them to be voiced.

Mum does that for me. 'It might be the baby. Let's call an ambulance.'

'No! Just let me have a minute. I'm okay,' I say more to convince myself than her. 'The pain's going off a bit now.' I straighten up and give her a weak smile.

'Come on, love. Let's get you to the car,' Dad says after a few moments, coming to my left side, and my parents support me to the car. He says to Mum, 'We'll get her to the hotel, it's only five minutes away. Sit her in a quiet room to rest. God knows what that bloody man said to upset her.'

In the car, the pain eases even more, and I take some deep breaths. Dad drives off and Mum's fussing and putting her hand on my brow. As if that will help. Then Dad's asking me who Donaldson was and Mum's telling him to shut up about that at the moment, and can't he see I'm upset? I tell him briefly, because I want them both to shut up. I want my life to go back to how it was. I want Leo. And I want my baby.

In the hotel's private room, Mum brings me a glass of orange juice and Dad hovers around like a spare part. He's shoving his hand through his grey curly hair and sighing a lot. Then he says, 'So you said in the car that man was Donaldson, Leo's boss?'

'Yes, Dad.'

'What did he say to make you so upset, love?'

'Tim, can we do this later? Kerensa's only just getting her colour back,' Mum says, giving him "that" look over the top of her specs. She takes a swig of wine she's got from the bar and pats her strawberry-blonde bob.

I look at them both and my heart swells. They're doing the protective parent thing because they love me so much. I stroke my almost non-existent bump and get where they're coming from. I guess you never stop trying to protect your baby even when they are thirty-two.

I'm about to answer Dad when the cramps come back with a vengeance. I almost drop the glass of juice as I set it back on the table and double over, a moan escaping. This is worse than before. Far worse. Then there's a sensation of damp between my legs and I yell, 'Mum, help me get to the loo, quick!'

Mum starts babbling but helps me up. Dad too, and they hurry me along the corridor to the Ladies. Once inside the cubicle, I sit down and look at the blood on my knickers with horror. The cramps continue and I look into the pan. Blood. So much blood. 'Nooo!' I cry. And then the tears come.

Outside the door, Mum yells, 'You all right, love? What's happening?' There's a tremor in her voice and I can tell she's only just holding it together. I think she's guessed.

It's a few moments before I'm able to say through a hiccupping sob, 'I think I've lost it, Mum. I've lost my baby.'

8

FOUR MONTHS LATER

I turn the calendar's page to November and can't believe it's over four months since Leo's funeral, since losing my child. The scene on the page is of a woodland path winding between tall trees; across their roots, a thick carpet of yellow and brown leaves. Beyond that is a bridge over a little stream where a couple of kids play Poohsticks. It certainly looks like late autumn, so it must be. The passage of time is lost on me though. Every day feels like the day after it happened. I wake. Open my eyes, and for a wonderful second or two, I don't have the weight of grief in the centre of my chest. For a second or two, I'm Kerensa Pethick, wife of Leo and mum-to-be. I have a good life. I am happy. Then I remember, and the grief weighs in, pinning me to the bed, crushing. Savage.

Despite this, the last six weeks or so, I have been forcing myself into a daily routine. This apparently is very important to establish a way forward. Normality, the mundane, the ordinary, are like route maps to follow. Cooking, washing-up, vacuuming are valuable anchors – signposts if I will, to progress through the day. This is what the counsellor tells me. She knows these things. And some days I might not follow the map and signposts. Some days I might hide in bed, and that's okay too. It is to be "expected".

Outside my window, the Atlantic waves have turned themselves into shouty turbulent crests, pummelling the rocks on the shoreline with huge salty fists. It's blowing a hooley and there's just one lonely dog walker on the beach, a man I think, judging by his height. He's being pulled by the dog in one direction and pushed by the wind in the other. The man, obviously tired of the game, slips the lead, and the dog barrels through a pool of standing water on the sand, scattering a huddle of seagulls like skittles. They squawk their anger at such a rude interruption and fly low along the beach, struggling against the wind. Perhaps I'll wrap up and go for a walk too. I've managed a vacuuming signpost so far today and made a sandwich. A walk will get me out of the house. Put some colour in my cheeks.

If I spread my arms and lean forward, the wind almost supports me. Almost. I try again and stumble forward a few paces and then I laugh as the wind whips back my fur-trimmed hood and wraps my hair about my head. I actually laugh. It's a wonder I remember how to. This must mean I'm getting there. I'm not sure where this "there" is but getting it is thought to be very important by most.

By the shoreline, I stoop and pick up a few flat pebbles, try skimming them and am ridiculously pleased when some do a few bouncy bumps. I don't think I've tried this since I was a kid. Such an important skill never leaves you. As I skim, I think I might attempt to open my shop over half-term. My counsellor would be ecstatic, as would my parents, brother and friends. Cousin Anna would be pleased too. She's been a stalwart, resolutely opening *Sea Treasures* three days a week come rain or shine during the summer season and only closed up around four weeks ago. Amazing, given that she has two children, a husband and three dogs to look after. She says anyone would do the same in the circumstances. But they wouldn't. They don't. It's not as if I need the money – Will sorted out the life insurance and I'm very comfortably off. But I want to keep *Sea Treasures*. It's the only thing I have left of the dream. Of how my life used to be.

Will is another amazing person. Throughout, he's been there to answer questions, sort things. All the tedious official stuff associated with a person's death. Stuff I never knew existed. The lead up to the funeral was a case in point. How many death certificates do you need, for goodness sake? Lots apparently. One for the insurance, one for the bank, one for the pensions people and one for the little boy who lives down the lane. The trouble with amazing people is you start to become dependent on them. Will's been over once a week since the funeral. Sometimes to help with a tedious bit of paperwork, sometimes to offer advice and often, just to be there for me. The stories he tells about Leo when they were boys always lifts me. He's a busy doctor, so I can't be number one on his priority list, but he always makes me feel like I am.

I brush my hands clean of sand, shove them in my pockets, hunch my shoulders against the wind and set off up the beach. Perhaps it's time to wean myself off amazing people. Time to stand on my own two feet again. As I'm thinking this, Will pops round the side of my house, a huge grin on his face, waving his arms like windmill sails. Dark clouds at his back, he sets off at a jog towards me – the wind ruffles through his yellow hair – a dandelion head brightening the grey day.

'Kerensa! I was about to leave until I spied you on the beach,' he yells, coming to a stop a few feet in front of me.

The wind snatches my hood and whips my hair across my

eyes. I wrest it free and say, 'I didn't know you were coming today.'

'I said today or tomorrow in my last text. I finished my list early, so decided to pop over.' He puts his head on one side, turns one corner of his mouth up. 'That okay?'

I look into his dark blue eyes and the frown of uncertainty he's wearing over them. 'It's more than okay. I could do with some company. Wanna cuppa?'

Will looks at his watch. 'It's almost five... a bit early, but we could nip to the pub down the road?'

I'm not one for drinking at this time, but his cheeky smile wins me over. 'Okay, as long as it's just the one.'

An hour later, and I'm happier than I have been since before... Before will do. I don't want to spell it out to myself – to leak misery out into this happy atmosphere. The wine is helping too, but the pub's bright, vibrant. There's a hum of not-too-loud chatter and laughter, and the smell of the sea and autumn has been brought in on everyone's hair and coats like a second skin. The conversation has been easy too between Will and I. There's been no talk of Leo and the past, just of Will's time in Australia and my love of art, coupled with my ambition to raise more awareness of sustainability and saving the planet.

'You should get a T-shirt printed and sell those in the shop too. Will points to his chest and draws a line across it as he says, '*Sea Treasures* – The Art of Saving the Planet is Beautiful.'

'Hey, that's not half bad.' I smile and drain my glass. 'Might have to cut it back a bit. Or get extra big T-shirts to fit it all on.'

He laughs. 'It might need a few tweaks, but I think it's a winner.' Will nods at the *specials* board on the wall. 'I could do with something to eat. How about you? The sea bass looks nice.'

My growling stomach answers him. I say I'll have the

chicken casserole and he goes to order. I sweep my eyes over his tall lean figure as he stands at the bar, then a rush of guilt makes me look away. I shouldn't be here having a drink and a meal with a man, should I? Not so soon after Leo. There's no romantic involvement, it's only a meal with a friend, but I feel so happy and carefree. I take a moment to cut myself some slack. It's about time I had some respite. I'm doing nothing wrong.

Will sets another large glass of Merlot in front of me, but I don't drink it yet. I need some food to soak up the other glass. There's a silence between us and it feels awkward. Maybe my doubts about being here have escaped into his head somehow. Stupid. Of course they haven't. He looks at me and smiles, takes a sip of his pint. 'Obviously I know that the name Kerensa is Cornish. But what does it mean?'

'It means 'love',' I say and feel embarrassed. I do like my name but wish I was called something else at times like this. 'Mum and Dad have a lot to answer for... seems a bit pretentious.'

Will shakes his head. 'Not at all. I think it's wonderful. Your mum and dad chose well.' There's another uncomfortable silence and Will shuffles in his seat, plays with a beer mat. I have to think of something to say.

'Tell me about your job,' I blurt, making it sound like an order. I take a gulp of wine and then remember I'm supposed to wait for my food.

Will brightens, looks relieved the awkwardness has passed. 'My job is wonderful, stressful, pressured, rewarding and...' He looks up to the left as if the next adjective is on the *specials* board. '...exciting.'

'A mixed bag then.'

'Yep. Certainly that. I do love it though, wouldn't want to do anything else.'

'It must be tricky remembering all those conditions.'

'Conditions?' He frowns slightly.

'Well, yeah. GPs have to have a wide knowledge of medicine, don't they?'

Will shakes his head. 'I'm not a GP, I'm a surgeon.'

This is news to me. 'But you told me you were a GP?'

'Nope. I said I was a doctor, so you just assumed, I guess.'

Maybe I had. But then you would, wouldn't you, if someone said they were a doctor. 'Why did you not say you're a surgeon?'

Will gives a sheepish shrug. 'Some people assume we're a breed apart. Snooty even, or boffins. I thought it was more...' He does the looking up thing again. 'More acceptable, if you like, to say I was a doctor.'

He's right to an extent, but I feel talked down to a bit. Maybe he thinks I'm not intelligent enough to cope with being friends with a surgeon. This rankles. 'You're a human being who does an incredible job. I'd be shouting about it if I were you.' I'm rewarded with a relieved smile. Then I add, 'But then I couldn't be you, could I? I don't have the brains for it.'

Will purses his lips, blows through them. 'That's exactly what I'm talking about. People assume we are all eggheads. Yes, of course you have to know your stuff, but it's mainly hard work and perseverance.' He takes a pull on his pint. 'And for the record, you are one of the most intelligent people I know.'

A flush of embarrassment floods my cheeks. 'Well, you can't know many people then!'

'Don't put yourself down, Kerensa. You're smart, funny, caring and... lovely.'

The look in his eye brings my colour up again, but luckily, I'm saved from a response by the waitress arriving with our food. God knows what I would have said anyway. I'm finding the whole situation a bit too much. Something has shifted in our relationship tonight. It's subtle, hard to explain, like a dream upon waking. But we *are* different together, and I don't like it. I don't want to feel different. We tuck into our food for a few moments. It's delicious, and mine is half gone before I look up again. He's watching me, an amused light in his eyes.

'What?' I say through a mouthful of potato. 'I'm hungry.'

'I can see that.' He laughs and continues with his meal.

'What kind of a surgeon are you then?'

'One that operates on people.'

'Oh. Ha ha. Can you sew up my sides for me, they're splitting here.' I try to keep my expression deadpan, but he laughs out loud and a smile betrays me.

'Love your humour. I have worked in a few different areas. Paediatric for a while, now I'm mainly orthopaedic.'

'Right.' I push my plate away. 'Why private? NHS no good?'

'No, I'd love to work in the NHS one day, they need all the help they can get. It's just that when I returned home from Australia, I needed a job that earned me big bucks. I also needed a place to live, and I want to fly my parents here a few times a year too. That's not cheap.'

'Might they come back for good?'

He shakes his head.

'I can't believe anyone would want to leave Cornwall permanently.' I shrug. 'But then I am hopelessly in love with it.'

'Me too. That's why I came back.' Will puts his fork down and shoves his plate to one side. 'Don't get me wrong. Australia is wonderful. It's just not home.'

'Where is home, exactly? Truro?'

'No, that's where the hospital is. I used to live there but now I'm in a house overlooking the beach in Mawgan Porth.'

'Oh, I love that beach – and just down the coast from me.' Why I made that sound like a bonus for him, I don't know. He nods and smiles, swirls the last third or so of his beer round the glass. It occurs to me that he's had two pints and shouldn't be driving back, even though it's only about fifteen minutes away.

Besides, the conversation feels like it's come to a natural end. I've enjoyed being with him very much, but time to call it a night. 'Best make a move, eh?' I say, sitting back in my chair.

Will frowns, looks at his watch. 'It's only just gone seven.'

'Not working tomorrow?'

'I'm not operating until after lunch. So time for another?' He looks hopeful.

'You're driving.'

'I could get a cab.' He lifts his gaze to mine.

'But then what will happen with your car?' The way he's looking at me is making my pulse race.

'I'll get a cab back and pick it up tomorrow on my way to work.'

Part of me wants to say yes. The other part of me is screaming *no*. Luckily, it's the stronger part and I say, 'Another time perhaps. But I think I might need an early night. I want to look in at *Sea Treasures* tomorrow. It's half-term in a few weeks and there'll be more visitors. It's important that it's looking ship-shape for then.'

There's disappointment in his eyes, but he covers it well with, 'That's brilliant! So glad you're feeling ready to open the shop again.'

'Not sure I am. But I have to try.' My counsellor would be proud of me. I get up to go and take my purse out.

Will stands up too. 'What are you doing?'

'Giving you my half.'

'No need. My treat.'

'That's nice, but I'd rather–'

'How about you make me a coffee at yours before I go? That make you feel better?' He shrugs on his coat.

I'm not sure if it will make me feel better. In fact, there's a jittery feeling in my stomach and I wish he wouldn't look at me in that way. If I was asked to define it, I'd say a cross between longing and curiosity. But then I could be reading stuff in his face that isn't there. He might just be looking out for me as his best friend's widow. Making sure I'm being cared for. As a friend. I say, 'Okay, coffee it is.'

How did it get to be nearly ten o'clock? Will found an old game of Trivial Pursuit on a shelf below the coat hooks. He was so enthusiastic about playing that I couldn't refuse. We drank coffee and played the game, then we talked, and somehow, now we're sitting beside each other on the sofa in front of the log burner, with glasses of brandy in our hands. It's been such a lovely evening and I don't want it to end. It must though. I nod at the clock. 'Better ring a taxi for you. They'll be coming from Newquay so it will be at least half an hour before they get here.'

Will sighs and closes his eyes. 'But I'm so comfy here. Can I just sleep on the sofa?'

This is a surprise. What do I say now?

He opens one eye. 'Pretty please? You wouldn't throw me out into the snow, would you?'

I laugh. 'It's not snowing! A bit blowy and possibly wet, but that's about it.'

'Oh let me stay. I'll be no trouble, and I'm house-trained.' He gives me puppy dog eyes.

What can it hurt? 'If you really want to. I have a spare room or two to choose from, no need for the sofa.'

'Thanks, Kerensa. I'm too tired to be buggering about with a taxi now.'

'I'll go and put the radiator on in the room. It's not been used for ages.' We stand at the same time and do an awkward shuffle as I try to step round him. We laugh and then he gives me an intense look. His eyes are really unusual close up. Sapphire, like the deep ocean out there. Before I know what I'm doing, I lean in and brush the corner of his mouth with my lips. 'I had a lovely time tonight, thank you.'

'So did I. And it was my pleasure.' Will puts his hand to my cheek and lowers his face to mine, but I come to my senses and duck round him, then hurry to the spare room.

A few minutes later, I go back into the living room with some clean towels over my arm. He's sitting on the edge of the sofa with his head in his hands. I've turned the radiator on, got the towels from the airing cupboard, but have mostly been racking my brains about what the hell to say to him now. I hadn't read him wrong at all, had I? There is a mutual attraction between us, but it can't happen. Certainly not yet. It's too soon. Maybe not ever, with him having been so close to Leo. Maybe it's *because* he was so close to him. He's a link between me and my Leo. Or maybe it's because Leo deceived me for years, stole money from his boss and then left me alone. God, I don't know. The counsellor's voice whispers, *Expect the unexpected. Chill your beans.*

'I've got some towels for you here, Will. I'll put them on your bed. It's the one next to the bathroom.'

He stands and looks at me. Hangdog. 'I'm so sorry, Kerensa. I don't know what came over me. We were getting along so well, and I had the best time. Then I went and ruined it. Can you forgive me?'

'Nothing to forgive. Let's pretend it never happened, eh? I like being friends and I don't want anything to come in the way of that.'

Will nods, but I see a flash of disappointment in his eyes. 'Thanks, Kerensa. And thanks for letting me stay.'

I smile and he takes the towels from me and goes to his room.

. . .

As I go to my own room and settle down into my too-big-for-me empty bed, I wish things were different. I wish Leo hadn't had the accident, or taken his own life. I guess we'll never know which. I wish he'd never got mixed up with that evil bastard Donaldson, because he'd be here with me now if he hadn't, and so would my baby, probably. Again, we'll never know. Would I have had a miscarriage anyway? Perhaps. Though my gut says no. I lost it because of the trauma of Leo and then having to face that disgusting thug at the funeral. I still can't get over the cheek of him. He'd sent a sympathy card after he found out I'd miscarried. Said he wasn't that bothered about the money really, he had more than enough, and it was the betrayal that rankled. He also said that I'd suffered enough and wished me well. Nice of him, that.

I wish lots of things. But wishes don't come true, do they? I'll never get Leo back, so I'll have to make the most of what the future holds without him. I have a good family and friends, and tomorrow I'm going to the shop to start as I mean to go on. I pull Leo's pillow into my arms, hold it to my nose and try to catch a sniff of his cologne or even the scent of his skin. I haven't washed his pillowcase, but all traces of him are gone. I throw the pillow at the wall and close my eyes.

9

It's been a good day. I haven't thought about the awkward situation with Will, my loss of Leo and the baby, or anything remotely sad. I've given the shop a good clean and organised the items for sale to make sure they're displayed to their best advantage. My paintings and wall hangings were all wrong. The cool blues and greens clashed with the brighter colours and it looked like they were all jostling for dominance along the back wall.

They look more at ease with themselves now and flow together in colour order. I've decluttered the window, and my driftwood models placed on a bed of sand have more space around them to really show off what they can do. I know it's daft to imagine inanimate objects as full of life, but the little dog I made and its owner look like they're really strolling along the beach.

About to give the counter next to the till a final wipe before heading home, the shop bell tinkles and in walks my friend Sally, from the cake and coffee shop. She opened it about the same time as I opened *Sea Treasures* and I haven't spent nearly enough time with her as I'd like. We are similar ages; Sally's four years older, I think. She's always cheerful and never has a bad word to say about anyone. I put the cloth down and walk round the counter to give her a hug. 'Hi, Sal. How's tricks?'

'Oh you know, not so bad.' She smiles, but her bottom lip wobbles and her dark eyes brim with tears.

'Doesn't look like it.' I put my hand on her shoulder. 'Want to tell me what's wrong, love?'

'Don't be nice to me, or I'll collapse in a snotty heap and that's not a good look.' She flaps her hands in front of her face, twists her chocolate curls round her hand and lets them fall again. 'I promised myself not to get upset when I came round, not with everything you've had to deal with lately.'

'Hey, what are friends for if we can't share our woes?' I hand her a tissue and she dabs at the corners of her eyes. 'Wanna cuppa? I'm about to close for the day.'

'I've closed up too. Yes, that would be great... if you don't mind. I mean it isn't something terrible – not like you've been through. It's not even about me, it's just...' Sally shakes her head, bites her lip and dabs her eyes with the tissue again.

'Come on, come through to the kitchen and let's have that drink. I might even have some custard creams going begging.'

After a few sips of tea and a custard cream, Sally takes a breath and says, 'It's my twin sister, Rachel. We don't seem to have much luck on the happy-ever-after front. She's recently finished with her husband of fifteen years and he's being a proper bastard to her. Marcus has always been controlling and a habitual liar. I've never liked him. I told her she could do so much better when I first met him, but you can't tell someone when they're in love, can you?'

'No. I don't suppose you can,' I say, wondering if Leo had flaws that I couldn't see. Maybe Mum noticed, but didn't say. She was a bit lukewarm when I first brought him home. So was Dad, come to think of it. But they were okay with him as the years went on and we got married. Perhaps they didn't want to upset me.

Sally points a biscuit at me. 'You could always tell when he was lying, he had a sly look on his face and wouldn't look you in the eye. Mind you, most of what came out of his mouth was a lie. My husband Rob used to say, "You always can tell when Marcus is lying, because his lips are moving."'

We laugh at this. Then I sigh when I see the sadness in her eyes. Poor Sally lost her soldier husband to a roadside bomb three years ago. She told me not long after we met, and said she was coping. But the grief is still fresh from time to time – it's to be expected. I ask, 'So how come she decided to end it?'

'He was just being his usual self. Bullying her verbally. Controlling the money. Telling her she couldn't do stuff. Swearing at her and the children – every other word with him is the F-word. And Rach decided that was it. She wouldn't put herself or the children through it anymore. Of course, she realised that the children would have to see him on his weekends, but at least they'd be protected from the worst of it.'

'So has he moved out?'

Sally gives a brittle laugh. 'No. Only decent men do that. He's neither decent, nor a real man. He prefers to see them all sharing a room at our parents' house. It's tiny so there's Rach and the two kids squashed into a box room. Marcus says it's her fault for leaving him. He wants to punish her, but he's punishing the kids too. He's either too dumb to see that, or he doesn't give a toss.' Sally takes another biscuit and snaps it in half.

'Hmm. That's bad. So how long ago did this happen?'

'They've been separated about four months. And the stuff he's done. You wouldn't believe it.' She shakes her head. 'He's changed the locks so she can't get in to collect any of her things. Then after much pressure from Rach and a call from the police, he eventually gave her a key. Then he changed the locks back again without telling her. He's like a child. Worse than a child. They're going through a divorce, but he won't pay maintenance. Again, he does this to punish her, but he's punishing the kids. There's not enough money for their clothes and school trips. Rach works but it doesn't pay much, and she has to borrow money from Mum and Dad.'

'What a bastard,' I say while thinking all the time about what Leo did to me. Sally doesn't know about that though, and I don't feel able to tell her. She might think I'm a bit stupid not to have realised about the money. But then why would I? He'd been so careful and secretive. Which of the two men was worse. Marcus or Leo?

'Then he took her car away. They have two but they're both in his name. He gave her three days to buy it from him or he'd cancel the tax. She wouldn't give him the satisfaction. So she bought her own with the bit of savings our grandparents left her. Mum and Dad helped too. She couldn't get to work, or pick the children up otherwise. She had no choice. And what really got me upset today is that I found out that he's not even living in the house. He's got a girlfriend already and he's living at hers! So the matrimonial house is empty but Rach and the kids can't live in it. Also, when he sees the kids, he forces them to spend time with this new woman and her child who is a law unto himself. It's such an awful mess. God knows what the kids are making of it. They will realise what a complete waste of DNA he is though before long. Can't fail to.'

I nod and eat a biscuit. Maybe it was for the best that Leo and I never had children. They would have been devastated by what he did, and of course his death. If there is an upside to all this, that would be it. So perhaps Sally has done me a favour telling me about this vile Marcus creature. I look at her puffy brown eyes and faraway expression and remind myself that she needs comfort and the world doesn't revolve around me. How selfish of me to think about her doing me a favour when her and her sister are obviously going through a really rough time. 'Is there anything I can do, Sal?'

She pats my hand. 'You listened to me, that's what I needed. And these biscuits and tea of course.' She flashes a big smile. 'I'm feeling better now I've got it off my chest.'

'Glad to be of help.' I consider again telling her the truth about Leo, but what would be the point? Best to let sleeping dogs lie... in the past where they belong. We talk about my new display, and then she goes to collect her children from school.

Mum pops round to mine as I'm putting a lasagne for one in the oven. She's come to bring me a jacket she'd bought that was too small for her. She'd told me about it over the phone yesterday. I said it probably wouldn't be my thing, but it is. Just a casual hoodie in a deep green. I offer to give her the money, but she won't hear of it.

'So how are you doing, love?' she asks, head on one side, arms folded.

For some reason her question and body language annoy me. It's as if she's talking to a sick person. I copy her stance, and frown. 'What's that supposed to mean?'

It's her turn to frown. 'Nothing, love. I'm just asking how things are with you these days. You know, after everything you've been through.'

'Eh? It's not as if we don't see each other. We often meet up or talk on the phone. You don't have to ask how I am, as if you've not seen me for months!'

'Hey, what's wrong? It's not like you to fly off the handle.' Mum's voice is gentle, full of concern.

I don't know what's wrong, or why I'm being such a cow. I shrug and stare at the floor.

Mum comes over and gives me a hug, and all of a sudden, I'm sobbing as if my heart will break. Mum guides me to a kitchen chair and hands me some tissues. Then she puts on the kettle. I'm reminded of the reverse situation with me and Sal earlier, and wonder if that conversation is at the heart of it all. 'Now, tell me what's upsetting you, sweetheart. Is it just the situation? You know, the sadness over Leo and the baby building up again. Because if it is, it's to be expected. It's only been just over four months after all.

I blow my nose and take a moment. 'I honestly don't know what it is, Mum. Yes, I suppose it's the situation. But I thought I was coping so much better lately.'

'You are.' She places a mug of tea in front of me and sits opposite. 'But you're bound to get a wobble now and then.'

'Yes.' I twist the mug slowly round and round and my thoughts follow suit. Why am I so upset all of a sudden? Might as well share my thoughts. 'I had a visit from Sally from the cake shop earlier and she told me about her shit of a brother-in-law.' I tell Mum what Sally said.

'Oh, poor Rachel and the children.'

'Yeah.' I take a sip of tea. 'Mum, did you like Leo... or did you think he was no good from the off?' I watch her face closely and she has that shifty look when she's trying to hide stuff.

'Erm. What do you mean by no good?'

'As we now know, he fiddled a shedload of money from Donaldson. The fact that Donaldson is as bent as a fishing hook is neither here nor there. The fact is, my husband went behind my back. He lied to me for months. Years probably, because he'd worked for him for five. I was wondering if he'd always been dodgy, but I'd not seen it. You know, a bit like Rachel and her husband. She'd not listened to her sister, because she'd been blinded by love.'

Mum's cheeks turn pink and she sighs. 'Me and your dad did think he was a show-off. Liked to "big himself up" as the youngsters say nowadays. Maybe he did exaggerate a bit too, like this Marcus bloke.'

My mouth drops open. 'Why didn't you say anything, Mum?'

She shifts in her seat, looks out of the window. 'I did try a few times, but you didn't want to know. You made excuses for him and changed the subject.'

'I don't remember that. What did you say?'

She looks back at me. 'I don't remember everything I said, it was only a couple of things anyway. I could see how much you loved him, so it would have been pointless. But I do remember saying he seemed to have all the say over when you would start a family, and I didn't think it was fair. I could tell how much you wanted a baby.'

Did she? I cast my mind back and remember something to that effect. 'What did I say?'

'You said it was only because he was working so hard to make sure there'd be enough for the baby, and for you to start up *Sea Treasures*. So I left it. Anyway, why are you thinking of all this now?'

I shake my head because I'm not sure of the answer. I think for a few moments. 'It's probably because I'm feeling a bit stupid, not realising who I was married to. I must be a really poor judge of character. If I'd have seen what you and Dad saw in Leo, I might not have married him. I might have avoided all this heartache and be married to a nice guy and have a couple of kids by now.'

Mum reaches for my hand. 'It's no good thinking like that. And I'm not saying I thought he was that bad. Everyone has their faults. No good wondering of what might have been, Enza.

What's done is done, and you need to look to the future. There will be a nice man for you one day. I know you might not think that now, it's too soon. But it *will* happen. You're too lovely a person for it not to.' Her eyes mist over and she raises her mug to her lips.

She said it was too soon? I wonder what she'd think if she could have seen me almost snogging Will last night. I feel my colour coming up, so to hide it I go to check on the lasagne. I need to steer well away from Will for a time. I've already made a grave misjudgement with Leo. I don't want to step blindly in front of another speeding truck. Perhaps that's why Leo was able to call the shots. Because compared to him, I'm quite weak. I'm generally content to let others lead. I like the feeling that I'm being looked after. Leo obviously exploited that to the full.

Mum gives me a hug and leaves me to my dinner, and I promise her I'll ring if I need a chat. I pour a large glass of Merlot and think about Will. He seems so grounded and calm, completely different to Leo. Will told me recently that Leo always relied on him to help him out of sticky situations when they were kids. Perhaps he wouldn't be a speeding truck at all. I picture him laughing, his golden hair tousled by the salt air, his eyes the colour of the Atlantic on a cloudy day... and then I stop. It's just me now for the foreseeable, and I need to get used to it. I need to be stronger, more determined to stand on my own two feet. My life is right there, waiting for me to make something of it. Shape it. Mould it into something meaningful. Something good.

10

February is draining me. January is normally the month that gets on everyone's nerves, dragging on and on. But for me, January went quite fast. I spent lots of it picking stuff from the beach to recycle, or collecting pebbles and driftwood. I was glad to see the back of Christmas. The first one without Leo for nearly nine years. I went through the motions for my family, but I'd have happily hidden under blankets until the whole "festive" season had been packed into boxes and put in the loft for another year. When I was part of a "happy" couple, I used to think people who moaned about it, and generally rained on Christmas fans' parades, were proper old Grinches. But they aren't. So many have lost loved ones, or have no one at all. Christmas can be the loneliest time of year for those people. For me.

February feels dead though. There's nobody on the beach much, unsurprisingly given the squally weather. And the town feels like it's hibernating. In a way it is. Hopefully half-term next week will bring a few tourists down to Cornwall. It won't be heaving, but it will be worth opening the shop for more than three days a week. With any luck. Luck hasn't been my friend lately though, has it? I shake my head and sigh at the misery I'm dredging up. Wallowing. I'm wallowing again. This needs to stop. Right. Now.

I close the blinds against the twilight shadows racing up the beach and put all the lights on. Time to start thinking positive. Just because I'm on my own, doesn't mean I am alone. I have friends and family and a lovely place to live. I've also stuck to my guns over Will. He's still popping over about once a week to see how I am, but I have refused all offers of drinks or dinner. He says he understands and can see why I wouldn't want to. However, we chat about anything and everything over a cuppa, which I must admit I really look forward to. It's great to hear about what he's been up to and the patients he's helped. Must be so fulfilling to know that you've got people walking again, able to live an independent life.

On occasion when he's popped round, I have had to pretend I was off to see a friend or my parents, because I felt myself being drawn to him. We get on so well and I know it wouldn't take much to move the relationship on. He has "that" look in his eye sometimes, and I'm sure it must be reflected in mine. But it's no good. It would never work. There'll always be the ghost of Leo between us.

On the worktop in the utility room, my ironing pile is pretending to be Mount Everest. I'm in the kitchen and can see it through the door from the corner of my eye. I have steadfastly ignored it, only attending to the things I absolutely need, because I hate ironing so much. But on this dark rainy February evening, I might as well bite the bullet.

I heave the basket up, flick on the little TV in the kitchen and make a start on the foothills.

Five minutes later, the doorbell rings. Oh dear, what a shame.

Just when I was enjoying myself so much. I catch a glimpse of my reflection in the hall mirror as I pass. No make-up, hair like a haystack. Hope it's not Vogue come to do an interview. I smile at this image and open the door. *Oh shit.*

'Hi, Kerensa. Hope you've not eaten yet,' Will says, holding up two bags of what smells like Chinese takeaway. He gives a sheepish grin and inclines his head to a figure standing behind him to the side, his face obscured by darkness. 'Hope you don't mind Patrick and I showing up like this.'

I feel my colour come up. 'Patrick?'

The figure steps under the porch light and I'm even more conscious of my appearance. It might as well have been Vogue. The guy is fairly tall though not a tall as Will, has stunning green eyes, wavy jet-black hair, and chiselled features. His chin is square – prominent, though not out of place, and his smile is Hollywood white. 'Good evening, Kerensa, I'm Patrick, Patrick O'Brien.' He's got a lovely Irish brogue, so smooth and pleasant. Those green eyes hold mine intently, so I blink and pull my gaze away. He sticks out his hand and I take it. His handshake is firm, strong. 'You look a bit shocked. It was my idea to swing by and surprise you.' Patrick flashes the Hollywood whites again. 'Say you don't mind.'

What do I say? Because I do mind. I feel like a complete mess. I'm not prepared for this, I look a sight. I just want a quiet night with my ironing, beans on toast and Coronation Street later. But no. No, I've now got to be witty and charming to a man who looks like he's just stepped out of a film. Do I say all this? No. Of course not. 'Hi, Patrick, great to meet you. Why don't you come in before the takeaway gets cold. It smells delicious.'

I wave them through, and give Will raised eyebrows and mouth, 'What the hell?' as he scurries in behind Patrick.

'Patrick's moved to the UK from Dublin,' Will tosses over his shoulder by way of an explanation. He ushers Patrick down the corridor. 'Well, I say Dublin. We met in Australia, didn't we, Pat?'

'We did indeed, my good man!' Patrick says from the kitchen, whipping a bottle of champagne out from under his long navy-blue coat. 'This will go well with the Chinese, yes?'

Will smiles and places the bags on the table. 'If not, I have a bottle of red in the carrier here. I know it's your favourite.'

The two men look at me expectantly. Patrick in particular has a very intense stare. It makes me feel vulnerable. Naked. I look away, scrape my hair into a ponytail, secure it with a scrunchie I have around my wrist, and say, 'What brings you here, Patrick?'

'To your house?' he asks with a cheeky wink.

'Well yes, but I really meant to Cornwall.'

'I know. I'm only messin' with you, woman. Let's crack this open and eat. Then I'll tell you all about it.'

I ignore this seemingly condescending comment, because I think it's just the way some Irish people speak. Or is it the Scots who say stuff like 'away with you, woman?' *Does it matter, Kerensa?* I get plates out of the cupboard and glasses and then pretend to spill some water on my top. This is the excuse I need to hare along to my bedroom and throw on a clean pair of jeans, a red smartish top, dust some blusher on my cheeks and show my eyes the mascara brush. My hair will have to do as it is.

As I walk back to the kitchen, I ask myself why I'm going to so much trouble. What difference does it make? I suppose my confidence has taken a pummelling over the last seven months since I lost Leo and my baby. As long as I look half decent on the outside, at least then the two men won't see the crumbling wreck that's hiding underneath.

'Wow, a quick-change artist! You look gorgeous,' Patrick says, his mouth full of prawn crackers. He's taken off his coat and he's wearing blue jeans and a thin black T-shirt which does little to disguise a honed torso beneath.

My colour comes up to compete with my red top and I turn my back to pour wine. 'It's just an ordinary top. Nothing special,' I mumble into my glass.

William dishes up the Chinese, talking all the time. He sounds nervous. Perhaps he realises it wasn't fair of him to show up out of the blue with a stranger in tow. 'So Pat's here on business for a few months with a view to moving back permanently. I'm showing him the sights of Cornwall and so far he's loving it, aren't you?' He hands Patrick a plate.

'I *am* loving it.' He sticks a fork in his rice but doesn't eat. He gives me a long lingering look. 'The scenery is stunning.'

Dear God. Is he for real? How cheesy was that line? I pull out a chair and sit down, the guys follow suit. 'Cornwall is stunning. I would never live anywhere else.'

Patrick says through a mouthful of food, 'Don't blame you. And if my business venture takes off, I'll be joining you.' He swallows his mouthful and guffaws. 'Not in your house, of course. I'd buy one of my own.'

'I bought one down the coast not so long ago. I've moved twice since I've been back. Sold my house in Truro and shipped out here. This coastline is the best in the world,' Will says, sipping his drink.

'It is. A bit similar to the coast in Oz, and in California, come to think. But on a smaller scale. No less beautiful though,' Patrick says, and helps himself to more sweet and sour pork.

'You've travelled quite a bit then?' I ask, mainly to cover an awkward silence apart from the chomp of our jaws.

'I have. Most of Europe, Australia, obviously. California. In fact most of the west coast and the deserts too. Arizona-Utah. Monument Valley is a favourite of mine.' Patrick's voice takes on a wistful tone and he stares into the middle distance as if reliving the sights he's seen. 'Love being by the sea best though. It feels like home to me.'

'Sounds wonderful,' I say.

'Yes. But as I said, the coast feels like home, and Cornwall especially feels like it's in my blood. Maybe I was born here in another life?' Patrick's unusual green eyes twinkle at me over the top of his wine glass.

I look back to my food and repeat my question from earlier. 'Why did you leave Australia?'

'Homesick, pure and simple. I went there on an adventure about five years ago and then had enough.' Patrick dabs his mouth with his napkin and throws it down. 'I did think to go back to Dublin originally, but I thought I'd look up old Will here.' He slaps Will on the back, causing him to drop his fork. Patrick thinks this is hilarious, but I notice Will doesn't join in the laughter as heartily as he might. 'When I saw how beautiful Cornwall is, I decided to stay.'

'And what kind of business are you starting up?' I'm beginning to feel like the Spanish Inquisition, but Will's keeping strangely quiet.

'I buy and sell luxury boats. There are a fair few beauties in this county I can tell you. Falmouth is probably where I'll be based.'

'That's how Patrick and I met,' Will says. 'I went on a friend's boat one afternoon and he'd just bought it from Pat. Pat was giving him a tutorial and we became friends, both coming from this neck of the woods.'

I nod, but think that Ireland's hardly this neck of the woods. Then I guess it is, compared to Australia.

'We went out a few times after that in my boat,' Patrick says. 'The marine life out there is stunning, isn't it, Will?'

'Yep. We saw dolphins, whales... and a few sharks from a safe distance.'

'As to why I'm here tonight, Will thought it would be nice to introduce me to a few of his dear friends. Help me settle in, you know? I am a poor lonely Irish boy after all.' Patrick turns his bottom lip down and pretends to be sad.

I give a quick smile. 'Oh, you'll meet new people soon, I'm sure. You're friendly and outgoing.' I get up to clear the plates and Patrick goes over to the fridge, pulls out the bottle of champagne.

'Let's open this and celebrate my new friendship with you, Kerensa.' He grins and pops the cork. I don't really want any, but have some just to be polite. He comes back to the table and pours some for Will and then raises his glass. 'Here's to us, my new life and many new friendships!'

We clink glasses and then the conversation's all about boats and Australia for a while. At least Will's a bit more animated now. Seems to have shaken his odd mood. I'm beginning to relax at last, partly due to the wine and champagne. And Patrick's good company and easy on the eye. But Will's more interesting, I decide. More genuine. There's something about Patrick that feels a bit fake. Contrived.

'Do you have family in Ireland, Patrick?' I ask.

'Yeah. My parents and a sister. I have a hundred cousins, aunts and uncles too. It comes with being Irish!' He laughs. 'They were chuffed to bits to find I was coming home – well, a bit nearer at least. Mum's not been doing so well health wise lately and I can nip across to see her from here in no time if I need to. Or I'll sail across on a fine day.'

'That will be nice for them. Family is so important.'

'Yeah. Will told me you lost your husband recently. Sorry about that.'

Patrick's words punch me in the gut. He said it as if it was a minor setback. As if he were just playing lip service to being sorry. 'Um... yes.' I take a gulp of champagne to wash down a knot of emotion forming.

Will glares at Patrick. 'Kerensa was devastated. Still is.'

Patrick looks suitably chastened. 'Oh, of course. I'm sorry if you're not up to talking about it yet. You must have loved him very much.'

At least this time he sounds genuine. 'I adored him.' And then from nowhere comes, 'But I'm also furious with him. Has Will told you what he was up to behind my back?' I'm almost as shocked as Patrick looks. Why did I say that?

'Erm, yes he did. He must have needed his bumps read, doing that to such a lovely woman. If I had someone waiting for me at home like you, I'd make sure I looked after her.'

Will says, 'Leo could be impulsive. An act first, think later kind of guy.'

'But aren't we all a bit like that?' Patrick answers, running his fingers quickly through his hair and then stroking his chin between forefinger and thumb a few times. Leo used to do the same thing when he was talking, and the knot of emotion resurfaces. 'Thinking about it again, it's intention in the end that matters. I expect Leo wanted to do the best for you, Kerensa. Set you up for life financially – start a family?'

I'm not having that. Especially from a bloody stranger. Did he think he knew my husband better than me? 'Will didn't tell you all of it then? Because I was pregnant at the time. I was waiting for my husband to come home so I could tell him that we were going to have a baby. He never did though, did he? No. He was too busy playing cloak and dagger and running from his shit of a boss who he'd stolen from. The same shit of a boss who threatened me at Leo's funeral and helped my miscarriage along. The same miscarriage that started because of all the fucking trauma of losing the love of my life.' I stand up, stare down at the men's shocked faces. 'But I couldn't really have been the love of his, could I? Because if I had, he wouldn't have done what he did in the first place!'

Will jumps up and puts his hand on my arm, muttering soothing words, but I shake him off. Patrick looks at me, white-faced, open-mouthed. This suddenly strikes me as funny. He looks like some landed fish gulping air on the quayside. And I want to laugh, so I cover my mouth with my hands. Then I realise laughter is turning to tears, so I run to my room, slam the door and collapse onto the bed.

A few seconds later, Will knocks on the door. 'Kerensa? Kerensa, are you okay?'

'Go away. Go away, Will and take Patrick with you.'

'Hey, he didn't mean to upset you, I'm sure. It's–'

'I know. I know he didn't. I'm just not ready to talk about Leo casually over dinner. Tell Patrick I'm sorry, but I need to be alone now.'

There's a bit of mumbling and shuffling outside the door and then, 'It's Patrick, Kerensa. I'm so sorry for upsetting you. It's the last thing I wanted.'

I sigh into Leo's pillow, hug it to my chest and try to make my voice light. 'Don't worry, Patrick. I'll see you another time. Bye for now.'

They say goodnight, and then after a few moments I hear the front door close. On the one hand I'm relieved I'm by myself again with my memories and thoughts. On the other, I feel desperately alone. Everything was fine until Patrick mentioned Leo. And no matter how much I like to think I'm coping with his death, getting stronger, I'm obviously not. I'm not ready to have his name dropped into some idle chatter, because like a pebble in a pond, the ripples go far, wide and deep.

Through the open window, the ocean sings its eternal lullaby, shushing me to sleep, whispering with the wind. My mind begins to calm, and I concentrate on my breathing. In.

Out. In. Relax. This is to be expected. I *am* winning at life overall, and tomorrow is another day. It's too early to go to sleep now though. I'll make myself a hot drink, wash up the plates, empty the bin and have an early night. Then I will awaken refreshed, recharged and be ready to do battle once more. I am a strong woman who will *not* be crushed under the weight of misery and despair. I will do this. I can do this. I must do this.

An hour later, I look at the full moon from my bedroom window. It's suspended in a hammock of stars, its face peeping between scraps of dark cloud as they scud across an ink-black sky. The moonlight splashes dabs of silver along the horizon, and I imagine myself to be in a little boat upon it. I am the captain of my destiny and the slave of none. My hand is on the tiller and I'm sailing to safe harbour. The more I say things like this to myself, the more it is likely to be true. My counsellor says so, and she knows stuff like that. I smile at the moon, close the curtains and go to bed.

11

Will flops down in a chair in the changing room. He barely has the energy to get out of his scrubs and drive home. He's tempted to sleep in one of the private rooms reserved for relatives of patients tonight. Three operations today might have been a tad overoptimistic. And his mind had been all over the place during the last one. Luckily it had been straightforward. If it hadn't been, he might have asked his colleague to step in.

His mind is always so full of Kerensa. Has been since the first time he saw her standing in Plymouth Hoe, out of her mind with worry about Leo. Leo who risked everything for money. If Will had the love of Kerensa, he would live on the streets if it were necessary. How could Leo have done such a thing? Will often thinks of Kerensa's face crumpling in grief when he told her Leo was dead. He should never have agreed to be the one to tell her. He hates himself for it, and for many other things.

In the shower he lets the hot jets of water massage his tired muscles and soaps his body. Why had he got involved with Leo again after all those years? He was trouble – always had been when they were kids. And soft-touch Will had always pulled him out of it. They'd had fun though as teenagers, bouncing off each other with the quick banter and crazy stuff they'd got up to. But leaving Kerensa alone, pregnant and scared was a despicable trick. Okay, Leo hadn't known about the baby. But Will knew he still would have done what he did, regardless. Because for Leo, everything always had to be about Leo.

The trouble with Will was he could never say no to Leo. He always managed to pull on the heartstrings, make it impossible for him to refuse help. Because inevitably it *was* always help that Leo needed. Will had tried to suggest that Leo just disappear, begged him even. He'd argued that he could stay away a few years, holed up somewhere, until Donaldson had forgotten about him. It had all fallen on deaf ears. Leo had to take it one tragic step further, didn't he.

No use thinking about all that now. Leo is gone. Kerensa is making a new life for herself and Will is keeping an eye on her, making sure she's all right. Being a good friend. Will flicks off the shower and grabs a towel from the rail. He rubs himself down and scrubs at his hair as if trying to punish his brain. He ought to be punished, shouldn't he? Because he isn't being just a good friend at all. No. He's in love with her and he's hoping that Kerensa will feel the same one day. Unlikely, the way things are.

Despite trying to shove any negative thoughts to the back of his mind, once through his front door, and he's sitting with a microwaved meal on his lap in front of the TV, Kerensa's back at the forefront again. Kerensa *and* Patrick. Patrick really buggered everything up at Kerensa's last night. Patrick tends to do that. Bugger things up. Just got rid of Leo, but now he's saddled with Patrick. But this time Will has no choice but to do Patrick's bidding. He has far too much on Will. He's told him he'll have no problem dropping him right in the shit either, if Will doesn't do exactly as he tells him.

Will switches off the TV and closes his eyes. Immediately,

Kerensa's lovely face is there – her laughing green eyes, beautiful smile... It's a good job Patrick doesn't know how Will feels about Kerensa, because Patrick has the same aim. To make her fall in love with him. Will can't bear it. But what can he do? There's no way he can refuse. How did he get so tangled up in all the lies and deception? If Kerensa ever finds out he's lied his head off to her, he'll never win her round. Will's a bright guy, but he just walked into it. Right into Patrick's trap, like some unsuspecting child. Will never saw it coming. He sighs and heaves his weary bones off the sofa, turns out the light. He feels so stupid. So desolate. Leo and now Patrick. Will can't decide which one he hates the most.

12

February half-term has been better than I could have ever expected, businesswise. I have sold so many of my little driftwood figures that I'll have to make some more, pretty sharpish. I even sold a large sculpture of a shark I'd made from part of an old rubber tyre, some tin cans, a shoe, some plastic bottles and various other bits and bobs I'd found washed up. Another customer was in the shop when I sold the shark, and was disappointed when I told her I had no more ready. She commissioned one, and I said it would be ready in a month. She paid a deposit of fifty pounds, so I'd better get my beachcomber wriggle on.

Opening the door to the shop this morning feels like a breath of fresh air. I have so many new ideas, and I must admit I'm feeling more positive than I have for a while. Not just about my business, but about everything. Will phoned the day after my outburst and apologised again. He said he'd keep away for a while if I liked. I told him it wasn't necessary, but perhaps a few days to get my head together might be useful. I haven't seen him for well over a week, and I miss him, strangely. Patrick had apparently asked if he could pop by and see my artwork soon, so I've been expecting him to appear over the week. Maybe he will today as Will had mentioned something about Friday, I think.

It's getting on for one o'clock when the bell jangles and in walks Sally wearing her trademark big grin. I have seen her a few times recently and she seems much more herself. Her sister has managed to get a small place to rent for her and the children, and Marcus has gone to work away, which is good news all round.

'Hello, Rens.' Sally holds a white cardboard box out to me. She'd taken to calling me Rens lately. People often shorten my name, but I don't really mind. 'Thought I'd bring a few cakes over and we could have a cuppa?'

'I like the sound of that. Have you closed the shop?' Odd if she has, as we've been so busy and it being a Friday, too.

'Don't be daft. Lily's holding the fort.'

'Thank goodness for part-time assistants, eh?'

'Wouldn't be without her. Gives me chance to sneak in here for a natter.'

We chat about anything and everything as we wait for the kettle to boil in my tiny kitchen, and my mouth waters as I lift the lid on the cardboard box. There's a selection of éclairs, chocolate slices and fresh cream doughnuts. Decisions, decisions.

Just as I bite into a large fresh cream doughnut, the shop bell tinkles again and I go out to see who it is. Great. Patrick and Will.

'Kerensa...' Patrick stops and stares at my face, tries to hide a smirk but doesn't succeed. 'I hope you don't mind us stopping by.' He's still staring with amusement at my face. My nose, to be precise.

Will opens his mouth to say something, but at the same time I touch my finger to my nose and find a dollop of cream and jam left by the doughnut. How humiliating. Heat floods my cheeks and I dash back to the kitchen to get a damp cloth.

'What's up with you? You look like a scalded cat,' Sally says through a mouthful of chocolate cake. I roll my eyes, scrub at my nose and then point into the shop. Sally frowns and goes in that direction. 'Oh hello. Will, isn't it? We met near here once, outside my shop, I think.'

I follow her in and Will's nodding, but I can tell he has no clue who Sally is. 'This is Sally, Will. Sally owns the cake and coffee shop two doors down.'

A flicker of recognition dawns in his eyes. 'Oh yes, I remember. You have fantastic cakes!'

Patrick guffaws. 'Good job you didn't say she has great buns!'

Sally laughs too, turning pinker than her top. It's obvious Patrick's stunning looks is having an effect on her. Though not too much to prevent her sticking her hand out and saying, 'I don't believe we've had the pleasure?'

Patrick gives her the pearly whites, shakes her hand. 'If we had, I'd have remembered, Sally. The name's Patrick.'

Dear God, Sally giggled. Actually giggled.

I say, 'Patrick's a friend of Will's over from Australia, Sal. He's hoping to make a life for himself here and start his boat business.'

'How wonderful! What kind of boats?'

He tells her, and for the next while we talk about boats. Well, Patrick talks, and we listen. Apparently, his boat business is almost a dead cert as he has some good connections who have pulled a few strings. He certainly has been blessed with the gift of the Blarney Stone and Sally's lapping it up. Then having exhausted the all-about-me spiel for now, Patrick turns my way. 'And Kerensa, what a fabulous place you have here. Such a talent!' He strides over to a framed collage of butterflies made from sea glass, painted bits of plastic bottles and flattened metal, and points at it. 'Can I buy this? It's phenomenal!'

I smile, but wonder if he's noticed the price tag. That's one of my more expensive pieces as it took me ages to make. Really fiddly. 'Thank you. It's two-hundred-and-fifty pounds though.'

'Never mind the price tag. And it should be twice that, more.' He stares at the collage intently. 'Stunning.' Then he pulls a fat wallet from his jacket and counts the amount out in cash on the counter top. He throws in an extra twenty. 'A bit more to show how much I love it. Great talent should be rewarded.'

I say thank you, but for some reason I feel uncomfortable, not flattered. Patrick's obviously loaded and it's as if he's showing off. Buying my friendship in a way. I take the money and put it in the till. Sally's still standing there gawping at Patrick with a daft grin on her face. But he's looking round the shop, still oblivious. Will's watching me watching them and says quietly, 'How's things with you?'

'Really good, actually. I'm spending lots of time here and have some new ideas. I got a commission the other day too.' There's pride in my voice and I feel a bit cringy.

'That's brilliant!' He steps forward and gives me a big hug. He smells of sandalwood and sea air, and his arms feel good around me. It's a long time since I've been held.

When we break apart, Patrick's right next to us, a flash of what looks like jealousy in his eyes. Then it's gone and he's smiling again. He beckons Sally over. 'I've just had a fantastic idea! If the weather's good on Sunday, let's go out on my boat. I bought her last week. I'll organise a picnic, champagne, the works! We'll go up the Fal river and moor up. Do a spot of fishing. What do you say?'

Sally looks like she's won the lottery and beams back at him. 'What a fantastic idea.' She stares at me pointedly, but I say nothing and rack my brains for an excuse. 'It's not every day we get asked out for champagne lunches, is it, Rens?'

Her big brown eyes are shining with excitement, and I know her having a lovely day out depends on me. But I don't really want to go. There's something about Patrick that I can't put my finger on. He's good-looking, charming and funny. But there's the overarching falseness about him that I noticed the first time we met. Sometimes first impressions prove to be unfounded, but this is the second time, and I feel no different. He wouldn't be the man I'd pick for Sally, that's for sure, but it's clear she fancies him. There's been only one casual boyfriend in the three years since her husband died, but it didn't last, as he didn't take to her having children. She needs someone dependable and honest. Patrick strikes me as neither.

I scrunch up my nose and try a placatory smile. 'I was planning to open the shop this Sunday – it being half-term.'

Sally frowns and Patrick's forehead borrows it a second later. 'Oh, what a shame. But couldn't you open in the morning and close about noon? We'd still have time to get to Falmouth for that fab lunch!'

Patrick brightens and pats her on the back. 'An excellent idea! You can't say fairer than that, can you?' He looks at me, head on one side, does the pretend sad face with the bottom lip turned down he did last time. That face is not endearing. It just gets on my nerves.

Will says, 'All work and no play. I'm free Sunday too. Not had a free weekend for ages.' His lovely blue eyes crinkle at the corners as he gives me a hopeful smile.

'Oh, I don't know,' I say, biting the corner of my thumbnail. How can I get out of this?

'I do,' Sally says, slipping her arm through mine. 'We'll go and have a great time. My mum will have the kids. I need a break!'

She looks at Patrick. I'm guessing she's trying to gauge his reaction to her mentioning the kids. He says, 'Oh you have kids. That's grand!' Then they chat about how old they are, their names and so forth, while I wonder how I've been so easily railroaded into spending an afternoon with Patrick. I catch Will's eye and he gives me a conspiratorial wink. At least he'll be there, so it won't be all bad.

As luck would have it, Sunday morning hasn't been at all busy in my shop, so when Sally calls round for me, I can't say I'm sorry to close up. I still have more than a few misgivings about going down to Falmouth on Patrick's boat though. I expect he will be all showy-offy and extravagant as usual. But the thought of seeing Will again makes me happy. I can't seem to help it, because the more I see him, the more I want to.

We walk towards my house to collect my car. I'm not going to drink. Champagne goes straight to my head if I have more than one glass. I pop inside to get my coat, in case this unusually sunny weather turns, and when I come out there's a flashy BMW outside. Sally's talking to the driver through the open window. Then she hurries over to me, all big-eyed and flappy hands.

'You're not going to believe this. But Patrick has only sent us his driver. I mean "his driver". Have you ever heard of such a thing apart from in films?'

Oh dear Lord. I know he's a show off, but this is ridiculous. 'No, Sally, I haven't. And how the hell did he know we wouldn't have gone by now?'

Sally smiles. 'He's been keeping in touch by Messenger and asked how we were getting there and what time we were leaving.' She sighs and puts her hand on her chest. 'Bless him. He's had this guy waiting round the corner for the last hour so not to miss us. Isn't that sweet?'

'That's one word for it.' I set off for the car.

'What's up with you?' Sally asks, hurrying along behind.

'Not sure. I suppose I don't like being controlled. Leo did that, and I didn't realise it until I thought back over our life together.'

'But how's Patrick controlling us?' Sally keeps her voice to a whisper as we climb into the back seat.

I say hello to the driver and thank him. Then I whisper back, 'Because we're like little pawns on a chessboard. He decides how we travel, and he's already made us beholden to him.'

Sally screws up her face. 'Eh? That's a bit dramatic. Don't you like him?'

It's obvious she's feeling disappointed with me and I don't want to ruin her day. Maybe I *am* going too far. I heave a sigh and tell myself to relax. 'He's okay. I just find him a bit full on I suppose. Let's give him the benefit of the doubt.' I smile at her and look out of the window at the fast-disappearing Atlantic.

Once more she lowers her voice. 'I wouldn't mind giving him a bit more than that.' Then she snorts with laughter and I have to join in, despite my misgivings.

The "boat" is a fifty-foot navy and white motor cruiser called *Ocean Phoenix*, the driver, Ken, tells us as we park up in Mylor Harbour. I can only imagine how much such a vessel would be worth. I'm still not prepared for the sight of her, however. Sally and I stare almost opened-mouthed as Ken leads us along the jetty. *Ocean Phoenix* is huge. The afternoon sun gleams off the hull as she bobs gently in the water, and along the silver rail and ladder waiting for us to board. As I place my foot on the bottom rung, Patrick appears on deck waving like a loon. He is wearing a navy hat with the word *Captain* across it. Such a child.

'Welcome aboard, pretty ladies!' he says, offering his hand as I reach the top. I take it because I'm unsure of the step down, otherwise I'd manage on my own. I stand on deck to look around and can't believe how gorgeous it is. There're two white leather high stools, under a blue canopy, and a huge steering wheel attached to a wooden panel, inset with various dials and a radio. There's white leather seating areas all the way around the deck and storage underneath. In the middle of the two stools, there's a door to below deck and I can just glimpse a table laid with a white cloth upon which sits a large picnic hamper and a bucket of champagne.

Sally's on board now. Unlike me, who's tried to keep my face from betraying what I think of the boat, she turns in a circle, taking everything in, her hand over her mouth. Then she giggles and says to Patrick, 'Oh my good god! Is this actually yours?'

Patrick grins. 'It sure is. I know how you feel. I have to pinch myself some days. Can't believe I actually am this lucky!' He sweeps his hand down his attire which is over-the-top smart navy trousers, and a stripy sailor-type top. Then he points needlessly to the hat. 'I'm the captain!'

Sally laughs and says he looks the part. I say nothing.

Just then, William comes up from below decks, a glass of champagne in his hand, looking much more as if he belongs here than Patrick. He's wearing light-blue jeans and a shirt to match which really accentuates the blue of his eyes. He shoves his messy blond hair out of his eyes and strides over to give me a hug. I can smell the champagne on his breath and can tell the glass in his hand isn't the first. 'You look gorgeous,' he says to me, then goes to hug Sally. 'You too.'

Sally smiles and tidies her already-tidy hair. 'I wasn't sure what to wear, me not being used to boats. So I put on sensible shoes and jeans.'

I notice both men eyeing her top, which is red, low cut, and not sensible at all. Particularly because we're still in February – sunshine or no sunshine. Then I smile to myself. I'm thinking just like my mother.

Patrick says, 'You look perfect...' He turns to me. '...and Will's right, Kerensa. You do look gorgeous. The top matches your eyes.'

Hmm. That kind of talk won't go down well with Sally. I glance at her but she's still looking round the boat. And I don't feel particularly gorgeous in my jeans and thin green jumper, but the jumper's new and it hugs my figure. I say thanks for the compliment, but notice how Patrick's eyes are lingering over my breasts. I fold my arms and as I walk towards the door at the front I say, 'Let's have the grand tour then. I'm sure you're itching to show us round, Patrick.' ...*You big lecherous show-off.*

The inside of the boat is even more of an eye-opener. More leather seating but more sumptuous than on deck, a huge TV, big kitchen area and two separate bedrooms – one with en suite and a separate bathroom. If I didn't know I was on the water, I would think I was in a luxury apartment. Sally is gabbling about how wonderful it all is and how amazed she is, but I just keep a neutral expression. Patrick's pompous enough without more praise.

'What do you think of my little boat, Kerensa?' Patrick asks as he pulls out a chair put at the table for me.

'It's very nice. Must have cost the earth,' I say stiffly.

Everyone sits down and Patrick takes the lids off the silver platters. There's a selection of cold meats, lobster, seafood, salad, new potatoes and bread rolls. No expense spared on the food either. We help ourselves, commenting on how good the food looks, but Patrick seems lost in thought. He pours the champagne and then sits opposite me, rests his elbows on the table and his chin on his interlinked fingers. He gives me a long stare, his expression unreadable, then he says, 'You're right, Kerensa. It cost quite a bit, even though it's second-hand. It would have been a good few million if it was new. But I worked hard for my money. Gave up so much – made huge sacrifices.'

To my surprise, I see his eyes are moist and he wipes them on the back of his hand. I swallow a mouthful of lobster and say, 'Hey, I wasn't criticising. Didn't mean to upset you.'

He flaps my comments away and butters a bread roll. 'You didn't. But I can see you think this place is a bit...' He looks up to the left, taps the bread roll on his plate. '...let's say, over the top?' He doesn't wait for my response. Which is good because I'm stuck for words. 'The thing is, I'm from a humble background. My family come from the countryside not far from Dublin. My grandfather worked on the roads, cut peat too. Anything to put food on the table. My dad managed to get a trade boatbuilding. Passed some of it on to me – certainly a love of boats. I was the lucky one. Went to uni, got a degree in business and the rest is history.'

Sally puts her hand on his arm. 'I'm sure you deserve every penny, Patrick. You worked your way up, worked hard. So why not buy something like this if you want to?' She smiles at him and gives me a reproachful glance.

How did I get to be the bad guy here? I look at Will, but he's busy stuffing his face and guzzling the champagne. He'll be half-cut if he doesn't watch out. I take a breath and decide to clear the air. Perhaps I have been too hard on him. 'All I said was the boat must have cost the earth. I'm not begrudging you it, Patrick. It's truly nice to hear about your success story.' He gives me a watery smile. 'What does your mum do? And your sister. Is she still in the "old country",' I say in a rubbish Irish accent.

'No sister. I have a brother Connor. Good traditional Irish

names.' He laughs. 'He's a teacher in Dublin. A few years my senior. Lovely man.'

That's odd. I could have sworn he said a sister when he came round to mine that time with Will. I say as much to Patrick, but he says I must be mistaken. I'm almost sure I'm not. For some reason I think he's lying. Or perhaps hiding something? He's not giving me eye contact, he's touching his nose and shifting about in his seat. But why lie? Then a thought suddenly occurs. 'I wonder if you know my late husband's family on his mother's side? They lived not far from Dublin, and Leo's uncle was something to do with boats. Leo loved them too, though we never had the money to get one. Certainly not one like this...' My words run out because it sounds like I'm criticising again, and because Leo did have the money in the end, didn't he? He'd managed to amass a fortune behind my back.

Patrick laughs. 'I swear you Brits think we all live in little villages and know everyone else. Dublin's a big place.'

Patronising as well as pompous? Nice.

Sally shrieks as Patrick cracks a lobster claw and catapults a bit of shell into a corner. I realise she's had two big glasses of champagne already. Dear God. What with her and Will, I'll have my work cut out. 'Not at all, Patrick. It's just with the boat connection thing.'

'No. I don't know anyone with the surname Pethick.'

'Now who's being dim?' I smile to show I'm joking. 'Pethick is Leo's dad's surname. He's Cornish. His mum was over here from Ireland visiting friends when she met him. It was the holiday romance that lasted. His mum's surname was...' I struggle to remember. 'Lynch! Got it in the end.'

Patrick takes a sip of champagne and shakes his head. 'There's lots of Lynches in Ireland. Can't say I remember a Janice Lynch. But then she'll be a good few years older than me. Maybe my dad would remember her, or more probably Leo's uncle. I'll ask next time we speak.'

'How do you know her name's Janice?'

Patrick frowns. 'You must have told me last time we met.'

The feeling that he's lying or maybe hiding something is back. Big time. There's no way I talked about Leo's parents, let alone told him my mother-in-law's name. 'I didn't.'

The shuffling about in his seat is back too, the looking everywhere apart from me. He nudges Will who seems to have caught the shifty look from him. 'Hey, Will, did you tell me what Leo's mother was called?'

Will's face has a pink tinge. He spreads his hands and shrugs. 'Must have if Kerensa didn't. I probably mentioned her in relation to Leo's funeral.' He takes a forkful of food and says casually out of the corner of his mouth, 'It's not important anyway, is it?'

'No. Course not,' I say, and attend to my food.

The conversation is quickly turned by Sally to sailing. It then branches out into fishing and children, the weather, and I nod and smile, comment where appropriate. But there's something odd about Patrick. He's definitely hiding something. But what? Did he know Leo? Is that why he knew his mother's name? And if he did know Leo before, why is it a secret? Will could have mentioned Janice when he told Patrick about the funeral, like he said. But judging by Will's guilty reaction, I bet he knows the answer to those questions.

13

Two hours later we're moored up along the Fal and attempting to fish. Or rather Sally and Patrick are. Will and I are sitting with our feet up on deck enjoying some unseasonably warm sunshine. Patrick had been a bit grumpy when I said I'd no wish to thread a few ragworms onto a hook, just in order to catch some poor unsuspecting creature that we were unlikely to eat. But Sally had gushed about how she'd not been fishing since she was six, and while he was helping her with her fishing line, she kept leaning against Patrick or touching his hand whenever she could. I'm not sure Patrick's interested though. He seems to look at me quite often, particularly when he thinks I'm occupied. It's a bit creepy.

Will's nursing yet another glass of champagne – I've lost count of how many he's had. He seems quiet and a bit sad today, I think. It's as though he's trying to drown his sorrows, and I'd like to know what's upsetting him – throw him a lifeline. We've been talking about nothing much apart from the boat, the weather, and how nice it is to be out in the fresh air on the water. Now and again our hands have touched, or he's brushed my arm with his. I think it's deliberate on his part and it's sweet. It's obvious he's trying to show me he likes me, but in an understated gauche way. A bit like being back in school. Mind you, often when boys liked me then, they would push me or twang my bra strap. I hope Will doesn't go that far.

Why is it sweet anyway? I'm not supposed to be encouraging him. I decided it wouldn't work as he was Leo's friend and seven months is too soon anyway. Isn't it? I smile as Will's hand brushes mine again as he raises his glass to drink and he catches me. 'Something amusing, young lady?' he asks, and gives me a long lingering look.

The booze has obviously made him more daring, because there's no mistaking the signals in his eyes. And what do I do with that? Nothing. You do nothing, Kerensa. 'Amusing? Not really. I'm just relaxing, taking everything in.' I raise my glass of orange juice and take a sip.

'Me too,' he says with a slow smile, as he tucks a strand of my hair behind my ear the wind has blown across my eyes.

Just then Patrick yells over his shoulder from the end of the boat, 'Hey, you two, I think I got one!' He turns in his seat and the big smile he's wearing slips off into the water when he sees Will rearranging my hair.

Sally shrieks, 'I got one too!' So Patrick turns back to the task in hand. 'Rens,' she yells. 'Come and see, it's a whopper!'

I don't want to go and see, because the look in Patrick's eyes chilled me through. When I thought he looked jealous the other day when Will hugged me, I was right. There's no doubt about it. He just glared at Will as if he wanted to murder him. But why? Patrick's only known me five minutes. I hope it isn't love at first sight because there's no way I want a creepy stalker-guy as a friend. Sally yells again, so I go over and see they've caught two large fish and they're flopping about in a net on deck. 'What kind are they?' I ask Patrick.

'Pollocks.'

'No need to be rude, I'm just asking,' I quip, which sets Sally off laughing hysterically. She must have had a fair bit to drink, because it wasn't that funny. It warranted a chuckle at least though, didn't it? Patrick's face remains stony. No trace of a smile even. He unhooks one fish, stills it under his deck shoe and takes a cosh out of the fishing basket.

Sally stops laughing. 'Oh. I thought you said we'd chuck them back in.'

'They're big enough to make a meal,' he snarls and brings the cosh down twice on the fish's head.

Sally covers her mouth but a moan escapes and she hurries past me and below deck. She looked a bit nauseous. I turn away from the bloodied fish too. I'm convinced Patrick killed it because he was angry with Will. Will comes up behind and pokes the fish with the toe of his trainer. 'Pollock?'

Patrick nods and grabs the fish by the tail. 'Yeah. Want to gut it? Or shall I?' He shakes it in Will's face, dislodging one of the fish's eyes as he does.

Will shakes his head. 'No, you're okay. Knock yourself out.'

Patrick glares at him, kills the other fish, and stomps off below deck.

'What's his problem?' I ask quietly. Will shrugs and avoids my eyes, so I walk over to the other side of the boat, rest my arms on the rail and look across the river.

He joins me and points downriver to a huge house in the distance at the top of a steep hill which runs down to the water's edge. 'Is that Trelissick House up there? I recognise it.'

I think about the geography of the area and decide he's right. 'Yeah. I haven't seen it from the water before. I've visited a few times over the years though.' *Nice way to change the subject, Will.* We watch the water for a few minutes and a group of seagulls lands on a boat nearby. Start a squabble. I wonder if I should do the same with Will. Or at least raise the questions about Patrick

I've been dying to ask for the past few hours. I take a deep breath and say, 'Did Patrick know Leo?'

It's as if my words stab Will and he visibly flinches. His head whips round, shock evident in his eyes. 'Eh? Why do you ask that?'

'Well, did he?'

'No. Not as far as I know anyway.' Will swallows and his colour comes up. 'If he did he would have said, I'm sure.' He looks back to the water and angles himself away from me slightly.

'Hmm. It's just that I feel he's hiding something. He definitely said he had a sister the night I first met him, and he knew Janice's name.'

Will looks back at me. 'So, because of that, you reckon he knew Leo? That makes no sense.' Will shakes his head, seems more sure of himself now. 'You must have been mistaken about the sister. And I must have mentioned Janice at some point. Probably when talking about the funeral. I *have* already said this.'

I see his point, but I won't just let it go. 'I get the feeling he's not quite what he says he is – or at least he's hiding somehow. Lying.'

Will sighs. 'Lying about what?'

'I don't know.'

'Right.'

'I mean, why is he so interested in befriending me? Putting on a driver to pick us up, for goodness sake, this boat – the lunch?'

'As he said before, he knows nobody here. I thought it might be nice to introduce him to you and most people would be thrilled by being invited here.' Will shoves his hand through his hair, gazes away into the distance.

'Yeah, well, I'm not most people. I'm naturally suspicious of extravagance and too-smiley people. Ever since Leo died, I've had to harden my heart. Become tougher. Being soft got me nowhere, did it?' I don't like the way I've changed, but it's necessary for self-preservation.

'I don't know. You seem lovely to me.'

It's my turn to blush. He's giving me that look again. 'Yeah, well, your best buddy doesn't like us being close. You must have seen his expression when you touched my hair back then.'

Will purses his lips, shrugs. 'I didn't notice.'

'And I'm the Queen of Sheba.'

'Pleased to meet you, your majesty.' Will tries a smile, but it freezes when he sees my stony response.

'He's obviously interested in being more than just friends. Poor Sally's barking up the wrong tree there.'

'I'm not sure, Kerensa. Patrick's a generally friendly and outgoing chap. You might have misread the signals.'

Before I can talk myself out of it, I say, 'I haven't misread yours though, have I?'

The intense look is back, and he slides his hand along the rail, strokes my fingers. 'No. And how do you feel about that?'

How do I feel? Pleased, I think. Nervous. Unsure. Excited. Guilty. 'It's tricky, Will. It's not long since I lost Leo, so I'm worried that I'm attracted to you because I need to be comforted. Maybe subconsciously, I'm hitting out at Leo for doing what he did to me. My feelings are all over the place... but I think I might feel, let's say, a connection?'

He gives me a huge smile. 'I understand, it's complicated. That time when I stupidly nearly kissed you, you said you just wanted to be friends. Might I hope for more, eventually?'

I heave a deep sigh. 'I think so. But can we take it very slowly? I don't want it to be common knowledge either.' I incline my head towards the sound of Patrick's hearty laughter coming from below deck and roll my eyes.

Will raises my hand to his lips and drops a quick kiss onto my knuckles. 'That's a very good idea. If Patrick knows, I'll never hear the end of it.'

'Especially if he's got ideas in that direction too.'

'Who's got ideas in what direction?' Patrick's head pops up at the top of the steps.

I say, 'Just someone in the shop who wanted to commission a wall hanging the other day. I was telling Will about his ideas.'

'Nice. Anyway, Sally's made coffee and I have cake! Come and have some.' Patrick's happy-go-lucky Irish charm is back. It's as if he's two different people at times.

As we walk toward the steps, Will says in my ear, 'Quick thinking, Kerensa. I didn't realise you were such a good liar.'

Neither did I. Yet another change in me since Leo died that I'm not sure I like.

A few hours later and I'm trying to get Sally to agree to leave. Each time I suggest we should make a move, she tells me, in a minute, or just let's finish this game of cards. Thankfully, Patrick has behaved himself and has been politeness personified. His eyes haven't wandered below my face either and he's been good company. Will and I have shared a few meaningful glances when we've been sure the others weren't looking, and thoughts of what it would be like to kiss him have surfaced in my mind more than once this afternoon. Time to go now though, and I hate to spoil Sally's fun, but it's getting on for six.

'Sally, we need to get going. I have lots to do in the shop tomorrow and I'm sure Will and Patrick have busy days ahead too.'

'But we haven't finished this game of cards. Just a bit longer?' Sally sounds like a petulant child beseeching a parent, and I have to hide a smile.

Patrick says, 'I don't have a lot planned for tomorrow actually. I don't mind how long you stay.'

Sally looks hopeful, until Will says, 'I'm afraid Kerensa's right. Time to make a move. I'm operating at noon, and I have lots of notes to read and so forth beforehand. Might have overdone the fizz too.' He pretends to be drunk, slurring the last few words and does a fake hiccup.

Sally concedes defeat and stands up.

Patrick looks thoughtful and says, 'If you'd like to stay longer, I could have Ken come back for you later, after he's dropped Will and Kerensa home?'

'Oh that would be nice,' Sally says, and looks at me, a question in her eyes. Mine give a non-committal answer, though I think she should leave with us. The children are with her mum after all. It's as if she's read my mind. 'Mind you, I suppose I should get back for the kids. Mum's babysitting.'

Patrick nods. 'I understand. Perhaps another time.'

'That would be lovely!' Sally says in a breathy voice. 'I have so loved it here today! Such a treat from the boring stuff I usually do.'

Dear God. Patrick's head is big enough.

'It was my pleasure. I hope you've all enjoyed yourselves.' Patrick stands up and casually slides his arm across Sally's shoulder. She turns pink and gives me a knowing look.

'I have, thanks, Patrick,' I say, shrugging into my coat. 'It's been fab.' I hope I sound convincing.

'As always, Pat, my friend,' Will says, taking my elbow and escorting me to the steps.

Ken's summoned and a few minutes after, he arrives along the quayside. Just before we get into the car, Sally says, 'Hey, Pat. Can I have your number so we can arrange that get together?'

Patrick shoots her the Hollywood smile. 'Sure you can, honey.' He takes her phone and types his number into it while she gazes at him, shifts from one foot to the other, looking like she's a fangirl at a celebrity signing.

After we drop Will, Sally says, 'Thank God he's gone.' Then she drops her voice to make sure Ken can't hear. 'I've been bursting to talk to you about Patrick! He's so into me – did you hear him ask me to stay on after you'd gone. *Alone*, mind you?'

Is she mental? 'Er... yes, I was there. Remember?'

'What I wouldn't have given to have stayed. God, he's so perfect, don't you think?'

'He's okay.'

She looks at me as if I'm nuts. 'That's it? Okay? What do you want in a man?'

I don't answer and scroll through my phone, pretending to check emails. Will is what I want in a man, but I can't say that, can I?

'Sorry, love.' Sally pats my arm. 'I wasn't thinking. I feel so bad 'cos it's not that long since your Leo died. Me and my big mouth.'

I tell her not to worry and she needn't be sorry. Truth is, it's me who feels bad. Missing Leo hasn't even crossed my mind. Maybe that's a good thing. I think about it as we near home and decide it is a good thing. No use in living in the past. Will might be my future. Let's just wait and see.

14

Three days without hearing a peep out of Patrick is unprecedented. Will guesses he's been "punished" for his little show of affection to Kerensa on Sunday. The drink had made him reckless. The wind had flicked a strand of hair across Kerensa's eyes, and thoughtlessly, he'd tucked it behind her ear, just as Patrick turned from wrestling with his fish and saw him.

Will knew immediately he was in the shit. But it had felt like the natural thing to do. Her hair was silky, soft, and he couldn't help himself. He curses Patrick. God knows what he'll do when he finds out he and Kerensa have agreed to move their relationship on. If everything works out and they get together properly, Will knows they will have to move far away. Away from Cornwall, even from the UK, if they are to have any peace. And that will *not* be an easy task.

Negativity settles heavy across his shoulders like a leaden cape. So Will decides to have another cup of tea and listen to some uplifting music before he sets out to the surgery. Music normally does the trick, and he selects some Vivaldi. As the first notes swirl around his living room, the phone rings. Great. He turns the music down and pulls his mobile out of his pocket.

Patrick's normally soft Irish brogue has hard edges. 'We need to talk.'

Will clears his throat. 'Morning to you too, Patrick. Thought you'd died.'

'You'd love that, wouldn't you? Leave the way clear for you to get your paws on Kerensa.'

'Oh for God's sake. You're delusional.' Will hopes the guilt he feels isn't apparent in his voice.

'I don't think so. I saw the way you were stroking her hair on the boat the other day. The look on your face told me everything I needed to know.'

'Don't be ridiculous. I can't even remember doing it… but if I did, I was just moving it out of her eyes. Yes… the wind blew it.'

Patrick's humourless bark down the line sets Will's teeth on edge. 'Kerensa couldn't do that for herself? You're such a liar, William.'

'No. You're the master at that, Patrick.'

'Only because I've had to be.'

Will sighs. 'Whatever. Now is there a reason for this call or–?'

'Yes. Number one, you're going to back right away from Kerensa. If I so much as see you even give her a friendly hug, I'll be on you so fast you won't know what hit you. And two, I'm going to change my tactics. She's clearly not impressed with the way I'm trying to get her onside, so I'm going to have to be more like Leo.'

Will sits on the edge of the sofa and sighs. Is there no end to this man's stupidity? 'What exactly do you mean? Leo isn't her most favourite person anymore, is he?'

'What exactly do *you* mean, William? He was her fucking husband and she loved him. They were happy!'

'Yes, until Leo swindled his boss, fucked off without a word and then killed himself!' Will knows fighting fire with fire's not a good idea with Patrick, but he's just so angry.

'You think you know Kerensa, but you don't. She loved Leo, still does. So if I make myself more like him, she'll come round. She'll realise I'm the one to make her smile again. Make her want to love again. She doesn't want you, Will. You have no chance there.'

Will squeezes the phone hard, wishing it were Patrick's neck. 'I told you, I have no designs on her.'

'Yeah, well, you'd better make sure you haven't, or I'll tell Kerensa what a cold calculating monster you are. I'll tell her you manipulated Leo, forced him to do things he'd never dream of. Pushed him into an early grave. Then I'll tell her you did the same to me. I'll tell her you tried to keep me away from her. I'll tell her you schemed to put yourself in the forerunning instead of me. I'll make all sorts of shit up, Will. You have no idea what I'm prepared to do. Or what I'm capable of. You will lose her forever, *and* you could end up in jail. Because I'll say you're the one who pulled the strings behind the scenes with scamming Donaldson. Used poor Leo as a puppet and–'

'Shut up!' Will's heart is thudding in his chest. It's a good job Patrick isn't here because he'd punch him in the face. Dammed little weasel. 'That's all lies, and you know it. You'd never get away with it!' Even as he says it, Will can't be certain that he wouldn't. Patrick is clever, and after all, Will is involved up to his neck in it, isn't he? Patrick's twisted everything, but there's no getting away from his own culpability in the whole sordid nightmare.

'Want to try me?'

Will says nothing.

'Didn't think so,' Patrick says, a smug tone in his voice. 'Now this is what's going to happen. You're going to arrange a dinner one week, a theatre trip the next, and so on. We'll invite Sally too, so Kerensa won't feel outnumbered, and I'll pretend to be interested in Sally, so Kerensa won't be scared off. We will take it very slowly. I'll be a complete gentleman, but I'll become more like Leo as time goes on. She'll be confused, puzzled at first. But she'll come round. She'll realise how much she's missed Leo, and because I'm like him, she'll grow to love me. I won't be Leo, but I'll be second best. Any romantic ideas about you she might have, will be snuffed out like a candle in the wind.'

Will snorts. 'I've never heard anything so ridiculous in all my life. She won't fall for a plan like that. It's more likely to freak her out – switch her off.'

'Just wait and see, William. You'll see I'm right. Now, run along and organise something for next week. Ring me when it's done.'

The line goes dead and Will stares at the phone in his hand. What a bastard Patrick is. And poor Sally. It's abhorrent the way Patrick plans to mess with her head, her heart. Will won't allow it. He won't go through with this madness. Then he thinks about everything that's happened since Leo got back in touch with him that fateful day. Thinks about what Will's done in the name of friendship. How could he have let Patrick trick him like that? Because he trusted him. Because he'd trusted Leo too. More fool him.

15

A spring barbecue they said. It will be fun they said. Fun for them, not so great for me having to slave away organising it, making lists of things that people can't eat. There's three gluten free people and two vegans. Then I had to buy new garden furniture because the old deckchairs I thought were okay have somehow rotted away in the shed. Maybe it's April 1st today, not the 10th, after all? Sally said she'd help, but everything has kicked off again with the hateful brother-in-law, soon to be an ex-brother-in-law. Marcus has, in his infinite wisdom, arrived back on the scene from working away, and thrown everyone's emotions into a cement mixer. He's lying to the children and promising them the world on a string. Sally's sister Rachel knows he won't follow through with these promises, but if she says anything, she's the bad guy.

I put a row of chicken breasts on the baking tray and brush them with marinade. A quick blast in the oven will make sure they're cooked through when they go on the barbecue. I bet poor Rachel has more to worry about than uncooked chicken. Thank God my life is so calm now compared to hers. I have a new relationship. Well, of sorts. Will is following "taking things very slowly" to the absolute letter. In fact, if it was any slower it would grind to a halt. We have kissed once or twice, but no more. I've made it clear more was on offer, but so far, he's not taken me up on it. Maybe he's gone off me in that way. It's nice though, having him around. We talk endlessly about everything under the sun. Leo never talked much. It's lovely to have someone to share things with.

And Patrick is a changed man. He's not showy-offy anymore and seems really nice and considerate. Sally is over the moon that he's showing an interest in her, but so far their relationship has been platonic too. They haven't been out alone together even once. It's always the four of us. Apart from when Will sneaks over now and then in the evening on his own to see me. More than once, Sally has told me she's given Patrick strong hints that she wants more, but he's oblivious. He's given her a couple of chaste kisses and that's it. Perhaps she'll have to spell it out in flashing neon lights.

I don't know what to make of it. Patrick seems to like her and no longer looks at me in a lecherous way. Maybe he wants to take it slow. Seems the "in thing" nowadays. I've not told her about Will and me. Not that there's much to tell. And because Will insists it has to be top secret, particularly from Patrick. If Sally knows, then so would he. She'd find it hard to keep a secret from him as he is very persuasive. This barbecue for example. He insisted we hold it and invite everyone we know. He's paying for the food and drink, but that's not the point. I'm not sure I want everyone over. It's the first "do" since Leo died, and I'm not used to being "the widow" yet. William convinced me it would be fun. So I went along with it.

I take out three lettuces and chop. Maybe I should have bought four, because there are around twenty people coming. Might be a few more depending on plus ones. Then I look at the mountain of dips, other salad ingredients, garlic bread, new potatoes, crisps, and of course chicken, sausages and beef burgers, and decide I'm worrying about nothing. I tend to err on the side of worrying. I think I get it from my mother. She always says it's not exactly worrying however. She says it's all about forward planning. If you fail to prepare, you prepare to fail. I decide she's right and count the red peppers waiting to be cut up.

As I slice, I think about Patrick and the change in him, because there is another thing about Patrick that's different too. I do wonder if it's my fanciful imagination, but recently his mannerisms are so like Leo's. I noticed it first on that disastrous evening he and Will popped over with the takeaway, but that was the only time. When he was chatting, he did the running his fingers quickly through his hair and then stroked his chin between forefinger and thumb a few times. Leo always did this when he was talking and thinking about what he was saying.

And lately he has other mannerisms of Leo's that take my breath away. One time at dinner, he tapped his fingernails on the side of his empty plate while waiting for the waitress to take it away. Another time, he stretched his arms above his head, clasped his fingers together and cracked his knuckles. The phrases he uses alongside mannerisms are so Leo too. Sally said something a bit risqué last week and he pinched the bridge of his nose and said, "Oh please. Do we have to sink to those levels?" There have been others too, and I asked Will if he'd noticed. Will dismissed it, saying lots of people crack their knuckles and say similar stuff. Perhaps he's right. Perhaps I'm just seeing things that aren't there.

An hour later and I'm ready. Good job because the first guests are arriving. Sally and Rachel plus all four of their children, my cousin Anna and her husband Ray, Mum and Dad, my brother Edward and his new boyfriend Mike, Leo's parents Janice and

Derek, and bringing up the rear, Lisa and Carl along with their teenage kids from the gift shop three doors down from mine. Everyone mucks in and soon the tables and chairs are set up on the beach, the barbecue is smoking hot and the drinks are flowing. There's wall-to-wall sunshine, a gentle breeze, the ocean's behaving itself, rolling politely in the distance over an obligingly soft and golden sand. Cornwall at its best. I must admit I'm beginning to enjoy this and concede it was one of Patrick's better ideas.

Thinking of which, he and Will arrive, lugging a huge crate of wine and beer between them. They are pulling and pushing, cursing and blaming each other for going the wrong way down the steps. I have to laugh, they remind me of a double act. I ask Ed to take over on the barbecue and go to help them. 'You'd have been better leaving that in the house. The white wine especially is no good on the beach – needs to be in the fridge. The beer too really,' I say, picking out a few bottles.

Will spreads his arms, glares at Patrick. 'What did I tell you? But no, you wouldn't listen as usual.'

'Away with your wittering, man. The wine and beer are cool enough, just out of my fridge at home and all.'

I shake my head. 'But it's hot on the beach, Patrick. Let's take the crate back. I'll help you.'

Will nods, but Patrick sighs, looks heavenward and puts his hands together in a praying motion. 'For the love of St Michael and Mother Mary, will you two stop worrying and relax?'

Will sighs, grabs a few bottles of beer and wine and hurries up the steps. I stare at Patrick opened-mouthed, a bottle of wine in each hand. Leo used to say that, do the same thing with his hands and look heavenward. It's so uncanny. Patrick's giving me an intense look. So I hold up the wine and say, 'Um... can you put the crate in the shade, Patrick. I'll pop these inside.'

He frowns. 'What's up? You look like you've seen a ghost.'

I don't answer, because I've noticed Janice, standing nearby, is wearing a similar expression to mine. I wave at her, as well as I can with a bottle of wine in my hand, and she comes over. 'Hi Janice, this is Patrick, a friend of Will's. And mine now, of course,' I add quickly. I say to Patrick, 'And this is Janice, Leo's mum.'

When I look up at Patrick, I nearly drop the wine because his face is a mask of sorrow. He holds his hand out to Janice. 'Pleased to meet you, Janice,' he says with a sniff and a tremor in his voice.

Janice's eyes fill too, and she shakes her head. 'Hello, Patrick. It's great to meet someone from home... and just then when you were messing about with Will, you sounded so like...' She drops Patrick's hand and composes herself. 'So like my boy.'

'I'm honoured. My heart goes out to you, Janice. I'm so sorry for your loss. I've heard so much about Leo, and you of course from Will. Is Derek here?' Patrick looks about, his hand shielding his eyes from the sun.

'He is. Come on, I'll introduce you.' Janice steps to one side and Patrick slips his arm around her as they walk down the beach.

I'm flabbergasted. What was all that about? Why did Patrick look so upset? And thank God Janice said what she said. I feel vindicated. I watch as Patrick shakes hands with Leo's dad and then all three fall into a lively conversation. I can't hear what they're talking about from this distance though. I'm torn between joining them and taking the wine to the fridge.

As I'm deliberating, Will calls me from the balcony. 'You bringing that wine up here, or what?'

In my kitchen, Will leans his hip against the worktop, raises a glass beaded with condensation and takes a long pull. Then he releases a slow breath. 'I needed that.' He puts the glass on the side and wipes his brow with the back of his hand.

'Been working hard?'

'You could say that. Patrick is always hard work. He's done my head in this morning. Should he bring this wine, or that? Will this lager be okay, or should he get more? Such a fusspot. Then he insists in lugging the whole lot down onto the beach.'

I pour myself a glass of red and down half of it immediately. Will raises his eyebrows and I say in answer, 'I needed that too, because fusspot or not, he's a reincarnated Leo.'

Will's expression is both distant and guarded. Then he tries a chuckle that sounds forced. 'Yeah. Because they look so similar, right?'

'As you know, they look nothing like each other, but lately he reminds me so much of Leo. His mannerisms... his way of speaking.' I walk over to Will and stand next to him, take another sip of wine. 'I did mention it to you, but you dismissed me, said lots of people have similar mannerisms.'

'That's because they do.' Will slips his arm about my shoulder and I like the weight of it. I feel secure. Safe. He smells delicious too, a mixture of salt air and spicy cologne.

It's easy to be distracted by his closeness but I want to have my say. I tell him about what Patrick said on the beach about St Michael and the praying thing. 'Janice was so shocked. That's how I know it's not just me.'

I feel Will's body stiffen. 'Janice and Derek are here?'

'Yeah. I thought it would be nice for them, and they get on well with my folks. Why?'

He relaxes against me. 'No reason. Just not seen them since the funeral and feel a bit guilty for not keeping in touch.'

'Right. But never mind that. What do you think about what I just said?'

'About Patrick?'

'No. About the Pope.'

Will laughs. 'I think it's understandable that you're a bit freaked. Janice too. But Leo used to say things like that because his mum is from Ireland. He'll have got it from her, and you might have noticed that Patrick is Irish too. I rest my case.'

I take another sip of wine and ponder a few moments. 'I see where you're coming from, but there's too many similarities lately. It's just weird.'

Will sighs. 'Okay. What exactly are you saying? That Patrick really is an incarnation of Leo. Because if you are, we need to book you in with my psychiatrist friend. He has reasonable rates.'

I elbow him and he pretends to double over in pain. 'No. I know it's impossible, but I think Patrick *must* have known Leo. He was visibly upset when I introduced him to Janice and said he was so sorry for her loss and stuff. It felt like he'd been an old friend of Leo's.'

'Kerensa, as I said, the two men never met.'

'As far as you know.'

'As far as I know. But why would Patrick keep it a secret?'

'I have no idea. Patrick is a complex character. He's made a change for the better these last few months, but I still don't trust him. There's something I can't put my finger on.'

Will shakes his head but says nothing. We sip our drinks in silence for a few moments and then Will takes my glass away and pulls me into his arms. 'Let's not think about Patrick anymore. Let's concentrate on us.'

Then Will kisses me. It's a deep, passionate kiss, far more intimate than any of our other few kisses, and I'm lost in the moment. I feel his hands travel down to cup my bottom and one of his hands slides back up to my breast. Then the front door bangs and we spring apart.

'There you are!' Sally says, hurrying in with a tray of empty glasses. 'Patrick sent me to find you. Your guests are clamouring for more beef burgers. Are they in the fridge?'

Heat in my cheeks, I check my clothes before grabbing the tray from her. 'Yeah, on the top shelf, I think.'

Will mumbles something about going to the loo and hurries out.

As I'm pulling the tray of burgers from the fridge, Sally comes up behind me and whispers in my ear, 'I get the feeling I was interrupting something there, matey.'

I play dumb. 'What do you mean?'

'You and Golden Boy.'

Sally always calls Will that because of his looks and hair colour. He'll catch her one day. 'Don't be daft. We were just chatting.' I turn and hand her the burgers without meeting her eye.

'Your nose is growing.' Sally puts her face close to mine and pulls a silly expression. 'I saw you all over each other. When I came in just now, I wedged the door open so it wouldn't bang on me as I carried the glasses through. I came down the corridor and saw you. Then I tiptoed back for the glasses and let the door slam to give you time to sort yourselves out.'

Oh shit. 'Great. You got me.' I take Sally's grinning face between the palms of my hands and look into her eyes. 'But you can't tell anyone. Nobody. Not even your sister, and especially not Patrick, okay?'

Her eyebrows arch up to her chocolate curls. 'But why not? I think it's lovely. He's a great bloke and–'

'Promise me, Sal. I need your word.'

She puts the burgers down and gives me a quick hug. 'Of course, if that's what you want. But I don't understand.'

'It's complicated. Some might think it's too soon after Leo. I do, to be honest, but I can't deny there's a connection. His mum and dad will be really hurt for a start. It's only been nine months. Besides, I don't want to have to justify myself every few minutes. And me and Will are very early days. It might not go anywhere, so–'

'Okay, Okay. I get what you're saying. Don't worry about it. Your secret's safe with me.' She picks up the burgers again and makes her way to the door. Over her shoulder, she says, 'I need a blow-by-blow account of every single thing that happens, yeah?'

Will comes in right as she says this. She giggles, winks and leaves. He raises a questioning eyebrow at me, but I just shrug. Then we load ourselves up with more food and go down to the beach.

16

Back on the beach, Patrick is spending loads of time with Janice and Derek. Sally keeps hovering around him, but he swats her away from time to time like she's an annoying fly. When will she wake up and smell the indifference? Will keeps giving me meaningful looks whenever I catch his eye, so I try not to. I wonder what would have happened if Sally hadn't barged in and interrupted. Who am I kidding? I know what would have happened. I can't remember Will being so passionate before. It's as if he's been holding back until today. And where does that leave us now?

I'm interrupted in my ponderings by my brother Edward, bounding up the beach like an over-excited puppy, closely followed by new boyfriend Mike. Today's the first time I've met Mike, and he seems so much more laid back than Jason, Ed's previous boyfriend. He and Ed were together three years, but Jason's unfounded jealousy and clingy nature drove Ed to end it a few months ago. Mike is five years older than Ed and a lecturer at Truro college. He looks the part; tall, with messy longish auburn hair, keen dark intelligent eyes which frequently peer at the world over the top of round metal-rimmed specs. Ed picks me up and spins me round like he always does, for the second time today, and I shriek when he pretends to stumble.

'How's my big sis?' he asks, setting me back on the sand.

'I'd be better if you stopped doing that every time we're together.'

Mike laughs and shoves his glasses up the bridge of his nose. 'He's very boisterous around you, isn't he, Kerensa?'

Ed shoves his floppy dark hair from his eyes. 'That's 'cos I used to do that to her when we were kids. Tormented the hell out of you, didn't I?' He grins and ruffles my hair.

I slap his hand away. 'Yes. And you know I hate you doing that too.'

Mike smiles. 'It's great to see how close you both are. Your brother loves you very much, don't you, Ed?'

Ed nods. 'I do. But I think you're feeling a bit left out, aren't you?' Mike frowns at this, then lets out a yell as Ed squats, flings his arms around him and hoists him into the air.

'Put me down, you fool. People are looking!' Mike says, laughing.

'This looks like fun,' Patrick's voice says in my left ear, making me jump.

I look round. 'Bloody hell, Patrick. What with you and our Ed, I'll be a nervous wreck.'

Patrick laughs and sticks his hand out to Mike. 'I'm Patrick, Kerensa's friend. It's Mike, isn't it? I met Ed earlier when you were paddling, I think.'

Mike grins and shakes his hand. 'Yes. I think that was a bit ambitious, the sea's still too cold.'

'Not at all. It's grand to see people making the best of this weather.' He leans forward and winks at the two men. 'And Mike's a better sport than that old misery guts Jason ever was.'

I'm gobsmacked. How the bloody hell...? Ed frowns and voices my thoughts. 'He is. But how did you know about Jason?'

Patrick looks momentarily flustered. Then he runs his fingers through his hair and strokes his chin. Leo again. 'Oh, Will told me. Hope I didn't speak out of turn.'

Ed smiles. 'No, of course not. Yes, Mike's very different to Jason. He's good for me.' He gives Mike a peck on the lips and Patrick slaps them both on the back before sauntering off towards the sea.

'He's quite a character, isn't he?' Ed says.

'Yes. He's that all right,' I say, unable to shake of the feeling of disquiet settling in my gut. I must remember to ask Will about Jason to see if Patrick's story checks out.

We three chat for a bit longer and then the two men go off to get more food. From a distance, I watch Patrick and Will chatting as they walk along the shoreline, and then Sally joins them with Rachel and the kids. If Patrick doesn't change his attitude towards Sally, I might have to have a word with him. I couldn't bear it if she was hurt.

Mum comes over and puts her arm around me, distracting me from my ponderings. 'Penny for them?' she says, and drops a kiss on my cheek.

'Nothing much. Just thinking what a lovely get together it is. I hadn't wanted to, you know, with me being on my own now?' She nods and squeezes my shoulder. 'Leo and I always did things like this together. But I'm so glad I allowed Patrick to persuade me.'

Her face lights up. 'What a lovely man he is! So funny and warm.' Mum's face turns a bit pink. 'And handsome too, but don't tell your dad.'

I laugh. 'He is nice, I guess. He's changed over the last few months. He was very arrogant and showed off – extravagant gestures and stuff. But he's mellowed, seems kind and more normal...' My voice tails off. I'm unsure whether I should share more about how much he's like Leo. Though now Janice has corroborated what I feel, maybe I should.

'What aren't you saying?' Mum knows me inside out. Always has. Her intuition is like a heat-seeking missile. There's no hiding place. Even in the darkest recesses of my mind.

'You might think I'm crazy, but Janice has noticed too.'

'Noticed what, woman? Spit it out.'

'He has so many mannerisms, gestures and sayings of Leo's. It's uncanny.'

Mum furrows her brow and leads me over to a deckchair. We sit down and she says, 'What exactly do you mean?'

I tell her and finish. 'I don't know what to make of it.'

With the sun on our faces, we watch the kids playing ball and the adults talking, laughing, paddling. It's like watching an idyllic scene from a childhood memory. Then Mum says, 'Hmm. I can't say I've noticed. But might it be because Leo's mum is Irish like Patrick, and he picked up sayings from her?'

'That's exactly what Will said.'

'There you are then.' Mum twists in her seat and looks at me.

'But that doesn't account for the mannerisms and gestures, does it?'

'People have similar gestures, after all, love. There's only so many.' She stares at the sea for a bit. 'And anyway, what's your explanation for it then?'

I toss everything in my head again and acknowledge the fact that Patrick has loads of money, which has been bugging me too. There could be an explanation for that beyond the fact that he's a good businessman. I look at Mum and decide the idea I've had for a while needs a second opinion, so I go for it. 'God knows, Mum. This is where I draw a blank... but I did wonder if Patrick knew Leo before. Perhaps they spent time together and he picked up some of Leo's ways. Was Patrick involved with swindling Donaldson – were he and Leo in it together? Has Patrick got access to Leo's offshore account that nobody else seems to have? Is that how he's managed to afford his boat?'

Mum's puzzlement turns to shock. 'Bloody hell, Enza! Really? I can't see him being involved in all that. He seems such a nice man.'

'So did Leo.'

Mum folds her arms and sighs. 'But what would be the point of him making a friend of you? You'd think he'd stay far away.'

'Maybe he feels guilty... perhaps because he's alive and Leo...' As I say this, another thought slams into my mind like a sledgehammer. My voice is a whisper. 'Oh God, Mum. Maybe he had something to do with Leo's death.'

'Kerensa!' Mum hisses, her eyes flashing. 'I think you're going too far now. What evidence do you have for saying something like that?'

None. I have none, and I need to shut up about all this before my friends and family think I've lost it. 'Sorry, Mum. I think I just let my imagination run away with me sometimes, that's all.' I pat her hand and give her what I hope is an apologetic smile.

Her expression softens. 'It's only natural, in a way. You're missing Leo, so see him in Patrick, I suppose.' I think that's very unlikely, but keep it buttoned. 'And who knows? One day you and Patrick might hit it off. You could do so much worse.'

I think I could do so much better too, as I watch a shirtless Will in "goal" dive after a ball. He lands on the beach in a flurry of sand, clutching it to his chest, a look of triumph on his face. 'I don't think that will be happening, Mum. Patrick's not my type.'

By early evening, people start to drift off. It's been a wonderful afternoon. For the last hour or so I'd put all my misgivings about Patrick to the back of my head and relaxed, had fun for once. Will and I kept our distance as per, but we played a game of rounders with the youngsters. Sally, having had a few glasses of wine, plonked herself down on Patrick's knee as he sat on a deck chair. The whole thing collapsed, leaving them red-faced and the rest of us in fits of laughter. Sally thought it was hilarious, so did Patrick, apparently, but I noticed he avoided her more than usual afterwards.

As people leave the beach, they come along to say goodbye and to thank me for such a wonderful afternoon. Rachel tells me she's had the best day for a long time. 'It's been ages since I've really been able to let my hair down and bugger what people think. When I was with Marcus he'd always made me feel like I was doing something wrong if I had a laugh.'

'Why? What's wrong with having a laugh?' I ask.

'Nothing. But he was always embarrassed by my extrovert nature. I laughed too loud, or said silly things, according to him. He used to say people were looking at me.'

The sparkle in her eyes is dulled by a memory only she can see. I say, 'Sounds like a right piece of work if you ask me. There's nothing wrong with having fun and enjoying yourself. You're a lovely lady and worth ten of him. You should be very proud of how you've turned your life around.'

She gives me a quick hug and we agree to stay in touch.

Janice and Derek are among the last to leave. They come along and give me a big hug. 'We've had the best time, love,' Janice says. 'Thanks so much for inviting us.'

Derek nods. 'It was almost like old times... apart from one much-missed person.' He clears his throat and a lump of emotion forms in mine as I see his eyes fill.

Janice says, 'Come on, love. Don't upset yourself. You'll upset Kerensa too.'

'Don't worry. It's true. It has been very odd without Leo,' I say with a sigh.

We stand in silence and it all feels a bit awkward. Then

Derek brightens and says, 'That boy Patrick is grand though, isn't he?'

'He sure is!' Janice says, beaming. 'We talked about home a lot. He comes from quite close to where my family are from. And my goodness does he remind me of our Leo. He looks nothing like him of course, but the way he talks and acts sometimes it's just like my boy...'

Derek flaps his hand at his wife. 'That's an exaggeration, Jan. A bit similar maybe. Anyway, he's coming down to St Ives soon for a visit. We're going fishing.' He beams at me and then pecks me on the cheek. 'Must be off, got to get back to feed Bonny.'

Janice laughs. 'That cat will be the size of a house if you don't watch it, Derek Pethick.' She gives me another hug. 'We'll catch up again soon, Kerensa. And don't forget, you're welcome anytime.'

I watch them disappear around the side of the house and my heart lurches. I didn't realise how much I missed seeing them until now. We used to have some fun times, Leo and I, with them down in their lovely little cottage in St Ives. Janice is a phenomenal cook and we'd often go for Sunday lunch. We'd eat mountains of food and then walk it off along the harbour-side and beaches. Normally we'd end up in one of the pubs on the way back too. And what the hell is Patrick up to, going down to visit? I'm not sure I like the way he's insinuating himself into my life. He was a complete stranger to me a few months ago, but now everyone knows good old Patrick. My family, Leo's family, my friends. What a lovely man he is, how generous... how kind. Maybe he is. Maybe it's just me who's too cynical.

Will, Patrick and Sally are the only ones left now, and they wave at me as they head up the beach. I wave back briefly and turn for the house. There's a grumpy mood pushing the mellow feeling I had to the edges of my psyche. It's grey and heavy and it's intent on destruction. I tell myself to let it go. Chill out and stop overthinking the Patrick situation.

The Patrick situation? Hell, he's a "situation" now? It's ridiculous. He's taking too much of my headspace and it has to stop. Earlier I'd thought how much nicer he was overall lately, and he is. So I have to hang onto that. Perhaps I'm just seeing things that aren't there, allowing my imagination to run riot. Maybe I'm still looking for someone to blame for Leo, and the baby too, as my counsellor used to say. Maybe Patrick is it.

From the balcony I watch Sally, Will and Patrick link arms and do a silly dance as they near the house. They look so happy and my gloom lifts a bit. I'll try harder to accept Patrick and not constantly question his every move. Nevertheless, I'll keep both eyes open and be on my guard. I can't afford not to be now he's making himself part of my life, my family's life. One thing is for certain, Mr O'Brien had better be the genuine article, or he'll have me to answer to.

17

Will opens the door to a beaming Patrick, and his heart plummets. He was about to have a shower and an early night. His work schedule has been punishing lately and the last thing he wants now is to entertain a friend... Though he's no longer a friend, is he? More like a drain on his existence, a demon waiting under his bed. Patrick's gaze sweeps Will's face and then he pushes past and strides into the house, saying over his shoulder, 'You look *so* pleased to see me, mate. Not.'

'I'm just tired. I'm going to book a few days off soon, they owe me.' Will's dismayed to see that Patrick has gone into the kitchen and is rifling through his fridge.

'Got any beer?' Patrick asks through a mouthful of olives.

'Help yourself, why don't you?' Will grabs a beer from the cupboard and hands it to him.

'I can't drink warm beer.' Patrick shoves it back at Will and opens the fridge again, pulls out half a bottle of white wine. 'This will have to do. And that cheese looks nice.' Patrick grabs the cheese and olives, then goes to the cupboard for crackers and a glass. 'Want to join me?'

'No. As I said, I'm–'

'Tired, yes. But I need a bit of a chat. A bit of a barbecue analysis. I also have a great idea for our next outing.'

A groan of despair is waiting in Will's throat, but he swallows it. 'What do you mean by a barbecue analysis?'

Patrick sits at the kitchen table and indicates that Will should do the same. 'How our visit to Kerensa's at the weekend went, of course. I think it was the closest I've been to her. You ought to have seen her face when I said the thing about St Michael and did the praying. It was as if she'd seen a ghost. And then when Janice said I reminded her of Leo – jackpot! Kerensa was practically in bits.' Patrick tosses an olive in the air and catches it in his mouth. 'Mind you, it was a bloody shock to see Janice and Derek there. You could have warned me.'

'I had no idea they were coming.' Will yawns and wishes Patrick far away.

'It's wonderful that they both like me so much... more than I deserve after... Anyway, I'm going down soon for a visit. Derek and I are going fishing.'

Whoop-de-doo. 'Do you think that's a good idea?'

'Yes, absolutely. I remind them of Leo, they miss him so much. So I'm helping them come to terms.' Patrick gives Will a beatific smile that makes him feel nauseous.

'Right.'

'Right? You're a man of few words this evening, William.'

'That's because I'm tired.'

'Dear God, will you stop labouring the point? You're acting like an old man. So do you think being like Leo is getting through to Kerensa?' Patrick's expression is hopeful, almost childlike with the expectation of reward.

Will's not sure how to approach the answer, because it's not what Patrick wants to hear. But what else can he say? No use in lying. He's so sick of those. He opts for the truth. 'I'm not sure she feels closer to you, Patrick, but she did mention to me that your expressions were very like Leo's.'

Patrick nearly chokes on his wine. 'Why the bloody hell didn't you tell me?'

'I didn't get the chance yet – it's only been three days since we were there. And I know you find this hard to believe, Pat, but I *do* have to work for a living.'

'Ooh, unlike me, you mean?'

'Yes.'

Patrick laughs. 'If you remember, I offered you a cut, but you refused. You didn't want to sully your hands... And I think you'll find, my man, I've just started up a lucrative boat business.'

'You pretend to Kerensa and Sally that you have a business, while spending Leo's money and swanning about on your boat, you mean.'

A shadow flits across Patrick's face then he smiles. 'If you like. I deserve it after everything I went through to get that money.'

Will sighs and looks at his watch pointedly.

'Anyway. Tell me more about what Kerensa said.'

'She was really puzzled. Then she said that the only conclusion she could come to is that you must have known Leo, and his mannerisms must have rubbed off on you.'

'Bloody hell...'

'Yep. And she couldn't understand why you would keep something like that from her. So you see, I'm not sure you got closer to her.'

'What did you say?'

'I said you didn't know Leo. I suggested it might be because you're Irish and Leo's mum is Irish, and Leo picked up ways of talking and gestures from her. You have a similar way of being because you lived not far away from where she grew up.'

'Excellent!' Patrick slaps his hand on the table, making the dish of olives jiggle. 'You're a clever one, Will. I'll say the same thing if she asks me about why I'm like Leo. Because she might ask. Kerensa won't let things drop just like that. She's clever too.'

Will does a fake yawn and stands up. 'It's really time I got some shut-eye, Pat.'

Patrick's staring into space, obviously wrapped up in his own thoughts. Then he looks at Will. 'Yeah, of course you do. But let me quickly tell you about this idea for our next activity. Paddle boarding!' He does a wide-eyed expression and childlike grin. 'I phoned Sally and she's up for it. Now you have to call Kerensa and ask her.'

'Me? Why is it always me who has to ask?'

'Because she's not sure of me yet. I have to play it slow and gentle.'

'Have you ever been paddle boarding?'

'No.'

'Me neither. So why do you think it's such a good idea?'

'Because it will be fun! We'll all be learning together. We'll fall in the water, mess about, laugh a lot. What more could we want in a day out?'

Will shrugs. He just wants to see the back of Patrick and go to sleep.

'That's sorted, then. And afterwards we'll go back to mine and have a meal! I've rented a place a spit away from Kerensa's overlooking the ocean, just like hers. It's right near the cliff path too. She'll fall in love with it, because it has a bigger garden than hers and a fantastic loft room she could use as a studio. Much better than working at the back of her shop like she is now.' Patrick drains his glass. 'And then once we're together, I'll buy it from the owner and live there.'

The gleam of excitement in Patrick's eyes is almost manic and Will wonders if he can actually hear himself. Kerensa's just supposed to fall into his arms and move in with him? He's deluded. 'I think Kerensa loves the place she's in.'

'So do I. But it has too many memories of Leo. We need our own place. She needs a fresh start.'

Yes. Away from you. Having no stomach to listen to more of Patrick's ramblings, Will smiles and taps his watch face. 'That's great. Now if you don't mind?'

Patrick stands and makes his way to the front door. Before he goes through it he says, 'And I'm glad we're friends again, Will. All that nonsense about you and Kerensa is over and done. I can see that now. I made sure I watched you the other day, and you were being no more than a friend to her. Just like we always said you'd be.' Patrick's mouth turns up at one side in a shy smile. 'Thanks, my friend. And it won't be long before she realises me and her are meant to be together.' He slaps Will on the back. 'Let me know what she says when you call her about the paddle boarding. Bye, Will.'

'Bye, Patrick.'

Will shuts the door and leans his forehead against the wood. What a mess. He is so weary of being caught up in this shitstorm which passes for his life now. Patrick thinks Kerensa will realise she is meant to be with him. Maybe she will... when hell gets a bit chilly.

As he lay in bed a while later listening to the waves, Will decides he needs to be more decisive, more forthright, with Kerensa. Because she's not meant to be with Patrick, she's meant to be with him. He needs to let her know how he feels. He needs to find out if she feels the same... and soon.

18

Almost a week has passed since the barbecue, but I've only spoken to Will on the phone a couple of times. I'm beginning to lose patience with him. I mean, what's his game? At the barbecue he was all over me, and then nothing. Just a call to ask how I was, what I'd been doing on Tuesday, like he always does. A friend-type call. Then Thursday, an invitation to join Patrick and Sally paddle boarding at Crantock beach.

Paddle boarding was Patrick's idea apparently. Of course it was. It's so him. He's like a big overgrown kid in a playpen full of money. But at least he wants to have fun, which is more than I can say for Will. Sally was over the moon that Patrick asked her along, because she was getting nowhere when suggesting dates for just the two of them. I must say, I'm looking forward to it too. It's time I tried something new.

I pull my new wetsuit out of the bag and struggle into it. There's no way I'm putting it on when I'm there. I need time to get used to it. I look at my figure in the mirror and am relieved I look okay. I turn sideways. More than okay actually. I think I've dropped just over a stone since my life fell apart. Is there any wonder? Leo used to love my curves, but I feel better now. I still have curves, but not the wobbly bits. Then a fist of regret punches me in the chest. What I wouldn't give to have a few wobbly bits and stretch marks. Too often these days I dwell on what our baby would have looked like. Perhaps it's because I would recently have given birth. Would it have been a boy or a girl? Would she or he have my blue eyes, or Leo's hazel ones? What colour hair?

I turn from the mirror and my sadness, and twist my hair into a scrunchie. Then the doorbell rings.

It's Sally looking hot and bothered in a too-tight-around-midriff-and-knee wetsuit.

'Look at me!' she says, sweeping a hand down her body.

'What do you mean?' I say, knowing exactly what she means. I usher her through into the hallway.

'I borrowed this from Rachel and didn't try it on until just now. I reckon it's a size too small and I wanted the one with the full legs, not this cut-off monstrosity.'

'It's a bit tight, but not that bad.'

'You couldn't look me in the eye when you said that.' Sally looks ready to burst into tears. 'I mean look at you all svelte and fit-looking in yours, Will won't be able to paddle he'll be so knocked out. And then here's me. A vision in pink like some inflatable cupcake.'

'Me and Will are not an item. I've gone off him a bit, to be honest. I never know where I am with him... and come on... you don't look like a cupcake...' I bite my lip and strangle a giggle, but she spots my discomfort.

'That's why you're trying not to laugh, I suppose.' Then she gets the familiar twinkle in her eye and cracks out laughing. 'It's a shame about you and Will, but never say never. As for me... What's the point? I'm not going like this. Patrick would do the front crawl at a hundred miles per hour to get away from me.'

'Okay, if you're not going, neither am I. I've had to shut the shop early again, so I'm losing money.'

Sally sighs and turns her bottom lip down which she's picked up from Patrick. 'Can you imagine what Patrick will say if we cry off at the last minute. And this might be the only chance for us to have fun before the main season starts. Patrick hates being disappointed, and he was so looking forward to today and showing us his new house.'

'New house?'

'Yeah, he's rented a place just over in Treyarnon Bay. He's cooking for us there. Didn't Will say?'

'No. He said we were all having dinner, but I didn't realise it was at Patrick's new house. I didn't even know he *had* a new house.' *A new house that's just five minutes' walk away along the cliff path from mine. Marvellous.*

'Might have wanted it to be a surprise.' Sally examines her figure in the hall mirror and sighs. 'Hope I haven't spoilt it for Patrick. Look shocked when he tells you, for God's sake.'

'I thought we weren't going. You know – with you resembling a cupcake?'

'Rub it in, why don't you.' Sally blinks and I see there's more tears of frustration waiting. She really has got it bad for Patrick, yet he acts as if he doesn't know she's there most of the time. Love is a bastard sometimes and I wish I could make things better for her.

Then I remember something. 'Don't despair, Cinders. I have just the solution. You shall go to the paddle-boarder's ball!' I drag her along to my bedroom and dig out my old wetsuit. 'Here, try that on. I think it will be the perfect fit.'

. . .

Emerging from the bathroom five minutes later, she looks the picture of happiness. 'It fits brilliant! And I don't look too bad at all.' She turns this way and that, admiring her curves.

'You look gorgeous,' I say, and she does. 'The other one must have been two sizes too small, that's all.'

'Yep. I forget that Rachel has always been the slimmer twin.'

I grab my car keys and bag with my towel and change of clothes in it. 'Come on. Let's get this show on the road.'

I must admit I've had the best fun the last few hours. Patrick supplied the boards, and good ones they are too. The four of us have fallen off them more times than we could count, but it has been such a laugh. I didn't realise how much I needed a proper good old belly laugh. It's been far too long since I've let my hair down properly. We're all upright now though, and plan to paddle round to the next bay along. It's supposed to be more sheltered and can only be accessed from the water. Patrick and Sally are slightly more accomplished than me and Will, and lead the way, skimming across the thankfully calm ocean.

'I saw a seal!' Patrick yells over his shoulder after a few minutes' paddling.

'Me too!' Sally shrieks.

I think the seals will have done a runner before I can see them with all that yelling. But no. A few feet away to my left a grey seal pops its head up and regards us with large black eyes. Then another, and another. Wow! Will comes alongside and I say, 'Aren't they wonderful?'

He nods, his face beaming. Then his board nudges mine and we wobble a bit. 'Oops, sorry. Too busy looking at these adorable creatures.' Will paddles away and the seals disappear one by one.

Rounding the headland, Patrick points into the water and

jabs his other hand towards the horizon. This apparently means we should avoid rocks. He briefed us on his hand signals before we set off. I immediately correct my course and am pleased how quickly I'm picking up paddle boarding. I'll definitely do it again, especially now I know I can get so close to marine life like this. Perhaps we'll see something else later.

As if it was reading my thoughts, a large flat white shape surfaces about three feet away. It looks like a floundering upside-down turtle, but I remember what it is from a TV programme I watched recently. It's a sunfish. They have a very odd way of swimming; wiggling their fin above the water and flopping it back down again.

Patrick's spotted it and paddles away from it very quickly, jabbing his hand at the horizon. 'What the bejesus is that?' he yells.

I have to laugh. He's obviously scared to death. 'Sunfish! It won't hurt you!' Then I point to the little cove that's come into view. It's deserted and inviting in the sunshine, so I make for it. Will comes alongside a few feet away and it's not long before our boards bump up together onto the golden sand.

'Wow, what a lovely little spot,' Will says, pulling his board up the beach.

'Stunning. You could almost believe it's miles from civilisation.' I shield my eyes from the sun and look at the cliffs hugging the beach in a horseshoe. Nobody in sight. I turn back to the ocean and see that Patrick and Sally look to be having a paddle race and are disappearing around the headland which sticks out to the left like a thumb.

Will points at them. 'Looks like we've been abandoned.'

'They'll be back. Probably just trying to outdo each other.'

Will unzips his wetsuit and rolls the top down to his waist. 'Yeah. May as well catch a few rays, eh?' He shoves his blond mop from his eyes and smiles.

I try not to notice his ripped torso, broad shoulders and toned biceps but don't have much success. He sees me looking and gives me a slow smile. This is not the time or the place and the others will be back soon anyway. A distraction is needed. I turn towards the cliffs. 'Think there's a cave up there. I'm going to explore.'

'Can I come too?'

The sun's in his eyes and as he raises a hand to shield them, I'm afforded a nice view of a line of golden hair running down from his belly button, and how his muscles flex in his arm. *Stop looking at him, Kerensa.* 'Yes, of course,' I say in a small voice.

The cave turns out to be only about three metres deep and I step inside, tracing my fingers gently along the damp wall covered with barnacles. It smells strongly of seaweed and wet sand, and I'm about to come out again when Will's arms go around me from behind and then he unzips my suit a little way. I feel his hot kisses on my cool damp neck and turn to face him. His blue eyes are lit with passion and he strokes a finger across my lips while his other hand lowers my zip some more. I say, 'Are you mad? The others will be here soon. Besides–' He covers my mouth with his, halting further speech.

With an effort, I break from him and put my hands on my hips. Give him a disapproving glare.

'Hey, what's wrong?' Will asks.

'You're not listening. The others will be here in a bit, and as I was trying to say, I'm getting a little fed up of you blowing hot and cold. I never know where I am with you. You're like this with me, and then I don't hear from you for a few days. Then when I do, you're just friendly. What's going on with you, Will?'

He makes his mouth a thin line and looks out across the ocean. Then he heaves a sigh. 'I don't blame you for being angry,

Kerensa. But things are so difficult. I need to tell you about how I feel, and why I've been behaving like this. But not here. Not today.'

I wasn't expecting that. He looks so fed up. So... torn. 'This sounds worrying. Is anything wrong?'

He looks back at me and gives me a sad little smile. 'Yes. Lots of things are wrong... but how I feel about you isn't.' Then he lowers his lips to mine again and this time I don't stop him. I can't. It's only when my wetsuit is halfway down my back and his lips are on my breast that I snap out of it.

'Will, we can't. Not here. And certainly not in these wetsuits!' I laugh and so does he.

'No. I guess not. We'd never get them back on again in time.'

'Let's get out of this cave before Patrick and Sally come back or we'll never hear the end of it.'

'Okay. But there's one more thing I have to do before we leave.'

'What?'

'This.' Will pulls me into his arms and gives me a long tender kiss. 'We'll have that talk soon. I'll call you tomorrow and we'll arrange something.'

Hand in hand, we step out of the cave, blinking in the bright sunlight, to see Patrick walking up the beach, pulling his board behind and Sally's just arriving. We quickly drop hands, but Patrick stops and stares. He's a little way off so I can't be sure, but I think he's scowling. I raise my hand to give him a cheery wave. He returns a brief one, lets his arm slap to his side. Then he goes to help Sally with her board. Will and I walk down to meet them and Sally grins, her face flushed with excitement.

'You missed dolphins! Actual dolphins!' she says, spreading her arms and doing a little dance on the beach.

'They might have been porpoises, but you two missed them, whatever they were.' Patrick's voice is monotone, clipped.

'Oh no! Where were they?' I ask, avoiding Patrick's eyes. He looks like he wants to murder Will and me.

'Just round there past the headland,' Sally breathes, her voice full of wonder. 'They came really close, Rens! A big one and three smaller ones. The really little one looked at me.'

'Why did you two come in here on your own?' Patrick says, casually rolling the top of his wetsuit down like Will's. He has a little tattoo of a lion on his shoulder and is obviously no stranger to the gym. Sally practically dribbles all over him.

Will shrugs. 'That was the plan, wasn't it? To come round to this little bay and explore.'

'And what did you find?' Patrick points to the cave. 'In there.'

I'm getting sick of this. It's as if we're naughty kids and he's the parent. Maybe he saw us holding hands, but so what! 'Nothing much, actually. Just a little cave. If we had known we'd see dolphins we'd obviously have stayed with you two. Not sure why you're so bloody grumpy about it.'

Patrick finds his Hollywood smile from somewhere and touches my shoulder briefly. 'I'm not grumpy, sweet cheeks, just disappointed you missed out on those wonderful creatures. We might see them on our way back, if we're lucky.'

I grit my teeth and go over to talk to Sally about the dolphins. Sweet cheeks? How much more patronising can Patrick get? This really doesn't help my mood. I'm pissed off with missing the dolphins, fed up with Patrick, and worried about what the hell Will wants to say to me in his little talk.

After a few minutes chatting to Sally, I feel much better though. Her enthusiasm is infectious and I'm eager to see if we can spot the pod on the way back. After a little rest, we all set off back to Crantock beach.

19

We were unlucky with the dolphins this time. But despite Patrick's moodiness and Will's enigmatic reference to a chat, I'm so glad I tried paddle boarding. It was exhilarating and liberating. I felt so free out there on the water, so close to the ocean depths and the creatures who live within it. There was a gladness in my heart and a calmness of mind that I often get living by the sea, but actually being out on it heightened all those feelings. I'm going to buy my own board and try to get out on the ocean as often as I can.

After a quick shower, I get dressed for dinner at Patrick's. I honestly don't want to go, but Sally's tugging at my heartstrings as usual. If I cry off, the whole dinner might not happen, and she confided in me that tonight is the night for her to take the bull by the horns. The kids are staying over at Rachel's, so Sally plans to tell Patrick how she feels. I think about Will's plan to do the same with me tomorrow and a shiver of apprehension shows up in my gut. Why was he so serious? So sad about it?

. . .

I stand on the cliff path, the sea at my back, and check the details Patrick texted to me earlier. Not far away are two grand detached houses, one slightly grander than the other, facing the Atlantic, their huge windows glowing red in the reflected sunset. I've seen these houses loads of times on my walks and often wondered who lived in them. I know who lives in one now.

Predictably, Patrick's is the larger, grander one. It's a stunning art deco structure of white walls and glass. Sally opens the door to me and I catch my breath. I've never seen her looking so stunning. She's wearing a red clingy dress which leaves nothing to the imagination in the cleavage department and her chocolate curls have been artfully twisted up into a messy bun.

'Hell, maid. You scrub up well,' I say as I kiss her on the cheek.

'You don't look so bad yourself.' She leads me into a huge living room which looks at the ocean through wall-to-wall and floor-to-ceiling windows.

Patrick's there relaxing on a long black sofa, dressed in smart trousers and an olive shirt which enhances his unusual green eyes. He's gelled his dark hair into a spiky style on top and is obviously trying to impress. Hopefully Sally's luck will turn later.

'A vision in blue, my darlin', and a proper sight for sore eyes,' he says, standing up to kiss me on both cheeks. He smells of expensive cologne and a trace of whisky. 'Me and Sal are having a cheeky drop o' the Irish. Want to join us?'

'I'm not a whisky fan, thanks, Patrick.'

He thumps his fist against his heart and does a wounded expression. 'How can you turn down a drop from the old country?'

Sally laughs and slips her arm through his. 'Rensa likes a G&T sometimes, don't you, mate?'

'It has been known,' I say.

'I might have better than that.' Patrick unhooks himself from Sally and walks out of the room. 'Wait there,' he calls from presumably the kitchen. 'I'll surprise you.'

Oh good. I can hardly wait.

'What do you think of this house?' Sally asks, a dreamy expression on her face.

'Pretty amazing what I've seen so far.'

Sally comes over and whispers in my ear. 'I've been imagining living here. Once Patrick and I get together properly, I don't see what's stopping us. He's already said that he's looking to buy it in the near future, if all goes well.'

I think she might be jumping the gun a bit. No. A Lot. But I say, 'That would be nice, wouldn't it?'

She raises one eyebrow. 'Nice? It would be bloody amazing. It has six bedrooms, so more than enough room for my brood and even a few more little ones, if the gods smile on us.'

This takes me aback. I lower my voice. 'I didn't realise you'd taken things that far.'

Sally rolls her eyes. 'We haven't... yet. But tonight will be the night.' She winks and fans her cheeks as Patrick comes back in with a tall glass of something complete with ice and fresh orange slices.

'There you go, Kerensa! Fill your boots.' Patrick hands me the glass and then folds his arms, watches my face expectantly.

I sniff the liquid and can hardly believe it. I take a sip to make sure I'm not mistaken. The familiar kick warms a path to my stomach. 'Negroni... My favourite,' I mutter. Leo and I drank them in Rome on our honeymoon. After that, we drank them on special occasions... I haven't had one since he died.

'Is it your favourite? How clever of me!' Patrick smiles and then takes my elbow. 'Come on, let's do the grand tour of my humble abode.' Sally and I follow him around the place like little puppies while he babbles on like an estate agent. I'm barely paying attention. How the hell did Patrick know about the Negroni? Coincidence? No. Sally said I liked gin, I said I liked gin and Patrick just wanted to make me something a little different. With gin. I need to accept it for what it is, instead of always looking for the bad in him.

'Yes. It would, but it would also make a great place for a telescope to look at the stars too,' Sally says, looking at Patrick with cow eyes.

They look at me and I realise I have no idea what she's talking about. 'Sorry, I wasn't paying attention.'

Patrick smiles. 'I was just saying this loft room would make a fantastic artist's studio. What with the huge skylights across the middle.'

Looking round properly for the first time, I see the room would certainly be perfect for that. Another picture window overlooking the cliff path and ocean, white walls, clean lines and those fantastic windows in the ceiling, allowing natural light to flood the space. 'It would be an amazing studio.' I run my hand along the wall and walk to the window to look at the view. 'You're going to have a bash at painting, Patrick?'

Patrick laughs. 'No chance. I don't have an artistic bone in my body. But you're welcome to use this space anytime, Kerensa. I'll get it set up as a studio, if you like.'

Great. Sally would love that. Not. I turn from the view. 'That's a very generous offer, Patrick. But as Sally said, it would make a great observatory too.' I give her an encouraging smile as I can see she looks a little disappointed.

'Nah. I've no interest in all that stargazing.' He's gazing at me though. A penetrating gaze, as if he wants to reach inside my mind. I glance at Sally. She's not happy. Then thankfully the doorbell rings. 'That's Will, I expect. Come on, let's go down and I'll check on the food.'

Will looks good enough to eat as usual and I realise I am starving. Paddle boarding certainly builds up an appetite. He kisses me quickly on the cheek and does the same to Sally. Once again, back to being the dutiful friend. Patrick goes into the kitchen and we follow him, sit round the huge marble-topped table. Like the rest of the house, the kitchen is stunning. State-of-the-art this, that and the other, and instead of the ocean, a view of a little herb garden and then a field of cows. Idyllic.

Patrick refuses to let us help with the food, the smell of which is making my mouth water. He won't tell us what we're eating either, as it's his signature dish and a "surprise". He looks a very comfortable chef, calmly adding a dash of this and that to a big pan, stirring pots, whilst at the same time topping up the nibbles dishes and our glasses.

'Okay, you lot. It's ready!' Patrick puts two large plates of crispy bread slices on the table and then comes back carrying a huge flat black pan. He places it in the centre of the table and says, 'Ta-da!'

Sally claps. 'Bravo, Pat! I adore paella. It looks so authentic.'

Will says how colourful it looks and picks out a prawn.

'Oi, get your mitts off!' Patrick shoves two big serving spoons into the dish.

I say nothing. I just stare at the yellow rice, the prawns, the lobster, the mussels, the olives and all the other ingredients. Regular authentic paella, except this one has sliced red pepper set in a fan shape in the centre. This was Leo's signature dish. He hardly cooked, but when he did, he made this. He put the peppers around the edge of the dish though, not in the middle. But this is his dish. I know it is.

Patrick's looking at me, a knowing twinkle in his eye. I want to stand up, yell at him. Demand he tells me the truth. How did he know my husband? Because he *must* have. There's no question in my mind now. He must have known Leo really well. He told him about the Negroni and Leo must have given him this recipe. And he's hiding the fact he knew him because? I don't know. But my gut tells me it's not good. One thing I do know. I'm not giving him the satisfaction of a showdown here. Because that's what he wants. He wants to put on a fake concerned expression and say I'm imagining it, explain it all away in a rational manner. I'll look deranged. Stupid.

No. This needs careful handling. *Take it slowly, Kerensa, and he'll slip up one way or another.*

'Wow! Patrick, this looks delicious,' I say. 'Leo used to make paella from time to time, but this looks far superior. And the little strips of red pepper in the middle. Never seen that before. How unusual.' I help myself to a big plateful. A quick frown furrows his bushy black brows, but then he's all smiles again.

Annoyingly, the paella is just as good as Leo's. We chat about the day and all agree with Patrick that we'll have to go paddle boarding again. I want to spend more time with Patrick, get close to him. He has a dark secret about Leo and I'm going to find out what it is. I need to be careful, watch my back, because I think Patrick might be dangerous. Even though my mum told me off for suggesting that he might have had something to do with my husband's death, the more I think about it, the more I feel he could have. This feeling is growing all the time. In fact, there's no "might" about it. I'm sure he had something to do with my husband's death. I catch Will's eye and he gives me a little wink. *And what about you, Will? You must know more than you're letting on too.*

. . .

As the evening wears on, I can tell Patrick is a little merry. He was already on the whisky when I got here, and he's been knocking back the beer through dinner. I can also tell he's not pleased with Will. More than once during conversation, he's sniped at him under his breath when he thought nobody could hear. He repeated what Will said in a sarky manner. I'm sitting opposite and a good lip reader. Will's cottoned on to his mood too and has more or less stopped addressing him directly. Sally is oblivious to it, I think. She's concentrating all her efforts on trying her best to keep flirting with our host. She's not making headway. It's as if Patrick's got a "Sally-proof" force field around him.

After pudding is over, Patrick stands up and pats his belly. 'I'm stuffed,' he declares, smiling. He says to Will, 'Can you come to the garage to help bring up a crate of beer? Need some ice too.'

'You keep ice in the garage?' Sally asks.

'Yeah, in the chest freezer. I buy bags of it. Can't be arsed with those stupid little square ice trays. When I fill them I tend to spill water all over the shop.' Patrick laughs as if it's the funniest thing he ever heard and Sally joins in.

'I'll come and help,' Sally says, jumping up.

'No. I want Will to help. I want to show him some new tools I bought last week too. You know – man stuff.' Patrick smiles at Sally and then at Will. I'm reminded of a shark hunting his lunch.

'You go and do your man stuff while me and Kerensa clear the table. It's the least we can do.' Sally nudges me and picks up her plate.

'Yeah. We'll stay here and do women stuff,' I say in a fake high-pitched voice. 'There's nothing we women like more than being in the kitchen.'

Patrick laughs again and walks to the door. 'Come on, Will. We have man things to discuss.'

I watch them leave and my gut tells me that Will's going to get in trouble for something. I need to follow them, see if I can eavesdrop. Perhaps I'll get to know more about our mysterious host. I wait a few moments, then say to Sally, 'Back in a mo. Just going to the loo.'

I hurry along the corridor and remember from our tour that the garage is through an internal door off the laundry room. Luckily that is right next to the downstairs bathroom. I sneak in, tiptoe past the washing machine and little sink, and see that the garage door is open a crack, so I put my ear to this and hold my breath. I don't have to strain my ears because both men's voices are raised.

'What the hell do you mean?' Will says. 'We were just looking in the cave!'

'So why were you holding fucking hands with her when you came out then?'

'We weren't.'

'I saw you. Don't lie to me!'

'Because you never lie, right?'

'Fuck off, William. Don't try to turn this round on me. I trusted you to keep an eye on Kerensa, not try to get into her pants!'

'For God's sake, you're delusional! I have no interest in her beyond friendship.'

'You're a fucking liar. And to think I apologised for accusing you of flirting with her on the boat. I was right all along!'

Oh my god. What the hell? There's silence, and all I can hear is my heart drumming in my ears. What if they're walking toward me right now? I need to get away from the door before they catch me eavesdropping – but I'm compelled to stay. Then Will speaks again.

'Hang on, I remember now. I did hold her hand because she stumbled on a rock as we left the entrance. It must only have been for a second or two. That's what you saw.'

Patrick does a fake laugh. 'Yeah right. Nice try. But I'm not stupid. I can see the way you feel about her when you look at her. When you think nobody is watching. But I'm always watching you, William. I'm always watching her too.'

'How many times must I tell you I–?'

'You can tell me a million times: I still won't believe you. But hear this. You will never be with her *ever*. She's mine. And when I tell her what you've done. About Leo, about everything, she will be disgusted.'

A cry builds in my chest, so I clamp my hand over my mouth.

'What I did? What about you?'

'I could *never* have done what I did without your help! And like I said before. I'll tell so many lies that you won't stand a chance.'

'I only did what I did out of friendship to help you, but you twisted all of it. Tricked me. You're an evil bastard. Always have been, always will be. Shame I didn't realise it until it was too fucking late.'

'Yes it is. Perhaps you're not as clever as you think you are, eh?'

'I'm not staying here listening to this shit.'

'You'll stay until I've finished!'

'Get off me!'

I hear a scuffle and take a few hurried steps backward across the room. Their voices are closer now. They must be right behind the door.

'If you so much as look at her the wrong way in my presence, I swear you'll pay for it, William!'

'Then I'll stay away. You can see her on your own.'

'You know she won't agree to that.'

'I do. So this shit about you trying to be more like Leo to win her over isn't working? I told you it wouldn't.'

'Then you have to help me make it work another way, William. Because if you don't, I'll tell her everything.'

The door handle is suddenly depressed, so I make a run for the bathroom. I fly through the door and lock it behind me, sink down on the loo. My god. What the hell did I just hear? Patrick sounds obsessed with me. And what the bloody hell has William done? How has Patrick tricked him and where does Leo fit into all this? Is it Will, not Patrick who's to blame for my husband's death? Nausea rises in my chest and I take a few deep breaths. I sit there mulling everything over, until there's a knock on the door. 'Hey, Rens, you okay, love?' Sally asks.

'Not really. I feel a bit sick. Might call it a night, actually.'

'Oh no. I was hoping to stay a bit longer... but if you're unwell.'

If her chances of snaring a sleepover with Patrick weren't dead in the water before, they are now. The only woman he wants in his bed is me, by the sound of it. Then I wonder if I should tell her what I heard... But I'm certain the way she feels about Patrick will mean she won't listen to me tonight. I'll have to tell her tomorrow though. She can't carry on like this, holding a torch that will never be lit. Besides, he might be dangerous. I say, 'You don't have to come, Sal. It's literally a five-minute walk.'

Sally protests, but not too much and I come out of the bathroom and make my excuses to Patrick and Will. Predictably, they both offer to walk me back, but I'd rather poke my eyes out than have either of those two anywhere near me.

Once home, I bolt the door and pick up a photo of Leo I have on a table in the hallway. I look at him smiling out at me. Even though he plunged me into my worst nightmare, God, I wish he was here. He'd know what to do. He might even be able to tell me what the hell Patrick and Will are up to. I kiss his lips through the cold glass and hold him to my chest. 'I promise you, Leo. If those two bastards were involved in hurting you in any way, I'll find out. And they *will* pay. I'll make sure of it.'

20

Dawn arrives, tracing pale-pink and indigo fingers along the ocean's horizon. A beautiful path for the sun to follow. I wish I had a path to follow. I've been awake, sitting on the balcony wrapped in a quilt, long before dawn put in an appearance. Three hours of fitful sleep and staring at the ceiling drove me from my bed and out here around four o'clock with a huge flask of coffee. Since then, like clothes in a dryer, my thoughts have tumbled round and round, over and over, as I try to figure out what to do next, where to find answers.

The easiest thing to do would be to confront Will when he phones me later. But my heart tells me it wouldn't be the wisest move. Maybe I need to get Patrick and Will together and spring on them what I heard yesterday from the laundry room. At least then they won't have time to cook up some more lies and plausible excuses. Though how they can rationally explain away what I heard is frankly beyond me. I've considered setting them up too. Maybe I could record what they say in answer to my questions on my mobile phone. If it's incriminating, I can take it to the police.

The more I think about that one, the more I worry about

how safe I'd be. If it's true that Patrick and Will were involved in Leo's death, they wouldn't think twice in getting rid of me, would they? Let's not forget that a huge sum of money's involved. Nobody would commit murder otherwise, would they? Leo stole and hid, I'm guessing, millions of pounds in this offshore account somewhere. Will and Patrick must have access to it. Patrick sounds like he's got the upper hand over Will, but it's clear Will's involved, so must have benefitted from some of the money. But I need proof. Solid proof.

The remaining coffee is lukewarm because I left the top off the flask. I drink it nevertheless, because ironically, now it's almost time to get up, I'm starting to feel sleepy. I need my wits about me today. I stare out over the ocean and watch a red fishing boat crisscrossing the bay, expertly avoiding the submerged rocks. My feelings for Will surface and twist my gut into a tight knot. I really like him... or did. How could he turn out to be such a shit? I thought I was a good judge of character. Clearly not. An inner voice speaking in his defence reminds me that he said Patrick had lied and tricked him. Even if that's true, Will should have come clean to me. Whatever it's all about, I would think more of him for being honest than going along with Patrick's schemes. But if it involves murder...

Moments later, I'm dragged out of my turmoil by my mobile going off in the kitchen. I hurry inside and see it's Sally. I glance at the clock – 6.30am. Why is she ringing so early? Shit. I hope nothing's happened to her because I failed to warn her last night. 'Sally? You okay?'

'Yes. But not very happy. Sorry to ring so early, did I wake you?'

'No. Been awake hours.'

A sigh. 'Me too. Two shitty things have happened. Will left just after you last night, so I had a chance to tell Patrick how I felt about him. I kissed him passionately first, or tried to. He pulled away so fast he must have got whiplash. You'd have thought I was the ugliest woman in the world by the expression on his face. I wanted to run out, get away from his look of revulsion, but I didn't. I needed to get everything off my chest...' Sally's voice becomes almost a whisper and I can tell she's struggling to hold back tears.

'Oh, Sal. What did you say?'

'I told him the truth. That I loved him.'

My heart sinks. 'What did he say?'

'That I was a lovely woman and a good friend but friendship's all that there can ever be. He loves someone else. Oh God, Rens, I felt such a fool. So humiliated.'

Poor Sally. I don't really know what to say. I'd like to say thank God. Because Patrick's a lying scheming shit, and might possibly be dangerous, but of course that's not what she wants to hear. Her heart's broken. 'I'm so sorry, Sal. But I suppose you know where you stand now.'

'Yeah. Out in the cold. I so wanted it to work between us... I thought I had a chance at real happiness. God knows who the woman is he's in love with. He wouldn't tell me – said her name wasn't important. Has Will said anything? You know, and sworn you to secrecy?'

Now I have to lie to my best friend. Thanks, Patrick. 'No. He hasn't said a word.'

'Okay. It might just have been an excuse to put me off. And then the second horrible thing was when I got back to Rachel's – she was in a right state. Marcus, as you know, was working away, seems he fell off a ladder and was killed.'

'Oh bloody hell. I'm so sorry.'

Sally sniffs and says in a tremulous voice. 'Yeah. He was a vile individual, but did he deserve to die? The worst thing is, we have to tell the kids when they wake up... they'll be devastated.'

'Sally. What an awful shock for you. First Patrick, now this.' I swallow down tears and take a moment. I can't dump all I know on her now. Even though I want to tell her everything, I need my best friend to help me through – but this time I'll have to go it alone. I can't tell anyone until I know exactly what I'm facing.

'Yeah. And they're flying his body home, but there'll be an inquest. There often is for an unexpected death. Something to do with risk assessments and red tape.'

'There is? I don't think Leo had one... or at least I was never told.'

'But Will sorted all that for you, didn't he? The funeral, getting the body... I mean Leo, home from where he had the accident and stuff?'

My memory of all that is very hazy. I was in such a state I might not have taken it in even if Will told me. 'I don't remember... I suppose he must have.'

'Yeah. Well, thanks for listening, and sorry to burden you with my troubles. I feel so flat now that any chance with Patrick has gone. Serves me right for getting carried away – imagining I could share that wonderful house with him.'

'No, it doesn't serve you right. It was only natural. I mean, he did encourage you, didn't he?' I say this not really meaning it, but I have to try to make her feel better.

'Yes and no. Mostly I think he was just being a friend, when I look back. It was all in my head... I think there's a chance for you and Will though, even if you always tell me you're just good friends and your romantic liaison didn't work out. I've seen the way he looks at you sometimes.'

'He's not for me, Sal.' *Sadly. Not now I've found out he's up to his eyes in lies and deception.* 'In fact I think I might keep my distance for a bit. I don't want him getting the wrong idea.'

'Hmm. Shame, but okay. You know your own heart.'

'If there's anything I can do today please let me know, Sal.'

'I will. But I don't think there is. As long as you're there for me to listen to my woes?'

'Of course. Anytime.'

We end the call, and then I eat a hurried breakfast and walk down to open my shop. On the way there, my brain torments me with unresolved questions and half-baked plans about what to do next. Once inside, I go over to examine my half-finished shark sculpture that's under commission. I realise I only have until next week to finish it as the woman is coming from up country to collect it. As I work, I think about the huge loft room at Patrick's. He was right. It would make a fabulous studio. While it's nice letting customers see me creating things in the shop, it's not without problems. It can be noisy and messy, and when customers are looking round, that isn't ideal.

Then it hits me. I'll take Patrick up on his offer of the studio. What better way could there be to have to snoop around his life? I'm sure I'll find out far more about what he's done than I would if I confronted him. I'll do the same with Will too. Try to be as normal as possible and slip in a few searching questions under the guise of idle curiosity. My idea of getting them together and springing on them what I overheard feels wrong. They would try to lie their way out of it and even clam up altogether. Probably they'd cut all ties with me, disappear and then I'd never know what happened to Leo and their part in it. This way, though more time-consuming, feels better. I don't know if this will work – but it's early days. If Patrick and Will want me, I can play one off against the other. Patrick especially sounds like he wants to make sure there's nobody else in my life. He warned Will off in no uncertain terms last night. And Will's at pains to keep his affection for me a secret. He's obviously worried to death about Patrick finding out.

I hammer a tin can flat on my wooden board with a mallet. It's exactly the right colour and texture for the shark's fin. I release a slow breath and hold it up to the light. I'm beginning to feel stronger now I have some semblance of a plan. The more the two men dislike each other, the better my chances are to get to the bottom of what they did. They'll be anxious to put the blame elsewhere and win my favour. I shake my head. That sounds like I'm a medieval princess in a castle waiting for rescue by a brave knight. Except I'm not, am I? I'm a strong woman who's been wronged. Whose dead husband has possibly been wronged in the extreme. I have to believe I can get the upper hand. And for that, I'll need my own suit of armour and sharp lance ready and waiting.

Half an hour later, my mobile rings. It's Will. 'Hey, Kerensa, how's tricks?'

'Not bad, you know. I'm making my shark sculpture and it's going fairly well. What are you up to?'

'I'm about to scrub up for an operation. Shouldn't be a long one though... Listen, can we have that talk I mentioned yesterday, later? You could come over to mine?'

His voice sounds like it's been coated with longing and I don't want to get into an uncomfortable situation at his place. After yesterday, I prefer to meet him on my own turf. I also don't want him at mine very long, so I won't ask him to dinner. I'll need an excuse to get rid of him too...

'Kerensa?'

'Yes, sorry. Just working on a tricky bit of the sculpture with my mobile clamped to my shoulder. Can you pop over about five thirty? I have a few things to sort out later this evening.'

There's no disguising the disappointment in his tone. 'Yes... that's doable. I should be done here around four. You'll be too busy for dinner then?'

'I will, sorry. Sally has had some bad news. Her ex-brother-in-law has died and her sister's in bits. I think she needs me over there.' I cross my fingers and hope a thunderbolt doesn't strike me down.

'Oh dear God. Anything I can do?'

Yes, bugger off and leave me alone. 'I don't think so, thanks. Okay, see you later.'

I end the call and want to hurl the mobile across the room. Why did he have to turn out to be the bad guy? I really liked him. Still do. You can't switch your feelings off just like that, can you? But this is exactly what I must try to do.

Another half an hour has gone by and another idea has blossomed. Stage one in driving an even bigger wedge between the two men than there is already. I pick up my mobile again. 'Patrick, have you got a moment?'

'Kerensa!' He sounds ridiculously pleased to hear my voice. 'I always have a moment for you, lovely lady.'

Excuse me while I throw up. 'You know the offer of letting me use your loft room as a studio? Did you mean it, or were you joking?'

'Of course I meant it. It would be a great pleasure to have you put that space to proper use. Tell me what you need. I'll get things ordered straight away.'

'Fantastic! You're so generous. Can I come round this evening to have a better look? I'll know what I need when I see the place again.'

'Come round anytime. We could have lunch!'

'No, this evening is fine. I'm in the shop now and I've

arranged to meet Will at mine about five thirty. So let's say... six thirty?'

'Um... yes. That's perfect. Will's coming to yours?'

'He wants to have a chat about something. No idea what.'

'I see.' I can sense the fury Patrick's feeling towards Will crackling down the line. Then Patrick puts his cheery voice back on. 'Okay, Kerensa. See you later, me darlin'.'

I smile to myself as I picture his brain working at a thousand miles an hour trying to figure out why Will's coming round. Patrick might even ring him, but Will's probably in the operating room by now, so Patrick will get no answers.

I've not been too busy in the shop today. The Easter break is over, and then there'll be the quiet time before May half-term. But the silver lining to all that is I have made really good progress on the shark. It has no eyes as yet, but I have some nice dark shiny sea-glass I gathered on the beach recently that will do just perfectly. A pain in my back from constantly bending over the workbench tells me to call it a day. I have to get back soon for Will anyway. Something I'm not looking forward to in the least.

On my walk back, I consider the way Leo left, almost without a trace. It's disquieting. And something else that's bugging me is Sally's mention of an inquest into unexpected deaths. Did Leo have one? Did Will handle that, just as he handled the transporting of Leo's body, the funeral and everything official? At the time I was drowning in grief for both Leo and my baby, a walking zombie, and was thankful for everything being taken out of my hands. But what if Will took over because he wanted to hide things? To brush things under the carpet. Maybe Patrick was helping him too.

. . .

In the kitchen, I sort through the mail. Chuck them on the side – just junk. There's never anything important apart from bills. Then this thought, as well as my ponderings on the way home, jogs my memory. I did a perfunctory shuffle through Leo's important document box not long before the funeral to see if he had left anything for me. He was a fastidious planner, and forward thinker, so I thought I'd check for a request or instructions for his cremation or burial. There was nothing like that in there. Just old school certificates, his accountancy certificates, house deeds, birth certificate and the like. Maybe now I'm thinking straight I should check again. Perhaps I could find some clues about Patrick or Will. It's worth a try.

I make a quick cheese sandwich, take it into the study, and place it on Leo's desk, which is by the window and looks out over the ocean. I remember when he worked from home sometimes, he spent more time gazing out at the view than he did accounting. I sit at his wheeled chair and swallow a lump of emotion with my coffee. If I close my eyes, I can almost see him sitting at this desk, lost in a world of his own. But was he really plotting how to steal more money from his boss? All the time I thought he was daydreaming, he might have been planning, scheming. And look where that got him. It got him dead. He was driven to kill himself, or maybe someone else helped him out with that. Maybe two people did.

Okay, enough. I push these disturbing thoughts away and turn the little key in the side cupboard. I take a bite of my sandwich and pat my hand around on the top shelf, hoping to grasp the wooden box. That's odd. I can't find it. I get off the chair and kneel down on the carpet, look on the shelf. There's just an old magazine and some pens. Maybe it's behind something in the main cupboard. Unlikely though, because I'm sure I put it back where Leo always kept it.

No. No, it's not behind the box files of computer paper and

A4 ring binders. I rack my brain, try to think. Was I so out of it before the funeral that I put it somewhere else? That's even more unlikely. Leo liked things just so – why would I have taken it elsewhere?

I eat my sandwich without much enthusiasm and stare out at a flock of seagulls sweeping across a grey ocean. A shocking conclusion is pushing for acceptance at the edge of my consciousness. The box has gone. It's been taken. But by whom and why?

21

Will's hands are shaking as he buttons up his shirt. It's a good job they weren't like this a few hours ago as he was sewing up a patient. But then it's hardly surprising he has the tremors, because the next few hours could be make or break for him and Kerensa... and if it's break? He checks his hair in the mirror and shoves that thought to the back of the drawer with a pullover he's decided not to wear. Downstairs, he grabs his car keys and an agapanthus plant that he bought on the way home. He remembered Kerensa had said she wanted one for her garden.

Behind the wheel of his car, he sets the plant in the footwell of the passenger side, and discovers the make-or-break thought has somehow escaped the drawer, and lodged in his head again. Kerensa did seem a bit odd on the phone earlier. It was as if she was preoccupied with something else. Okay, Sally needed her, but it wasn't just that. The warmth in her voice he's been used to was absent too. Unless he was imagining it. It's a possibility, because he's about to open his heart for acceptance or rejection and so he's bound to be nervous and worried. And bloody

Patrick hasn't helped. Leaving malicious voicemails and texts every second of the day – that's enough to make anyone nervous. He's got a bee in his bonnet about Will going round to see Kerensa. God knows why she told him. Will texted back that he wanted to chat to her about a surprise for Patrick's birthday, and to stop pestering.

Outside Kerensa's front door with the agapanthus nodding in the breeze, he feels like he's trying too hard. The last thing he wants is to come across as needy and desperate. But then that's what he is. If she doesn't feel the same, he couldn't face it.

'Hi, Will,' Kerensa says upon opening the door. Her expression is neutral and then she looks at the plant and brightens. 'Oh, is that for me? How thoughtful, thanks.' She takes the plant and he follows her inside. She seems pleased, but the spark of connection in her eyes when she looks at him wasn't there just now.

'I remembered you said you wanted one for the garden,' he says, leaning against the work surface as he watches her pull out a little watering can from under the sink.

'I did. That's so nice of you.' She waters the pot and asks if he wants tea. She's polite and courteous, as if he's someone she's just got to know, not an almost lover.

Will's so nervous he drops his jacket on the floor as he's hanging it on the chair back, and his wallet falls out. It skitters all the way across the floor under the table and out the other side. Kerensa, unsmiling, picks it up for him, hands it back. Will feels like a dumb kid. He sits at the table to wait for his tea and makes small talk. He's no idea how to start now. The change in her has thrown him, and he's not imagining it this time. She's distant, removed. 'How's Sally?'

'Oh, you know. Getting there. Patrick didn't help yesterday...' She puts a mug down in front of him and sits opposite. 'Do you know about that?'

'No, what did he do?'

'She basically spilled her guts out to him. Told him she wanted them to be together and he said he didn't feel the same. He said he was in love with someone else. Any idea who?' Kerensa takes a drink, her keen green eyes watching him carefully.

Shit. Will hopes he's not in for the same fate as Sally. And he's going to have to lie, isn't he? Again. 'Oh no... poor Sally. And no, I have no idea who he's in love with.'

Kerensa sits back, tosses her hair over her shoulders and folds her arms. The body language is loud and clear. She doesn't believe him. 'Odd. Him not mentioning anything, with you and him being besties.'

Will snorts. 'We aren't besties. Far from it.' Then he wishes he hadn't let his mouth run away with him, as Kerensa leans forward, rests her elbows on the table.

'Really? Why's that? Has something happened between you?'

He has to think quickly. 'Not really. He's just annoying sometimes. For example, he's left me voice messages and texts asking why I'm coming over to yours tonight. He seems to think he should be invited every time. I said we were talking about a birthday surprise for him to shut him up.'

'Hmm. He can be a bit overbearing. When's his birthday?'

'In a few days. Can't remember what date.'

Kerensa sits back again, sighs. 'Leo's is in three days. He would have been thirty-five.'

This is not going the way he planned. 'So sorry. You must spend the day keeping busy... We could do something?' For the second time this evening, Will's said the wrong thing. Kerensa's mouth becomes a thin line and she looks away.

'Not sure spending my dead husband's birthday with another man is the right thing to do, Will.'

'No. No, of course it isn't. Everything's coming out wrong tonight.' He takes a breath to continue but she speaks first.

'Talking of Leo. How come there wasn't an inquest? Sally says there always is one when it's an unexpected death. She found this out recently, with all this stuff going on regarding Marcus. Also, how did you organise for his body to get here? Must have been tricky.' Then her voice becomes less interrogatory. 'I was on a different planet during that time as you know. Just curious, I suppose.'

And now this... Things are going from bad to worse. 'That's okay. There's not always an inquest. It was clear what had happened with Leo... and as far as the transportation of him here, I ordered a private ambulance through work. They took him to the funeral directors in Truro.'

'I see. Well, thanks again for everything you did,' Kerensa says with a little smile.

Will smiles back. That went smoother than he expected.

As he gathers his courage to say how he feels again, she continues. 'So what have you come to say? Only I said I'd be over at Patrick's in a bit. Sally doesn't need me after all.'

This news hits him between the eyes like a sledgehammer. Not just that Kerensa's going over to see someone who she says she's suspicious of and isn't keen on, but it's the way she brushes Will off like he's unimportant. She must have an inkling what he's come to say to her. Yesterday in the cave he'd dropped a huge hint as to what he wanted to say... hadn't he? 'Um... well, it was about what I said in the cave... and why are you going to Patrick's?'

'I'm taking him up on his offer to let me use the loft space as a studio.'

Will's heart plummets. Patrick and Kerensa alone, spending lots of time together, is not a good combination. 'That's unexpected. Thought you didn't like him much.'

'I don't have to like him to use the studio, do I?'

'No. I guess not.'

There's an uncomfortable silence as they sip their tea, stare at the table, the wall, anywhere but at each other. Kerensa takes the mug to the sink. Her back to him, she says quietly, 'What have you come to say, Will?'

He's not sure anymore. It's as if he's talking to a stranger. But if he doesn't say it, he'll always regret it. He gets up and goes over to her. 'I want to say I'm sorry for blowing hot and cold – causing you to wonder where you stand. It's just that I need to keep how I feel away from Patrick.' Will dries up and so he places his hands on Kerensa's shoulders. She turns to face him.

'This isn't news. You said this after that day on the boat. We have kept our relationship – such as it is – a secret from both Patrick and Sally. From everyone. What's changed?' Kerensa narrows her eyes.

'What's changed is I think you're right about Patrick. He's weird around you because I think he has a thing for you. Maybe you're the one he's in love with, like he told Sally.' Kerensa's eyebrows go up and she shakes her head. 'But the thing is... The thing is, Kerensa, I love you too.' There, he said it.

Kerensa gives him a sad little smile and moves away, walks through the living room and onto the balcony. Great. Not exactly what he'd envisaged when he'd gone over and over the scenarios last night as he lay awake.

Will joins her on the balcony and they stare out at the navy horizon underlining the sky, confining the ocean. He's booked a few days off work in case it went well so they could spend some proper time together. Looks like he shouldn't have bothered. There's a few couples and families walking on the beach and one little girl is splashing in the breakers of the incoming tide. Will prays things will all work out and that he and Kerensa might have children one day.

Kerensa shifts position and half looks at him from under her long lashes. 'I'm not sure how to say this, so I'll just be honest. I thought we had something a little while ago, Will. Our friendship was blossoming into more, and we both knew it. But then you would keep changing the way you were with me, and I found that irritating. But... yesterday in the cave, I almost gave in to you. Then I came to my senses. You see, I'm not really sure you can love me if you're either ashamed or frightened of showing it around other people. Around Patrick.'

Damn it. Patrick will swing for this. 'Hey, Kerensa, I'm not ashamed, not frightened. But it is complicated. Patrick can be... let's say unpredictable. If he knew about us, he'd try to ruin it. Break us up... especially as I said... He feels the same about you.' Will slips his arm around Kerensa and kisses the top of her head. But instead of leaning into him as she has in the past, she stiffens. *It's now or never.* 'Look, I'll be honest. I think he's more than unpredictable. If he knew about us, I think he could be dangerous. So, Kerensa...' Will turns her to face him and swallows a lump of emotion. 'Kerensa, my darling. I'm asking you to marry me, come with me to Australia, away from him, away from the past. I know it's not long after Leo, so we don't have to get married straight away... but tell me that you'll think about it?'

Kerensa's mouth drops open and her face floods with colour. She starts to speak but then bites her lip. Will can't tell what she's thinking but he's worried that it's not going to be what he wants to hear. Kerensa touches his shoulder lightly and then tucks both hands under her armpits. 'Oh, Will. I'm afraid I'm going to have to say no to your proposals. Cornwall is my home and always will be. I can no more leave here than fly into space. I belong here... and as for marrying you, yes, it is too soon after Leo. Far too soon. And if I'm being honest, I don't trust you anymore. Let's just say I have new information about you, and about Patrick, that has made me very confused, suspicious. I think it's best that we don't see each other anymore... not even as friends.'

Will takes a step back as if her words are blows. They might as well have been for all the pain they cause his heart. Of all the scenarios he pictured, this was not one of them. Not even friends? And what new information? He takes a moment and then says, 'I'm not sure I understand. You have some confusing information about both of us, yet you want to cut ties with me, but are about to go round to Patrick's to talk about setting up a studio in his house?'

She shrugs and walks back inside, saying over her shoulder, 'It's for my benefit, not his.'

Will follows her. 'We can't leave it like this... let's talk it through. Tell me what you've found out at least.'

Kerensa leads the way to her front door, opens it and stands to one side. 'I think that would be a bad idea. Goodbye, Will, and thanks for all you did to help me in the first few awful days and weeks after Leo died. I won't forget it.' Her face is set. Determined.

Will wants to shout, yell, cry, beg. But he doesn't. He knows it would do no good. Instead, his feet take him outside, around the side of the house and along the path to his car. As he walks, he sees the little girl still jumping in the waves and he brushes away a tear. He can hardly process what's just happened. But he knows who's to blame. Patrick. Patrick is to blame and Will's a bloody fool for allowing himself to get dragged into this unholy mess.

Once more behind the wheel, he leans his head against the window and lets the tears come. Then he wipes them away with the back of his hand and thumps the dashboard. He won't give Kerensa up without a fight. And Patrick is going to wish he'd never been born.

22

After Will's gone, the house feels so empty. My heart feels similar, and I sit at the kitchen table in the chair he sat in and put my head in my hands. Why does everything turn to shit lately? What must I have done in a previous life to be visited with death, deception and heartbreak? A week ago, I might have considered Will's proposal, probably wouldn't have accepted it, but it wouldn't have filled me with sadness like it did just now. I certainly would have been pleased that he loved me. Nevertheless, even though I felt... feel deep affection for him, I would never leave Cornwall. Wild horses, and all that. But he seemed hell-bent on leaving here to get away from Patrick and the past. I need to find out exactly why, and what the argument I overheard in the garage is all about.

I realise my plan to play one man against the other fell through the minute I told Will to leave and that I didn't want to see him again. It wasn't planned, I just knew in my heart of hearts that it wouldn't work to keep on seeing him. I care about him. He's hurt me too much with his lies and half-truths. Patrick is the one who has the upper hand in their relationship, and getting on his good side is key to what I need to get at the truth. I hope. From my wardrobe, I select a green velvet top with a scoop neck. It's not too revealing, but it does show some cleavage. I pair it with some skinny black jeans and set off for Patrick's.

He opens the door and the way he looks me up and down makes me shudder. Can he be any more obvious? I ignore it and find a bright smile from somewhere. He says, 'Darlin', you look absolutely gorgeous. Come on in and I'll fix us a drink.' Patrick waves me through and I follow him into his kitchen. His head in the fridge, he says, 'I'm having a lager. How about you?'

'Just fruit juice, thanks.' I need a clear mind and my wits about me.

'Really? That's not like my Kerensa.'

I bristle inside, but carry on smiling. I'm not *his* Kerensa. The only person who was allowed to call me that was Leo. 'I'm going to do a bit of sketching when I get home. If I have a drink, I'll fall asleep.'

'It won't be long before you can make good use of your new studio,' he says, handing me a glass of orange juice and popping the cap off his bottle of lager. He flicks his vivid green eyes over me and then looks into the middle distance. 'I can almost see it all in my imagination. You sitting by that big window working on a piece, looking up at the ocean from time to time, happy in your work and in your life. I can't think of anything more lovely.'

The strength of feeling in his words and the adoration in his eyes throw me a little. But then I remember the way he threatened Will in the garage, and it all makes horrible sense. It's not obsession, or at least, not just obsession he feels for me – I think he loves me. Actually loves me... I take a breath and dredge up my best acting skills. 'You make it sound perfect, Patrick. Thank you so much. I can't wait until it's set up.'

He gives me a wink. 'The pleasure's all mine. I love your

work. Let's go up there now and you can tell me what you need. I'll make a list.'

Twenty minutes later he's made a long list of things I need. He's added loads to it that I didn't ask for. Materials such as paint, clay, a welding torch and brushes. Though I protest, because I know how much it will all cost, he says money's no object and it will give him pleasure to think of me working on my next masterpiece in his house. I thank him and say I have to get back, but he puts his hand on my arm, stops me as I walk to the front door. 'Did Will come round earlier? You said he was going to.'

'Yes, he did.'

Patrick gives me a shy glance. 'I must admit, I was curious about why, so I asked. It's kind of you both to organise a surprise for my birthday.'

'Ah yes…' I pause, unsure of what to say next. How much to divulge. I opt for a half-truth. 'Will and I argued actually. I said I didn't want to be friends anymore… I'd rather not go into why.'

Patrick's face can't decide if it's overjoyed or angry. 'Bloody hell. If he's hurt you or–'

I hold up a hand. 'No. Nothing like that. Can we leave it now, Patrick?'

'Do you want me to have a word with him?'

'No. As I said – let's leave it. I'm tired and I don't want to talk about it.'

He places both hands on my shoulders and I try not to flinch as he pecks my cheek. 'Of course, honey. But remember, I'm here for you whenever you need me.'

'I know, thank you.'

Once again behind my own front door, I heave a sigh of relief.

Forty-five minutes pretending to be nice to Patrick has left me exhausted. God knows what I'll be like when I'm actually working in the studio. If it gets too much, I'll ask him to leave. Hopefully he'll get the fact that the creative process needs quiet, not a loud Irishman continually rabbiting in my ear. The whole point of accepting his offer is so I can find out more about him, and hopefully do a bit of snooping if he leaves me alone in the house. Someone took Leo's document box. If it's there I'll find it. The box could be with Will, of course. That thought makes my heart sink. It's still hard to believe that he could turn out to be such a disappointment.

I start a sketch of a couple of leaping dolphins, but then think a sculpture, like the sharks that sold so well, might be the right medium instead. A scavenging trip to the beach will be needed and I close my eyes and try to remember what items I have left in the shop in my recycling bin. Then an idea of how to get Patrick out of the house slips into the mix. I'll have to orchestrate a situation whereby he'll be gone for a while. Maybe I'll buy him a birthday present and give him clues to where it is. That place needs to be at least half an hour from here. So, an hour there and back, plus the time it will take for him to jump around taking selfies like an overgrown child when he finds it.

The sketch of the dolphins is nearly finished by bedtime. I decided to carry on and use it as a reference when I make my beachcomber sculpture. The buzz I get when I'm working on something new is in full force and I'm feeling more settled. I have a plan, and though still hurting about Will, I know not seeing him again is the right thing to do.

The moonset over the Atlantic from my bedroom window shimmers silver across the water. I wonder if Will is lying awake puzzling about why I rejected him so cruelly. He'll get his explanation eventually, when I find out what the hell happened to my Leo.

'For fuck's sake, Patrick. What do you want at this hour?' Will says through the small gap at his front door.

'I need to talk to you about Kerensa.'

'It's nearly bloody midnight. It'll have to wait until tomor–'

Patrick sets his shoulder at the door and barges in before Will has chance to draw breath. 'We're talking about her and we're talking now!' Patrick marches into the living room and throws himself into an armchair. His face is dark with anger and his eyes are too bright – agitated.

Will takes a breath. He knows when Patrick gets like this, he needs careful handling. He smelled of booze when he stormed past. 'Look. Whatever's eating you, it can wait. You've probably had a drink and–'

'Yes, Sherlock, I've had a drink. Is there any wonder? My Kerensa comes round earlier and says you've upset her so badly that she's cut all ties with you. What exactly did you do?'

Why did she say that to him? 'I didn't upset her in the way you mean…' Will's struggling. He can't tell Patrick the truth, or he'll explode. If he explodes, Will is liable to as well. Earlier he'd wanted to go round to Patrick's and throttle him. He stopped himself, but only just. He'd done something else instead. Something that hopefully would land Patrick in hot water one day.

'Really? I'm all ears.'

'No. I'm not telling you. It's between me and Kerensa.'

'Tell me, or I swear I'll reveal everything.'

Dear Lord. Is he insane? 'There's no way you can do that. She'll run a mile – probably in the direction of the police station. We'll both be locked up. How many times have we argued about this now?'

Patrick thumps his fist down on the arm of the chair. 'She won't run from me. I could see affection in her eyes tonight.

Kerensa's coming round. She'll understand when I tell her. But she'll hate you. I'll tell her everything was your idea. *You* took advantage of *me* – I'll say that money motivated you. By the time I've finished spinning my tale, *we* won't end up locked up – *you* will.'

Will sighs. 'If you believe all that, then you're dumber than I thought.'

'I'm dumb? You're the one who nicked Leo's document box with the PIN numbers and passwords to his offshore account. It has your fingerprints all over it.' Patrick smiles, shoves his hands through his hair, strokes his chin. 'I expect the police will like that.'

For fuck's sake. 'I only took the box because you asked me to. I keep it here because you said it was safest!'

'Yes. You do seem to fall for the same tricks, don't you?'

Will ignores that. 'And anyway, it has your fingerprints on it now too.'

'No, it doesn't. Every time I come round here to access it, I wear surgical gloves.'

Will is boiling mad. His heart's racing and it's all he can do to keep from striding over to Patrick and punching him. 'I have some nasty shit on you too, don't forget. You were the one who came up with the crazy plan of telling her Leo killed himself. I can still see the hurt in her eyes when I had to break it to her that day in Plymouth. There she was, worried and pregnant, and not only did she have to learn her husband was dead, she found out it could have been prevented. Leo actively decided to leave her. All because of money! How could you spin such a story to a woman you supposedly love?'

'It had to sound authentic. It fitted with Leo's state of mind! You remember what he was like back then!' Patrick threw his arms up. 'And once again, William, I'll just say it was your idea. You were the one who told her. You were the one who did it all.

As I've said before, if you even think of telling her the truth, you'll be the one losing everything. Your job, your liberty. It wasn't me who used bribery and lies to get the ambulance sorted to pick up the body, was it? And similar for the paperwork. Need I go on?'

Will's incredulous and impotent all at the same time. 'You gave me the money – plus it was your idea!'

Patrick laughs. 'But there's no proof and you know it. I can see it in your eyes. For a surgeon you really are stupid sometimes. Too trusting.'

'How can you live with yourself?'

'Easy. My only concern is to win Kerensa and I will do whatever it takes to get her. I mean it. There's *nothing* I won't do – so you'd better watch your back.'

There's a manic gleam in Patrick's eye and Will can see he means every word. He's not thinking it through. Even if Patrick blames the entire debacle on Will, Kerensa would run a mile from him. From both of them actually, but it has to stop. It has to stop now. All of it. This has gone far enough: Will wants Patrick out of his house. Out of his life. Then he's going to tell Kerensa everything and face the music. Will tries to calm his erratic breathing and slow the thump of his heart. He musters a calm tone. 'Listen to me, Patrick. I'm going to go upstairs to get you your precious document box. Then you're going to fuck off out of my life. I don't want to hear from you ever again.'

'I don't think so, Will!' Patrick stands up, a nasty sneer turning his mouth down at the edges. Will judges Patrick's ready to do "whatever it takes", but he's past caring. Part of him wants a fight. He'd like to smash that handsome face to a pulp. Break him into a thousand pieces. But could he take him on? Is Patrick stronger and fitter? It's a close call... but sod it.

Will rushes from the room and up the stairs, two at a time. He hears Patrick bellow and then he's thumping up the stairs after him. Near the top, Will swings round and puts the flat of his hand on Patrick's chest. 'Stop right there! How dare you barge into my house, demand things from me – threaten me? After all I've done for you!' Will moves his hand because he's itching to give Patrick a shove.

Patrick puts his face inches from Will's. His eyes are wild, fury dancing in them like green flames. 'You've betrayed me. I can tell you're in love with Kerensa. Admit it.' He jabs a stubby finger into Will's chest. 'Admit it!'

Before he can stop himself, Will yells, 'Yes! Okay, I admit it. I told her I was tonight, but she didn't want to know. So I've nothing to lose. I'm going to tell her all of it! About Leo. Tell her exactly what kind of an evil monster Patrick O'Brien is! Satisfied now?'

Patrick's face contorts into a mask of rage. He leaps to the top of the stairs behind Will and hooks an arm around his neck, yanks him backward and squeezes so hard Will feels his eyes bulge. Fuck, he's strong. Patrick yells in his ear, 'No. But I'm satisfied now, you traitorous bastard!' Will grabs at Patrick's arm, but before he can get enough purchase on his bicep, he feels a row of knuckles and a hard shove in his back. He's tumbling. Will claws at the banister as he falls, but all he catches is air. Then the blue ceramic tiles on the hall floor race to meet him.

No. Please God, no!

Upon impact, there's a crack and searing pain... then darkness.

23

'I think I might get a dog,' I say, through a mouthful of Sally's famous coffee and walnut cake. 'Leo and I often talked about it, but what with me being out all day teaching, and him working away from home, it never felt right. I mean, it wouldn't be fair to leave a dog at home all day, would it?'

Sally wiped coffee cream from the side of her mouth with a napkin. 'No. But what's changed? You're in the shop all day now, aren't you?'

'Yes. But the dog could come with me. And I could take him or her for a quick sprint on the beach in my quiet times too. I could get a rescue dog who needs a break. We'd be good for each other. I do get lonely.' I look out of the coffee shop window at the passers-by and think of Leo. Then my mind drifts to Will, even though I don't want it to. It's been two days since I told him to go, and it's odd not hearing his voice on the phone.

'I reckon it's a great idea,' Sally says, getting up from our table by the window and dusting crumbs from her apron. She's grabbed a minute to sit with me but now the shop's filling up and she needs to help Lily behind the counter. 'When will you get one?'

Now the idea of a dog is becoming a real possibility, I'm not sure. What if it pees and poops everywhere? What if it bites me? What if it fights with other dogs? What if it runs off on the beach and leaps on poor unsuspecting people when they're having a paddle? I hate it when dogs do that to me. I blame the owners though, not the dogs. 'I'll have to have a think.'

Sally goes off, and I chase a few cake crumbs around my plate with my finger. Maybe I'll wait a few more weeks and then see if I still feel the need of a dog. Maybe a cat would work better. It could have a cat flap and go and come as it pleased. It would be there waiting when I got home, and we could snuggle up together on cold winter nights in front of the fire. Cats don't pounce on people on the beach or need walking. Mm. Yes, a cat might be the answer. We had a few cats when I was growing up, so I know how to look after one. Maybe I'll be a mad cat lady in years to come. Just me in that big old house with fifteen cats. I smile at the image and then realise I'm about to cry. Do I want to be alone for the rest of my life?

Mum phoned this morning and said she was a bit worried about me. She said I don't seem myself. What exactly is myself? I don't really know these days. Maybe I'm not myself because my husband died, killed himself or was murdered. Maybe I'm not myself because my baby died. Maybe I'm not myself because Will turned out to be a shit. Maybe I'm not myself because I'm currently on a mission to find out what he and Patrick had to do with Leo's death. And right now, maybe I'm not myself, because I am devising a list of clues for Patrick in order for him to be out of the house finding his birthday surprise, while I'm at his house rifling through his life.

I've ransacked my own house just to check one hundred per cent it wasn't there. So now it can only be with Patrick or Will. My money's on Patrick, because he's the trouser-wearer. But if I'm wrong, I'll have to make up with Will. Great. I look at the notepad in front of me. Five clues should be enough. I'm going to send him to Porth, Newquay, Crantock, Truro and back here to the pub. The barman has his present – a small painting of a girl on the beach – behind the bar. I'm going to hide the scraps of paper with the clues on them in various places at the locations. Each clue will lead to the next one and if he gets stuck, he has to ring me for help. What a shame this isn't for real. It's a nice idea.

Sally hasn't asked about Patrick, which I'm thankful for. I hate lying to her. She will ask sooner or later, I expect. But until then, I'm keeping the studio that's been kitted out for me, and the fact that I've banished Will, a secret. Because of my mission, I've had to close the shop for the afternoon. Patrick can't go clue-hunting at night after all. Still, I can make the time up at the weekend. I finish my coffee and say goodbye to Sally. I need to give Patrick a ring and hide these clues.

On the drive to Porth, I call him on the car phone.

'Happy birthday, Patrick.' I put a smile in my voice but feel anything but pleasant.

'Thank you, sweetheart! It's lovely to hear your voice, this fine day.'

'Yours too.' I cringe. 'Now here's your surprise.' I run through what he has to do and tell him the first clue.

'What brilliant fun! And *so* thoughtful.'

'Glad you think so. And Patrick, while you're on your treasure hunt, can I pop over to yours to do a bit of work in the studio? I know it's not quite ready yet, but the light in there is–'

'Of course! You don't have to ask. Mi casa es su casa. That's Spanish for–'

'Yes, I know what it means. That's so kind of you. Will you leave the door unlocked?'

'I will. I'll get you a key cut while I'm out too.'

Yes! I can sneak in any time. 'How nice of you. That would be ideal.'

'It's my absolute pleasure, Kerensa. See you soon, my dear, dear friend.'

I contain my revulsion and end the call.

After I've set the clues, I pop back home to grab a bottle of water. All that rushing around has made me thirsty. I take a big swig, then drag a kitchen chair out with my foot so I can sit down, and notice something little slide across the tiles. I reach down to pick it up. It's a credit card. Will's credit card. Odd. I turn it round and set it on the table. How did it get under my table? Then I remember he dropped his wallet the other day. I picked it up and handed it back. The card must have slipped out unnoticed. He must have been wondering where the hell it was these past two days. Why hasn't he phoned to see if he'd left it here?

I drink some more water and with a sinking heart, I realise the onus is on me. This means I have to get in touch with him. But why should I? Bugger him. I owe him no favours. But then if I don't, he's going to contact me sooner or later, isn't he? Or even show up. Shit. I really don't want to face him again. Then I have a brainwave. I won't ring him, I'll send it to his work instead. Buggeration. I don't know which hospital... but then how many private hospitals can there be in Truro? I get my laptop and Google them. Two. Good, it won't take long to find out. Grabbing my phone out of my handbag, I call the first one. No, they don't have a William Gray working in orthopaedics there.

Has to be this one then. A receptionist answers, reciting the name of the hospital and asks how she can help. She sounds as though she'd rather be anywhere but on the end of this phone. I take a breath and say, 'Good afternoon. Can you tell me if you have a surgeon called William Gray working in your orthopaedic department?'

'Yes, but not in orthopaedics,' she says curtly.

That throws me. 'Are you sure...?'

'Of course I'm sure, madam. I've worked here ten years and I know all our staff and which department they work in.' She does a little polite laugh, but I can tell she's not remotely amused.

So why did he tell me orthopaedics? 'Right. But to be clear, he does work there?'

'Yes... I can't divulge more due to data protection.'

I can almost see her rolling her eyes at the other end of the line. 'Okay. Thank you. He's a friend of mine and he left something at my house the other day. I'll address it to him and send it to you by registered post either today or tomorrow. Thank you.'

'I see. May I ask who's calling? Shall I ask him to call you back?'

Hmm. Now she's interested. A bit of gossip about a female friend of Will's to spread round the staff. 'No, thanks. I'm sure he's busy.'

'He was due back from a few days off today, but he's–'

I end the call. Thought she couldn't divulge much? I can't be bothered to feed her boring little gossip mill. And why would Will tell me the wrong department? In the end I decide it doesn't matter why he lied. I've done with him anyway.

On the cliff path to Patrick's place, a few butterflies show up in my belly. What if he comes back unexpectedly and catches me snooping? The bedrooms might be the best place to start, while he's at the beginning of the present hunt, and then I can search the rest of the place later. That way, if he does come back and catches me in the living room, it's easy to make an excuse. Bedrooms are not so easy. I stand on the path for a few moments looking out over the ocean and the craggy cliffs sheltering the bay. It's a long way down and not for the first time I wish I could just take off and glide through the air, calling to the wind like the seagulls.

Releasing a breath, I reluctantly turn from the scene and hurry across the grass to Patrick's house. The door is unlocked, but I still check round the front to make sure his car's not there. It could be in the garage though. What if he's inside waiting for me? He might have forgotten the clue and needs to check something. *Come on, Kerensa. Get this done.* I hurry back round and go inside. My trainers squeak on the highly polished wooden floor so I take them off and my jacket too. I wait and listen. No sign of life. In the kitchen, I hang my jacket on the back of a chair and open a cupboard or two. Nothing but pans and crockery. This is just procrastination. I get a grip and run up the sweeping staircase.

The loft room goes up some spiral stairs to the left of the landing, and there are six doors leading off. Patrick did give Sally and me a quick tour that first day here, but I wasn't paying that much attention. I hurry along, opening all of the doors and find five bedrooms and a spacious bathroom. Two of the bedrooms overlook the front of the house, the herb garden, the gravel driveway and the cow field beyond. Three of the bedrooms overlook the ocean. Four don't have a lot in them, just a bed each, and a few sticks of furniture – stripped-back guest bedrooms really. But Patrick's master bedroom is stunning. It's about the only one that made an impression last time, but now I examine it in detail. A large en suite, a huge bed, with what looks like a bespoke bedcover, in a Moroccan-type pattern of yellows and greens. A calming blue on the walls, the main one presenting my butterfly collage to its best advantage. I don't think I remember it from last time I was in here. On the stripped pine floor are various woven rugs to match the bedding. The furniture is sleek and inconspicuous and the floor-to-ceiling windows open out onto a long balcony, upon which sits a sun table and two chairs. The ideal place to watch the ocean.

At the foot of the bed is a large antique ottoman, strangely at odds with the rest of the décor, yet somehow it fits perfectly. It's to this that I go first. It has nothing of interest, just extra bedding and a few towels. The wardrobe doors slide back effortlessly and contain racks of shirts, trousers, jackets and jumpers. They are colour-coordinated, shoes to match too, placed in a line on the bottom rung. Leo used to like order, but he wasn't quite as neat as this. The dressing table and chest of drawers contain underwear, T-shirts, shorts, hairbrushes, a shaver, but no document box. Under the bed there's nothing. Not even dust. Patrick must have a cleaner. I can't envisage him doing housework.

I do a quick search of the other bedrooms, the bathroom too, and find nothing, once again. Okay, now to try downstairs. Then I remember the master bedroom en suite. Doubtful he's hidden a document box in it, but might as well check.

The usual's in here. A shower, toilet, bath, a few mirrored cabinets and a cupboard. Nothing apart from toiletries and toilet rolls in the cupboard. Same kinds of things in one cabinet and in the other; a few medical supplies and a pile of little boxes tucked to one side of the shelf. I know I'm supposed to be looking for pertinent items, but these little boxes have piqued my interest.

I sit on the loo, stick my fingernail under the lid of one of the boxes and gently pry it open. Contact lenses. Green-tinted contact lenses! How vain can you get? No wonder his eyes look so bright and unusual. There's more pairs exactly the same in the others, though I don't open all of them. I quickly put them back where I found them. Who'd have thought it? But it's not really a surprise, is it? Patrick is one of the vainest men alive. I check that everything looks just as I found it and leave his bedroom.

The living room has so many possible hiding places, it takes me a good hour to search them all. Cabinets, shelves, behind sofas, under sofas, in cupboards. The sideboard looks promising, and I do find the rental documents to this house and receipts for his car and one or two other utility bills, just no box. The kitchen cupboards prove fruitless too, as does the laundry room and downstairs bathroom. There's more contact lenses in there. He must buy them in bulk so he never has to worry about running out. Is his real eye colour so awful?

I sit on the arm of the sofa and go over everything and everywhere I have looked again in my head. There's nowhere left to look. Then something suddenly strikes me. Apart from the folder of bills and stuff in the sideboard drawer, there are no personal documents. Everybody has birth certificates, passports, academic qualifications, things like that. So where are Patrick's? Has he put them in Leo's box – keeping them all safe together? It's possible. What about a loft? There's the big studio loft room, but is there further storage anywhere? In one of the spare rooms to the front of the house there's a little square door set in the ceiling. This must be it!

I stand on a chair I drag from another spare room, pull open the hatch and lower a ladder. There's nothing in the loft apart from a huge spider, empty packing boxes, empty suitcases and some broken toys. Must have been left behind from the previous tenants.

Back downstairs, the clock on the wall tells me I'm running out of time. Won't it look suspicious if he comes back and finds me down here – not working? I've not even so much as put pencil to paper since I arrived. *Shit.* Racing up to the studio, I fling open the door to find a huge bouquet of flowers and a big box of handmade chocolates on top of the workbench. An envelope addressed to me is next to those and inside's a card with a seascape on the front. Patrick's printed in block capitals:

TO MY BEAUTIFUL AND TALENTED KERENSA. MAY YOU CREATE YOUR BEST WORK AND ALWAYS BE HAPPY IN THIS SPECIAL STUDIO!
LOTS OF LOVE – PATRICK XXXXXXX

Oh God, how over the top. And can't he do joined-up handwriting? I stand the card up and open the chocolates. No point in wasting them, is there? I grab a sheet of A5 paper and do a very quick sketch of the view. When Patrick comes back, I can say I started a sketch and then got lost in gazing at the ocean and eating chocolate. I'm getting too used to this lying. But what choice do I have? The chocolates are delicious and as my third one disappears, I have a light-bulb moment. I didn't check inside the washing machine in the laundry – nor the bloody garage! It's unlikely that the document box would be in either, but isn't that where he would hide it if he didn't want it to be found? In the most unlikely places?

Galloping back downstairs to the laundry in my socks, I nearly go flying along the polished wood in the corridor. *Okay, calm down. Be methodical.* I've already checked the bottom of the laundry basket but do so again, just in case. Then I look inside the washing machine. Nope. Then the tumble dryer and shelf space again. Nope. But then it's impractical to hide a box in machines which are in frequent use. Nothing in the big cupboard under the sink. Just soap powder, fabric conditioner, pegs, a washing-up bowl, cloths and a plunger. So the last chance saloon has to be the garage.

It's a sizeable space with a workbench, gardening equipment, tool boxes and a few large cupboards on the wall. There's nothing of note in one of the cupboards, just oil, a pressure gauge, a tyre pump and a handbook. I look at the final cupboard. The last place left I haven't searched. I fill my lungs and exhale. This is it. I stride up to it and pull the handle. It won't budge. I try again, it might just be stiff. No. Odd. I look around the side of the cupboard and see it has a metal strap latch and a padlock holding it closed. My heart's racing. This is the only thing that's been inaccessible in the whole house. If the box is anywhere, it's in here.

Now, think. Where can the key be? I cast my eyes about and soon see a little pot on the workbench. I pick it up and have a look inside. There are pens, bolts, screws, but no keys... It seems most likely that Patrick might have the key on his key ring. If it was me, I'd want it with me at all times. Bloody hell. So near and yet so far. Then I nearly scream out loud when the garage door starts to buzz open. Patrick's back! I race through the laundry door and then remember I've left the light on in the garage. I dash back and flick it off, just as I hear his car crunch along the gravel towards the garage entrance.

In the studio again, I sit at the desk at the window. I try the calming breathing technique taught to me by my counsellor in my darkest period before Leo's funeral. In through the nose for a count of five, out through the mouth for four. My pulse rate is almost back to normal and I've added a bit of shading to my sketch when Patrick comes in.

'There she is. Kerensa, artist extraordinaire and light of my life!' he says with a laugh and pats me on the back. Then he peers over my shoulder to see what I'm working on.

I laugh too and get out of my chair, move to the other side of the studio, ostensibly to get the chocolate box, but in actuality to keep my distance. 'Thanks for the compliment and for these.' I wave at the bouquet. 'And those.' I stuff another chocolate in my mouth and offer him one.

'Don't mind if I do.' He selects two and tosses one in the air, catches it in his teeth. I used to clap in admiration when Leo did that, but Patrick doing it just irritates me. Does he ever stop showing off?

I lean against the wall and fold my arms. 'Did you manage to find all the clues?'

'I did! And let me tell you it was the most fun I've had for ages. It took ages too – in Truro at least. The other clues were easy, but the one at the post office took some thinking through. The paper was covered in brick dust too when I pulled it from behind the window frame. I could only just make it out!' He does the big bellowy guffaw again.

'So where's your present?'

'Right here.' Patrick goes to the door and picks up the painting of the girl that he's left on the landing. 'I adore it. Thank you so much. Where shall we hang it?' He's wearing the overgrown-kid expression and looking expectantly at me.

'Um. How about in your room next to the other one of mine?'

His overgrown kid is folded under a grimace of suspicion, as it hits me what I've just said. 'You've been in my room today? I only put that picture up last week.'

Fucking hell. How stupid! Now what do I say? 'Er... I'm sorry. I only popped my head round on my way up here.' My face is aflame. 'What can I say? I'm just really nosy.'

Patrick smiles. 'It's only natural. No worries.' There's an uncomfortable pause until he gestures at my sketch. 'This is nice.'

'Thanks. I haven't done much. I got preoccupied with the chocolates and the view.'

'Great art needs thinking time.' He gives me a big smile. 'I love that you feel relaxed here. Think of this space as yours.'

'That's kind, Patrick. Well, I'd best be off.'

His smile disappears. 'But it's my birthday. I was hoping you'd join me later for a meal. You and me... we could go out?'

No way in hell. 'It might feel a bit odd, Patrick. I'm no longer friends with Will and we've always done things as a four. Then there's Sally. She'd be very hurt if she knew. After... you know?'

'After what?' Patrick has a knowing twinkle in his eye.

I'm not amused. 'I think you know. She was very upset when you said there was no future for the both of you.'

He shrugs. 'Can't help how I feel, Kerensa.'

'Maybe not. But you did lead her on a bit.'

'Hardly. She threw herself at me.'

'You encouraged her.'

Patrick puts his hands up. 'Whatever your point of view, I'm not interested in her that way. If that's hurt her, I'm sorry for that too. I like her, as a friend, but that's all. And as far as Will's concerned, he's helped me settle down here in Cornwall, but if you're not happy to see him, then neither am I.'

'But that's ridiculous.'

'Why?'

'Because he's been your friend for years. You've only known me two minutes.'

'Look, Kerensa. I'm not sure how to say this but...' He stops, gives me an intense stare.

Oh God, please don't let him declare undying love. 'Then don't say it.'

'I have to. The thing is, I am very fond of you. Very. And anyone who hurts you, hurts me.'

He does the scrubbing his hair thing and stroking his chin that Leo did, which just gets my temper up. When will he learn that imitating my husband will *not* win him my affections? I take a breath. 'I'm flattered, Patrick. But right now, there's no room in my life for any man. I'm still in love with my husband, even though he did a despicable thing. It will take a long time for me to be ready to love again. If I ever am.' I look out at the waves and swallow an unexpected ball of emotion. When I look back, I see Patrick's wiping tears from his cheeks.

'Oh God, would you look at me?' He sniffs and tries a wobbly smile. 'The strength of your love for Leo is humbling. He was a very lucky man.'

'Yes. It's a shame he didn't realise that.'

'Oh. I'm sure he did...'

'And you know this how?' I try to keep a lid on my anger but it's bubbling up in the pot.

Patrick frowns and avoids my gaze, folds his arms across his chest in a classic defence move. 'I don't really... but I'm sure he only did what he did for you both for the future.'

I'm sick of this. 'Did you know Leo, Patrick?'

'Um... no.'

Liar. 'Then please stop talking about him as if you did. It doesn't help, in fact I find it very annoying.'

He opens his fake green eyes wide and puts up his hands. 'Please, Kerensa. Let's not argue. That's the last thing I want. I'll have to accept that you're not ready for more than friendship, but I'm willing to wait until the day you are.'

Arrogant bastard. 'What if I'm never ready? And if I am, what if it's not with you?'

He heaves a sigh. 'That's a risk I'm prepared to take. Please say we can be friends.'

I want to tell him to shove his friendship up his arse, but the little key to the cupboard is jingling inside my head. In order to find that box, and how he and Will were involved with Leo, I need to play the long game, no matter how unpalatable it is. I also need to give him a few crumbs of hope to keep him interested. I force the edges of my mouth upward and say, 'Of course we can be friends. But I'm tired tonight, but why don't I bring some cake over tomorrow? A birthday-type cake.'

Patrick flashes the Hollywood smile. 'Fantastic! And I promise from here on in that I'll be your best friend and nothing more. You call the shots.'

'Okay. See you tomorrow.'

On my way home, I think about tomorrow and spending more time alone with Patrick, and my stomach rolls. It has to be done though, because I need to find out where he keeps the key and try to get my hands on it. If the box isn't in that cupboard, it has to be at Will's. If it's at Will's, then I'll have to get back on side with him. God, what a bloody mess this is turning into.

24

Mum pops round as I'm getting ready to go to Patrick's. She's got that pinched look she wears when she has something serious to say to me. I gird my loins and push Patrick's birthday cake to the back of the counter. I made it first thing before work and decorated it when I got back. It took longer than expected, because I had to keep stopping to dry my eyes and gulp water. Almost to the day I'd made a cake for Leo's birthday. Isn't life a bastard? Little did I know when I was piping the chocolate icing around the edge of his cake and wrote his name across the middle in vanilla, that it would be the last time I ever did.

'You look nice, love. Going out?' Mum says, her eyes scanning my kitchen and coming to rest on the cake.

'I am in a bit. Want a cuppa?' I ask, hoping that she doesn't.

'Who's the cake for?' She walks over and peers at it. 'Happy Birthday, Patrick? I thought you couldn't stand him.'

'I'm not over fond. I just think he seems a bit lonely – so I made him a cake.'

'Lonely? Thought he had lots of friends. And I know for a

fact he has Will, you and that Sally. I thought him and her were going out?'

Mum has swapped her pinched look for her Spanish Inquisition expression. I'm going to have to tell her a watered-down version of the truth, or I'll never get out alive. 'There's been a big falling out. Sally told Patrick how she felt, and he turned her down. I sent Will packing because he declared his undying love to me, and Patrick fell out with him too – but I'm not sure why.'

'Oh no.' Mum's pinched look is back with a helping of concern. 'That's why I came over. I've been so worried about you and I thought that Will could make you happy. I've seen how he looks at you, and like it or not, the way you look at him too. I wanted to tell you to try to put the past behind you a little, and give the poor boy a chance.' Her eyes fill. 'Because I hate seeing you so sad, my darling. Sad and... and lonely.'

Seeing her upset brings tears to my eyes for the second time this evening. Oh God. This is all I need. 'Hey, Mum. I'm not lonely, honest.' *Lie.* 'Yes, I did like Will, but I'm not ready for a new relationship yet.' *Half-truth.* 'There's nothing to worry about. I'm busy in my work and the shop's doing well.' *Truth.* 'Everything will be fine and I'm actually happier than I have been for a long time.' *Lie.*

Mum's expression doesn't change. 'Are you sure, Enza? You know you can tell me anything.'

'I'm sure, Mum. Stop worrying.'

She purses her lips, blows down her nostrils. 'I can't weigh you up sometimes, my girl. Why you've changed your mind over this Patrick, I have no idea. I mean, I thought he seemed nice, but at the barbecue you said you reckoned he might have been involved with Leo and swindling money from that evil Donaldson man. You said he was copying Leo's mannerisms and he might have even been involved in poor Leo's death. Now you're making him cakes!'

'One cake.'

'Don't be facetious. You know what I mean.'

'Yes, but I did tell you on the phone a while ago I was wrong about Patrick and I'd jumped to wild conclusions.'

'You say that kind of thing to shut me up. Stop me worrying about your state of mind.'

'My state of mind? Are you saying you think your only daughter is a fruit loop?' I laugh, hoping it sounds genuine. I need to get going.

Mum loses the pinched look and smiles. 'Well, you've always been a fruit loop. But you're my fruit loop and I love you.' She envelops me in a huge hug and I want to tell her everything. About the overheard argument between Patrick and Will, about Leo's missing box, and about the mission I'm on to find it, and about my determination to see both men punished when I find out what they did to my husband. I can't tell her any of it though. Can I?

'I love you too, Mum,' I say into her shoulder and inhale the perfume she's always worn, and I'm immediately comforted. With an effort, I step out of her arms. 'But I really must get this cake over to Patrick's. We'll have to meet up for lunch soon and have a proper catch up.'

'I'll hold you to that.' Mum gives me a kiss on both cheeks, looks into my eyes. 'You promise you're okay? Me and your dad don't have to worry about you night and day?'

I cross my fingers behind my back. 'Promise. Now off you pop.'

I wish I could have popped off with her, but instead, ten minutes later, I'm outside Patrick's house with a cake tin in my hands and a big grin on my face. He opens the door and hugs me and the tin. The metal edge presses into my chest and I say,

'Ow. Steady on, you'll crush me and the cake.' I grit my teeth and smile.

'Sorry, sorry! And what am I like leaving you outside in this nippy air?' He ushers me through, and I follow him into the kitchen, put the tin on the side.

'Hope you like chocolate cake.' I pull an anxious look out of the bag but couldn't give a toss if he does or doesn't.

'How can anyone not like chocolate cake?'

'No idea.' I ask for a plate and take the lid off the tin. 'Now go into the living room and I'll bring it through when I've sorted it. Tea okay?'

'Tea's fine. I can't tell you how brilliant this all is. Thank you. I'll go through and put on some music.'

It had better not be a love song. I put the cake on the plate and take a box of candles out of my bag. Then I notice Patrick's bunch of keys on the table and stride over, try to examine them without picking them up in case he comes back in and catches me. Car key, two Yales, various others but quite large, and there's a little one too. The padlock was small... this looks to be the perfect size. My heart's thumping in my ears. He might come in, but I think it's now or perhaps never. I might not get this chance again. With trembling fingers, I pick the bunch up and start to twist the key off, and then the music starts, and I drop them with a clatter on the table.

The Sweetest Thing by U2 snakes out of the living room and squeezes my heart. Leo and me loved that song. How the hell could Patrick know? He couldn't know. I tear off some kitchen roll and dab at my eyes, my thoughts grabbing at fantasy. Is this Leo's way of letting me know he's here and is telling me he's sorry for what he's done? I look out of the window at the herb garden, whisper – 'Leo? Leo, are you here?' I close my eyes, take a moment. God, I need to get a grip.

'Everything okay in there?' Patrick yells.

I swallow hard. 'Yeah, just coming!' I stick the candles in the cake and light them. Then I walk through into the living room. 'Happy birthday to you, Patrick. I'm not going to sing because my voice sounds like a creaky gate.'

'Ha! I'm sure it doesn't.' He points the remote at the stereo and turns the music down. He looks at the cake and beams at me. 'Ah, it's brilliant! Thanks so much, Kerensa. Will I blow out the candles?'

'Er, that's the plan.'

'Okay. I'll make a wish... after three.' He closes his eyes. 'One, two, three!'

The candles are snuffed out by his first puff and I clap. 'Congratulations. Many happy returns and may you have many more. How old were you yesterday, Patrick?'

'Thirty-five.'

I nod. *Same as Leo would have been.* I cut the cake and then remember I didn't make the tea as I was distracted by the keys. 'Just going to get the tea. Tuck in.'

I fill the kettle and switch it on. Do I dare try to get the key again while I'm waiting for the kettle to boil? I take a step towards the table, just as Patrick comes in, his mouth full of cake. 'My god, this is incredible, Kerensa!'

I sigh inwardly. No chance of getting the key now. 'Glad you think so.' I attend to the tea as his mobile starts ringing in his pocket.

Patrick puts his plate and fork down by me and answers the call. 'Yes, this is Patrick? Who? Oh yes, sorry. I remember you, James. How are things...? Yes, I left messages on his phone... No. No, Jesus, no.'

The anguish in his voice twists my gut and I turn to see him slump into a kitchen chair. He rakes his hand through his hair and shakes his head in bewilderment at me.

'What's wrong?' I mouth.

He doesn't answer, just shakes his head again. Covers his eyes with a trembling hand. 'Oh no. I can't believe it. How? How did it happen? What... a raised rug? Such a fucking stupid accident. A fucking stupid...' Patrick's shoulders shake and he's crying silent tears. He holds the phone away from his mouth and strangles a sob. I take a step towards him, but he holds up a hand. Composes himself, says into the phone, 'I'm sorry... yes, James, I'm still here. I'll be okay. Thanks for letting me know.'

Patrick ends the call and stares into space for the longest time.

I finish making the tea and place a mug next to him. 'I don't know what's happened, but it sounded serious.' I sit down opposite and wait.

He draws a long shuddering breath and says, 'That was James, Will's friend and work colleague. Will fell down his stairs they think at least two days ago. There was a raised rug on the landing at the top of the stairs and... somehow... somehow they think he got his foot under it and it tripped him. They think he went right from the top to the bottom.'

Patrick's voice is distant, like his stare, and the chill of dread is forming in the heart of me. I picture those stairs. They are wide and steep; the hall tiles are hard and ceramic. I can barely get my words out. I don't want to get them out. But I have to know. 'My god. How... how badly is he hurt?'

Patrick's eyes drift back from the far distance, alight on mine like timid butterflies and then fly away again. 'He's... Oh shit, Kerensa.' Patrick covers his face with his hands and moans through his fingers. 'He's dead.'

25

My eyes feel like they've been rolled in sand. But is there any wonder? I must have had an hour's sleep tops last night, and I've cried enough tears to fill a bathtub. Will's gone. He's actually gone and never coming back. Just like Leo and my baby. And I told Will I never wanted to see him again. So it's my fault, isn't it? If I hadn't have been so mean, he'd still be alive. But then I think of Patrick again and decide it's all his fault. These two thoughts have been chasing themselves around my brain all night, and just as one catches the other, it lets go and the other gains dominance, and the chase continues.

Logically, I can't be to blame because being mean to someone doesn't lead to their death. But what if he had got drunk because of what I'd said, and caught his foot under the rug at the top of the stairs because he was out of it? It would be my fault then. Maybe the police could tell me if he'd been drinking. But that might seem a weird thing for a friend to ask. Maybe Patrick could find out, but then why would I believe a word that comes out of his mouth? In the end, fault isn't the main thing. The main thing is that Will is dead. I don't know how to process it. I can't cope with much more tragedy in my life.

At seven o'clock I get up, splash some cold water on my face and puffy eyes, go downstairs to make some tea. It's a lovely morning, so in my pyjamas, I take my tea down the steps to the beach and sit on a rock, wiggle my toes in the wet sand, and try to clear my mind. A few dog walkers are striding along the shoreline, their dogs chasing balls and each other. The sun's been up an hour and has been busy along the dunes, banishing shadows and turning the sand white. I can hardly believe it will soon be May. Nearly ten months since Leo and my baby. I take a gulp of tea to submerge the knot of emotion and let my thoughts drift.Once more, the Patrick-being-to-blame scenario surfaces and this time it sticks. Not only did he have something to do with Leo's death, he's had something to do with Will's too. I know it. I have no evidence, just a few questions and a whole load of gut feelings. Last night, after he ended the call to Will's colleague James, he couldn't speak for a while and neither could I. I couldn't do anything, not even cry. I was feeling too guilty because of the way things had ended between Will and me. But then I eventually gained control and asked Patrick what this James had said. He told me, and then Patrick said he'd left a few voicemails on Will's phone because he'd not heard from him for a few days. It wasn't like Will not to answer his calls.

This felt wrong, because he told me he'd done with Will because I had. So why was he ringing him and leaving voicemails? But the main thing was, because I'd been in such a state, I set off for home without my coat, so I had to go back for it. When I'd left five minutes beforehand, Patrick had been the picture of depression. Head in hands, wiping his eyes with a tissue, asking why, over and over.

So I was a bit shocked to say the least when I knocked on the door and couldn't get an answer because of the sound of U2 being played super loud. I let myself in and caught Patrick wiggling his bum and singing along while doing the washing-up. Hardly the grieving friend! When he saw me in his kitchen, grabbing my coat from the chair back, he went bright red and started gabbling about music and how it helped with sadness. I just gave him a look, flapped his excuses away and hurried out.

I finish my tea and tell myself for the umpteenth time that these two things aren't enough to point the finger at Patrick. But what if he is involved? What if he went over to Will's house and threw him down the stairs? I think he did. I feel it. But that's a long stretch. Then I realise I'm tired, emotional and need a sounding board. Sally is the obvious choice, but am I ready to tell her everything? She's probably going to go against Patrick anyway – a woman scorned. Perhaps I should just mention to her some of my worries. I need someone to tell me I'm being overdramatic, fanciful. And Sally certainly is good at that. There's nobody I know who is more sensible or level-headed.

Even though it's only three in the afternoon on a Saturday, I have to close the shop and go home for a sleep. I can't concentrate, and the painting I'm working on is a mess. Like my head. I can't stop thinking about poor Will. I'll feel much more like myself if I get some rest and besides, I need to be fresh, because I called Sally earlier and asked if she wanted a break away from her family's troubles. I offered to cook her a meal here later and she jumped at it. The children are having a sleepover at her mum's so it couldn't be better.

Unbelievably, I slept for three hours. I honestly didn't think I'd be able to, but as soon as my head touched the pillow, I was out. Good job I'm cheating with dinner. I grabbed a chilli from Sainsbury's, a bag of salad and some garlic bread on the way home. I'm putting the rice in a pan when Sally arrives with a bunch of flowers in one hand and a bottle of Merlot in the other.

'It seems like ages since it's been just you and me for a good natter,' she says as she kisses me on the cheek, thrusts her gifts at me and breezes in. She looks pleased to see me and I hope she'll not regret it when I start my story.

'That's because it has.' I lead her through and get a vase from the cupboard. As I do, the agapanthus Will brought me catches my eye. It's still in its pot, waiting outside the patio doors to be planted in the ground. A macabre comparison between that and the resting place of its purchaser has my eyes brimming in seconds. Thank God Sally's chattering on about the shop and the kids while I compose myself. I put the flowers in water and pour us a drink.

Maybe I should have told Sally about Will's death on the phone and just left it at that. She's already had to cope with Rachel's grief, now I have another shock in store and a few madcap theories for her to juggle with. The poor love thinks she's coming for a nice meal and a catch up. Maybe I won't tell her. It's so selfish of me. But then if I don't tell her about Will and she finds out another way...

'You okay, Rens?' Sally leans her hip against the work surface and frowns.

'Yeah, why?' I ask, and realise my voice sounds forced, too cheerful.

'For one thing, that cheesy grin looks a bit strained, and you've been miles away ever since I walked through the door.'

I take a gulp of wine and check on the chilli then I wave her through to the living room. 'Let's sit in here on the comfy chairs until dinner's ready. It shouldn't be long now.'

She plonks herself down on the chair and holds her glass up to me. 'Cheers. Now spill what's bothering you. And don't even think of telling me there's nothing to spill.'

I sit down too, put my drink on the coffee table, take a deep breath and tell her about Will. I watch her blink away tears and do the goldfish act. I suppose I must have looked very similar last night. 'I'm so sorry, Sal. I didn't want to tell you over the phone.'

She continues to open and close her mouth and then eventually manages, 'So was he drunk or what? I mean how the hell did he manage to get his foot tangled in the rug unless he was?'

'God knows.'

'And how come you were at Patrick's? I thought you weren't that keen on him.' She looks suspicious. Perhaps she thinks we are getting it on behind her back.

'I'm not.' I pick my glass up and take a big drink. Where do I start? 'Look, shall we go through and eat while I tell you the whole miserable story? I know that news about Will might have ruined your appetite, but we can't let it go to waste.'

'There's a miserable story? God, this sounds ominous.' She stands up. 'Okay, lead the way.'

The miserable story is divulged bit by bit throughout the meal. Sally looks like she's about to choke on the chilli a few times, particularly when I tell her about the argument I overheard that day in the garage, between Will and Patrick. And that I suspect Patrick of being involved in Leo and Will's deaths. My heart is so much lighter having unburdened myself, but for reasons best known to my intuition, I don't mention the box I'm trying to find.

'Okay. So, you're telling me that Will and Patrick fell out over you. They are, or in Will's case, were, in love with you and they had something to do with Leo's death. Also, Patrick might have killed Will and made it look like an accident.'

'Yes. I know it sounds unbelievable but…' I sigh and break off a bit of garlic bread.

Sally frowns and forks the chilli into the rice. 'Hmm. Just a bit. And what is also unbelievable is that you knew both of the men wanted you, yet you didn't tell me. You let me go on thinking me and Patrick had a future. Let me make an utter fool of myself.'

I swallow a mouthful of bread. 'Oh, Sal. I didn't have time. I overhead the argument the same night you told him how you felt.'

'You made an excuse about feeling sick and went early and left me there with Will and Patrick.' Sally put her fork down and glared at me. 'Why couldn't you have taken me to one side before you left and told me what you heard? It would have saved my humiliation.'

'Because I didn't want to hurt you. I was in shock too. The things they said about Leo scared me.'

'Yeah. So you thought you'd bugger off and leave me with two dangerous men?' Sally pours more wine, bangs the bottle down on the table.

She has a point; I wasn't thinking straight. 'Now you put it like that, it does sound crap. But I was all over the place. And then the next day you told me you'd told him how you felt... and that it was over. So I didn't see the point in telling you. I would have told you if you'd kept on seeing him, honest.'

'Nice of you.' Sally's not looking at me now. She's got her arms folded and her mouth set. What do I expect? I've acted like an idiot.

'Sally. Please, let's not fall out. I was blinded by my mission to find out how they'd been involved with Leo and his death... I'm sorry if I hurt you. And then this. Will's dead and I think Patrick had something to do with it.'

'Yes, you said. And why?' She looks up to the left and puts a forefinger onto her chin. 'Oh yes, I remember now. Because Patrick rang up his friend to check if he was okay, even though he told you he'd washed his hands of him. And the other reason – he was listening to music when you came back for your coat. Obviously guilty then.'

Mockery and anger glint in her dark eyes and I realise how much she's hurting. She told Patrick she loved him, only to find out that he turned her down because he loved me. Furthermore, I knew about all this and the fact I suspected him and Will of a serious crime and kept it from her. 'I don't know what to say apart from how very sorry I am. I never meant to hurt you, Sally.'

She looks at me and her expression softens. Hopefully she can see I'm telling the truth. 'Right. Well, what's done is done. And the mission to take up his offer of the studio, so you can snoop around his house looking for clues about Leo – how's that working out?'

Her tone has lost the mocking edge, but I know my instinct was right to keep the box a secret. 'Nothing yet. But, Sally, I can't just let it all go. I want to get to the bottom of what that overheard argument was about. And I can't shake this gut feeling that Patrick hurt Will.'

'Kerensa. You can't go to the police with an overheard argument and a gut feeling.'

I manage to bite back my own mocking tone, even though it's raring to go. 'I know that. I need proof, and I hope to find it soon.'

'How?'

'Patrick's bound to slip up sooner or later.'

'Is he? And what if he doesn't?'

'Liars always do.'

'But what if you get hurt in the meantime. If Patrick has done these things, he's dangerous, no?'

'I suppose so... And I forgot to tell you that he wears coloured contact lenses.' My voice sounds little, unsure, as if I'm a child being challenged on a dodgy argument.

'Oh well, he must be dangerous then.'

'It's odd though, isn't it?'

Sally frowns and taps her fingers on her lips. Eventually she says, 'No, I don't think so. He's just vain. But if he *is* as dangerous as you seem to think, you could end up the same way as Leo and Will, if Patrick feels under threat.' She takes a sip of wine and gives me a level stare.

'I'll make sure I don't.'

'And you'll do this, how?'

Before I can stop it, anger forces its way up onto my tongue with a torrent of words. 'Bloody hell, Sally, I don't know. But what I *do* know is I can't pretend I didn't hear that argument, or see Patrick singing and dancing at the sink last night, only a few minutes after he was told his close friend was dead!'

Sally leans her elbows on the table and puts her head in her hands. Shit, I've lost a good friend now. I can't seem to do anything right lately. Just keep fucking everything up. I'm about to apologise again when she looks at me and says, 'No. I don't suppose you can. And if that bastard has done what you suspect, I'll help in any way I can. God knows how. But I'll help.' She stretches her hand across the table and takes mine.

I'm moved to tears and she's the same. We stand and hug each other. 'Thanks, Sally. Thanks so much. I'm truly sorry for keeping everything from you.'

'Let's put that behind us now and move on.'

I nod and wipe my eyes with a napkin. 'Yes. That's a good idea.'

'And where's the pudding? I assume there *is* pudding?' She raises an eyebrow and does her big smile, though it is a bit wobbly at the corners.

I laugh. 'How could there not be in a situation like this?'

In the kitchen, I serve up the chocolate mousse and can't get my head around how surreal my life has become. Will's dead and I think Patrick might have killed him, but here I am serving up chocolate mousse. Though now Sally knows almost everything, at least I'm not totally alone. She might not be able to do much to help me, nor would I want to put her in danger, but at least she's someone else to bounce ideas off and tell my worries to. And as the old saying goes, two heads are better than one.

26

The last two weeks have been unreal. I've been going to work, coming back, eating, watching TV, but it's like someone else is doing it all. It's as if I'm watching from a far distance. Of course, when Leo and my baby died, I was worse, but this feels a close second. I can't get my head around Will's death and the verdict. According to Patrick, who's been kept in the loop by Will's friend James at the hospital, it was just a tragic and accidental death. There had been alcohol found in Will's system, but not enough for him to be drunk. He'd just tripped on the raised rug and fell. Falling downstairs apparently is not an uncommon cause of death. Try as I might, I can't picture a rug along the landing at his house. It doesn't mean there wasn't one though. It also doesn't mean that Patrick didn't push him and then stage the rug afterwards either.

One thing I haven't been doing these past few weeks is going round to Patrick's. I have explained to him that I don't feel like creating things at the moment and need space. He was disappointed but said he understood. It's to be expected. I know I need to get his keys and open the cupboard in the garage, but not yet. Not now. Just thinking about going back into that house with him makes my stomach lurch.

Sally's been fantastic. She's popped into the shop with coffee and cake and generally been there for me. Mum, Dad and my brother Ed too. They said what a great loss Will was to everyone. Such a nice man and such a tragic and needless death.

Nodding and agreeing has become second nature to me when people say things like that about Will. What else can I do? Tell them what I know about him – such as it is – and have them look at me like I'm crazy? Will was a surgeon, an upstanding and respected member of his community. I'm a recent widow who lost her baby too, and clearly isn't coping. Biding my time is the plan until I feel strong enough to go back into Patrick's house. One good thing, if you can call it that, is if the box was in Will's safekeeping, it's now with Patrick. There's no way he'd let such an important thing be discovered at Will's.

For the second time in ten months, I'm getting dressed for a funeral. Will's parents are over from Australia. They considered having his body flown to Sydney, but when all is said and done, Will chose to come back to Cornwall. This was his home. They said they wanted people to wear bright clothes today to celebrate the life of their son. I look at myself in the mirror dressed in a blue and white flowery summer dress and feel ridiculous. Bright colours might be okay for the funeral of someone who'd had a long life, but black feels right for a man a few months short of his thirty-fifth birthday. I wonder what Patrick's wearing. A grim reaper's costume would be appropriate.

Sally picks me up and we drive in almost silence to the crematorium. There's nothing to say, is there? What's the point in small talk – too much effort. We pull into a space and get out. I feel a bit self-conscious because my feelings are in turmoil. At the back of my mind the argument I overheard plays through again and I want to find Patrick, demand to know what they did to my Leo and what Patrick did to Will. Instead, I take a deep breath and slip my arm through Sally's.

There're loads of people milling around outside. I don't recognise many, probably Will's colleagues. I notice a tanned couple in their late fifties talking quietly together by the door. The woman's petite with light brown hair pulled into a tight bun and she's wearing a salmon suit. She's dabbing her eyes with a tissue and holding onto the man's arm. The man is tall with grey hair and navy eyes. He's trying to comfort the woman, but his bottom lip keeps trembling and he stops talking. They're definitely Will's parents because his dad's an older version of him.

Patrick comes around the side of the building with Leo's parents. I hate how close they are with him. He's wormed his way into their affections like some alien parasite. Janice told me last week how happy he makes them when he pops round to see them. He always brings a little gift, and Derek and Patrick have been fishing a few times, like he used to with Leo. Janice was quick to tell me that of course he could never take the place of Leo, but he is so like him in his ways, it does help with missing him, even though her heart breaks for her son. Patrick waves and I wave back. He looks like he's about to come over, so I drag Sally towards the entrance. I'm not in a hurry to go in, but it's better than listening to Patrick waffle on about how wonderful Will was.

There's a big picture of Will at the front of the room and my breath catches in my throat. He's sitting on a wall somewhere in Australia with a beer in his hand, his blond hair flopping over one eye, looking happy and relaxed. There are a few kangaroos in the background and some unfamiliar trees stretching away across the red earth. What a waste of a life. I swallow hard and follow Sally onto a row near the back and close my eyes.

A few moments later, Will's immediate family come in and sit at the front. There's an elderly couple sitting next to Will's parents and I realise they must be his grandparents. The old lady's shoulders are trembling and she's crying uncontrollably. It's all I can do not to join her.

Sally nods over at them. 'God, I can't imagine what that must be like. To lose a child and a grandchild like that. Such a shock.' Her eyes are moist, and I have to look away. Then Sally nudges me. 'And guess who's sitting right behind the family.'

Patrick is leaning forward and whispering something in Will's mother's ear. She nods and he pats her shoulder. She covers his hand with hers. How bloody dare he! 'God, what a total bastard,' I whisper to Sally.

'Steady on. We have no proof he did anything to Will yet.'

'Oh he did. I know in here, he did.' I tap the left side of my chest. Then I feel a surge of frustration as I realise proof is going to be pretty impossible to get.

A few moments later the celebrant begins proceedings and we listen to a selection of eighties music not dissimilar from Leo's. The celebrant said Will's mum had chosen them because she remembered having to listen to these tracks over and over when he was a teenager in his bedroom. Then there's a reading from somebody who worked with Will, might have been James, I'm not really paying attention. My mind is elsewhere, thinking about how unfair everything is. Then Will's dad gets up and goes to the front to talk about his son's life. His eyes are red-rimmed and in his trembling hand, a piece of paper flutters like a captive bird.

This is too much. Too many memories and feelings are crowding in and I'm back at Leo's funeral. I look at my nails, the floor, anywhere but at the broken man at the front with Will's eyes, leaning on the rostrum, talking about his wonderful son and how proud he was of him. I switch my mind to the shop. Picture myself inside and imagine I'm looking through the recycling bin. I mentally count the pieces of fishing net and plastic bottles I collected yesterday. The netting could be used in an idea I have for a...

My attention is snapped back to the room by something Will's dad is saying. 'Of course, working in orthopaedics was rewarding for Will in the early days, but recently he told me he was so glad he switched. So many people were helped by my son's clever hands. Even as a boy he wanted to help others. He was generous to a fault and wise beyond his years. Sometimes other kids would take advantage of him. They might ask to borrow money, or take a toy or something, and I'd tell him to say no. But my boy would always say, their need must be greater than mine, Dad.' Will's dad takes a moment and sips some water. Then he goes on to talk about how well respected Will was in his work and then about Will's love of Cornwall.

This is all really moving, but what Will's dad said reminds me that the hospital receptionist I spoke to said Will wasn't in orthopaedics. Then with everything else that happened after, it had gone out of my head. Why would Will lie to me about what type of surgery he was in?

Will's dad sits down, and Enya's haunting *If I Could Be Where You Are* fills the room. There's not a dry eye in the house. Except mine. Sally nudges me. 'God, this is heartbreaking.'

'Hmm.'

'You okay? You look puzzled.'

'I am. I'll tell you why later.'

Will's mum gets up and places a rose on the coffin and then almost collapses, sobbing to her knees. She has to be supported by her husband and friends.

Outside, a bit later, his parents and grandparents stand by the flower arrangements, try to put on brave faces and shake hands or hug people as they go to pay their respects. It will look odd if I don't go over, but it feels so wrong. I really liked their son, but sadly I found out he wasn't as wonderful as everyone thinks. Only Patrick knows the whole truth. On cue, he goes over and hugs them, wiping a tear or two for show.

Sally sighs. 'We'd better go over and say something, hadn't we?'

'Not sure I can face it.'

'You'll have to. We'll go home straight after, if you like. No need to go to the wake.'

I think about this. 'No. We'll go, or it'll look like we don't care. Patrick might get suspicious. I know we'd fallen out with Will, but even so. Besides, we might get to find out something more.'

We go over to Will's parents and I shake hands with them and say who I am. Patrick's standing a little way off and I can tell he's listening to our conversation, cheeky bugger. Will's dad says, 'I'm Andrew, pleased to meet you. And it is such a shame that you and he didn't get a chance to...' Andrew blinks away tears. 'Get a chance to take your relationship further. Will told us so much about you and how much he thought of you.'

Bloody hell, I wasn't expecting that. Neither was Patrick by the look of thunder on his face. What do I say now? 'It's such a terrible thing to have happened. I was very fond of him.'

Valerie, Will's mum, says, 'You have had your fair share of tragedy this year too, my dear. How you're still in one piece I don't know.' Her kind blue eyes swim and she gives me a hug. This is not what's needed, and I make a sound in my throat that's a cross between a cough and a sob. She seems a lovely woman and in another life, I might have got to know her better.

'I have, Valerie. And some days I don't know how I keep going either.'

We say goodbye and I wait by the car for Sally. I've changed my mind about going to the wake. I'm feeling too fragile. Patrick makes a beeline for me and I look round for an escape route. There isn't one. Shit.

'How are you, Kerensa?' He puts his head on one side and gives me a little sad smile. 'I heard what Valerie said about Will. That must have been upsetting.'

'Not at all. It was quite comforting really. It's nice to think that he thought so much of me that he told his parents. Who knows, if he'd lived, we might have got together eventually.'

My words have the desired effect. There's a deep furrow across his brow and he's clenching and unclenching his jaw. 'I thought you said there was no chance for anyone because of Leo.'

'That's correct. Not at the moment.'

'So if Will had lived you might have given him a chance?'

'Maybe. I did have feelings for him quite early on, actually. I think my heart was hitting out at Leo's betrayal... Will was just what I needed.'

'I see.' Patrick narrows his eyes. 'You never did tell me why you and Will parted company.'

'No, I never did.'

'What can it hurt to tell me now? He's dead.'

'You seem strangely unconcerned about that, Patrick.' There's more waiting to erupt out of me, but I bite my tongue.

He does an indignant face. 'Of course I'm concerned. Will was one of my best friends.'

'He was Leo's very best friend.'

Patrick shakes his head. 'I know. What are you getting at?'

'Nothing, Patrick.' I sigh and lean back against Sally's car. 'I'm tired, emotional and have had it up to here with funerals and tragedy.'

He takes a step towards me, his arms out for a hug. 'Hey, come here and–'

'No.' I hold my hands up. 'I don't want a hug, I just want to go home and have a hot bath, watch some trash on TV and zone out.'

Patrick lets his arms fall to his sides, bites the inside of his cheek. 'Not coming to the wake?' I give him a look. 'Okay. I get that.'

I watch Sally take her leave of the Grays and walk over to us. Patrick folds his arms, gives her a curt nod. She glares at him. 'Hello, Patrick. Long time no see and shit.'

'Yeah. How are you?' He looks away across the car park.

'I don't think you honestly care, do you?'

Patrick looks back at her. 'What's up with you? You're not still upset because of that night, surely?'

Oh God. This is all we need – a huge showdown in the car park in front of the mourners. I interrupt Sally as she looks ready to tear his head off. 'Of course she's not. But listen, you two, I tell you what's weird. I was puzzling about it for ages in there.' I nod towards the crematorium. They frown at me together – bookends. Good. At least I stopped World War Three.

'Yeah, what was it?' Sally asks.

'It was what Andrew said about Will's job. He said he did another type of surgery – he wasn't in orthopaedics anymore. So why did Will tell us he was?'

'Oh yeah,' Sally says. 'I'd forgotten that. Mind you, Will never talked much about his job, did he? I'm not sure I could have told you that he did orthopaedics, until you reminded me just now.'

Patrick's looking down, dragging the toe of his shoe back and forth across the gravel.

'Why do you think he lied about the type of surgery he did?' I ask him.

'Hmm?' He looks up in a pathetic attempt to appear absent-minded. 'Sorry, I was miles away. God knows. Will was a law unto himself.' Patrick smiles and does a fake yawn. He's so transparent it's ridiculous.

I press him. 'So what kind of surgery *was* he doing exactly? His dad didn't say, did he? But then I wasn't really listening.'

'No, I don't think he did. And no clue about what Will did. As Sally said, he never talked about work.' Patrick looks away. 'Right, looks like people are off to the wake. You sure you're not coming?'

'No,' I say.

Sally just shakes her head.

'Okay. Take care and speak soon.' Patrick smiles again and hurries to his car.

'Couldn't get away from me quick enough,' Sally says with a shrug and opens the car door.

I get in the passenger seat and think it was actually me that he couldn't get away from quick enough. He's hiding something. Something about him, Will and Leo as usual. Then I suddenly get the unshakeable feeling that what I know so far is only the tip of the iceberg.

27

Three days after the funeral, I'm sitting in my house, staring at the TV but I'm far away. It's Saturday evening and I've had a good day in the shop, but how I got through the day I don't know. I was nice to customers. Tried my best to be witty, informative and pleasant, but all the time my mind was elsewhere. I can't concentrate on anything. Apart from Patrick. Patrick and my mission to find the truth. My futile mission, it seems.

All of a sudden, I can stand it no longer and flick off the TV. It's only seven o'clock. I could go over to Patrick's and hope he's going out – it is Saturday night after all. If not, I could do a couple of hours in the studio and maybe catch him out somehow. It's better than sitting here wallowing. I grab my phone and call him.

I'm in luck. He's going to see a man about a boat down the local pub in a bit, so I can get the key as he'll be walking. I say, 'That's great, Patrick. I'll pop over in a few minutes then.'

'You know I could cancel. It's ages since we've had a chat, apart from at the funeral. Hardly the place for a laugh and joke, eh? I could cook for us if you've not eaten yet too.'

My stomach rolls and I scrabble for an excuse. 'I grabbed something earlier, thanks. And when I'm working, I do like to be alone really. Chatting to you means I'd not get much done.'

He sighs. 'Okay. But I do hope we can get back to how we used to be. We're friends, Kerensa, and sometimes it feels like we're enemies.'

I wonder why, Patrick? 'I'm sorry, that's my fault. I have been quite down lately. But I'm sure I'll be more myself soon.'

'That's to be expected. And of course you'll bounce back before long. Let's arrange a get together when I get back from the pub, yeah? Maybe next week we could go out on my boat again.'

Over my dead body. 'Yes, maybe we could. See you soon, Patrick.' I end the call and grab my coat and bag from the kitchen. My heart's thrashing about in anticipation already, and I take a few deep breaths to calm myself. The blue sky and sunshine that I walked home in has turned to dark clouds and high winds. I zip up my coat and hood too. I'd forgotten the weather forecast said we had a storm coming, but that was supposed to be tomorrow. Great. I'll have to be careful on the cliff path on the way home if we get a downpour.

'Come on in!' Patrick says as he opens the door. Then he looks at the sky and rubs his arms. 'Blimey. Weather's turned a bit, considering the time of year! I might drive to the pub after all.'

No. Please don't drive! 'It's not supposed to get really bad until tomorrow. You'll be fine. People drive too much nowadays when it's not necessary.' I follow him through to the kitchen, hoping he's going to take my advice, or those keys will be out of reach yet again.

Patrick looks at me, head on one side. 'You think? It's not too cold?'

'No, it's fine, you big wuss.' I grit my teeth and give him a playful push to one shoulder.

He laughs and wags a finger at me. 'Nobody calls me a big wuss. I'll walk then. Just to please you.' Patrick grins and goes to the fridge. 'In here is a wide selection of mouth-watering delicacies to tickle your taste buds. We have chicken, olives, ham, salad, and for afterwards, some cream cake. There's plenty of other stuff too – the list goes on. Also, we have soft or hard drinks, otherwise known as alcohol, to wash it down.' He pulls a bottle of wine out of the fridge door and wiggles it at me to emphasise his point.

I give him a pleasant smile and hold up my hand. 'I'm not hungry thanks, Patrick. But I might have a glass of red wine later on, if you have it.'

'Indeed I do. There's a wine rack over there. I'll join you when I get back.' He closes the fridge door and shrugs on his jacket. 'I'll only be an hour or so. Two at the most.'

'Take your time.'

'Right you are. Okay, see you soon. And be good!'

Patrick pats his pockets and then goes to a cupboard in the kitchen and takes his bunch of keys from a hook on the inside of the door. Shit! Why the hell does he need those? He's walking and he doesn't have to lock up because I'm in the house! I try to keep my smile steady as he waves and hurries out the front door, but all I want to do is yell and swear and scream. Now what? First thing to do is to pour a glass of sodding wine. I'm so sick of shit going wrong.

I take the wine into the living room, perch on the arm of the chair and down half the glass in one. Damn Patrick. I could have had that bloody box in my hands by now if all had gone to plan. Still, no use moaning to myself. I'll go and see if by some miracle the cupboard in the garage is unlocked. It could be. Maybe he shoved the box in there recently and forgot to put the padlock on. Maybe I'll sprout wings and fly too. I take another sip of wine and walk down the corridor to the laundry room. I'm about to go through into the garage, when I notice a newspaper folded on the washing machine. There's a photo of William at the top of the page. It's an obituary. *Eminent Reconstructive Surgeon, William Gray…*

The front door slams.

'Kerensa! It's only me, I forgot my wallet! Can't remember where I left it either!'

No! I don't know where to go for the best. If he comes this way looking for it, what excuse can I have for being in the laundry room? If I rush, I might just get to the loo before he sees me. I grab the newspaper and set off for the door, but the rest of the wine in the glass tips in my hurry and spatters all over the floor. Fuck! If he sees this, he'll know I've been in here.

'Kerensa! You in the studio?' Patrick yells, his voice much closer now at the bottom of the stairs. I crouch down behind the washing machine and make myself as small as I can. If I don't answer, he might go upstairs and see I'm not there. But if I do… A jingly tune rings out right outside the laundry room doorway. The door is half open and I can see Patrick's arm as he reaches into his pocket for his mobile. 'Hello. Yes, this is Patrick O'Brien… Yes, I'm a friend of Derek Pethick… Oh Jesus. Dear Lord, no…'

Behind the washing machine, I close my eyes and put my hand over my mouth. *Please don't let Derek be dead. I couldn't bear it.*

There's a long pause and then Patrick says, 'What ward is he in? Okay, yes I'm going there now. Thanks for letting me know.'

Not dead but in hospital. Bloody hell, I hope he's going to be okay. I hear Patrick shuffling about outside and hope he goes soon, or goes upstairs searching for me. Once he's left the corridor, I can nip into the loo and pretend I didn't hear him calling. Lame, but what else do I have? Then I hear a thump. I peep around the corner of the machine to see him facing the laundry room slumped down, his back to the wall, head in hands. I duck back to my hiding place, drop the newspaper and hug my knees. I'm trapped. Then I hear him crying. Not just a few sniffs but wracking sobs. I peep at him just as his hands go to his mouth to stop the noise.

'Dad... Oh Dad. Please get better. I'll do anything. Anything! Please God let him live. I'm begging you. I'm so sorry for what I've done!' Then a few seconds later, Patrick gets up and runs off.

My pulse rate rockets and I can't get my breath. I try to stand and find my legs don't work, stumble to my knees in the wet patch left by the spilt wine. I mumble into my hands, 'Oh God. Oh God, I can't believe it. This must be some fucking disgusting nightmare.'

He runs back along the corridor and from the bottom of the stairs I hear Patrick shout, 'Kerensa! Derek and Janice's neighbour rang. Janice asked him to contact me 'cos Derek's had a heart attack. 'I'm off to Treliske! I'll keep you posted!'

Moments later, the front door slams.

I curl into a ball on my side. Sobbing, I wrap my arms around myself to try to stop the debilitating tremor running the length of me. I want to scream, pinch myself to snap myself out of it. Madness threatens to consume me. I take some deep breaths and try to make sense of what's happened out there in the hall. But it's incredible... impossible. My mind is telling me one thing, logic is telling me the opposite. My mind tells me that I just heard my dead husband Leo praying out there in the corridor. Patrick's Irish brogue had gone. It was Leo's voice. Leo was talking to God. Begging him to save his dad.

Logic tells me that's impossible. Leo is dead. Dead! I went to his funeral. Then slowly, little by little, an idea forms in my head. Snapshots of the weird things that have happened and all the things I've been puzzling over fly at me one at a time. Fast. Sharp. Deadly. Pieces of the last ten months slot themselves into place in my head, snap, snap, snap. Until finally, with the discovery of the newspaper obituary, the whole terrifying jigsaw is complete. Lying here on the cold wet tiles, I can no longer ignore the truth. The incontrovertible truth.

Leo never died... Patrick is Leo.

28

I don't know how long I've been lying here on the wet floor. Though it's uncomfortable, I'm scared to move. Because then I'll have to decide what to do next. I can't think. I can't do anything apart from lie here. I want my mum. I want to curl up on her lap like I did when I was a kid and cry on her shoulder while she strokes my hair. I want Mum to make it all better, but how can she? What he's done can't be made better. What he's done is pure evil. I can hardly comprehend it, but it all makes horrible sense now. I want him to admit it. I want him... I want my bastard pretend-dead husband Leo to stand there in front of me and confess what he's done. There's one last thing to do before that though.

Using the washing machine, I drag myself up from the floor and lean on it while I get the strength back in my legs. Then I walk to the garage and look in the cupboards and under benches until I find what I'm looking for. The crowbar is cold and I weigh it in my hand. This should do the trick. I take it over to the wall cupboard, drag a bucket from under a bench, flip it over and stand on it. I shove the metal-pronged end of the crowbar under the hinged metal strap and twist it hard. It comes loose surprisingly quickly, but it's still attached to the side of the cupboard by a few screws. I lean my weight on the crowbar and twist again. It snaps and the cupboard swings open.

Leo's box is on the bottom shelf covered with a few pieces of sandpaper. I grab it and take it out of the garage and into the living room. I place it on the sofa and then get the wine from the kitchen. I don't bother with a glass, just swig it from the bottle until my nerves feel calmer and then I set it on the coffee table. Part of me wonders if this is really happening. Maybe I'm trapped in a dream. I know I'm not though, I'm not that lucky. I look at the box and feel my hands still trembling... in fact all of me is trembling, so I sit down on the sofa, put the box on my lap, take a deep breath and open it.

There're all Leo's documents that were always inside. Birth certificates, accountant's and various education certificates, his passport. But on top of all these, there are two more passports, and driving licences. Two have Patrick's photo and name, the other two have his photo, but with the name Howard Fisher. Why? Is he planning to leave the country under that name if things don't work out for him here? There's a little red book at the bottom that Leo used to jot down important things like passwords because he could never remember them. I flick it open and see new entries. There's the name of a bank I don't recognise, details of two accounts, and PIN numbers and passwords. There's even a list of what I imagine are memorable words for security – how sentimental; one of them is Kerensa.

From nowhere, another ocean of tears waits for release and I wrap my arms around myself, let them come. How could he have done it? How could he have let me think he was dead? We loved each other, didn't we? We were going to start a family together. Leo threw that all away. All the heartbreak he put me through, the anguish. How *dare* he? He made me a widow, made me lose our unborn child. Then anger elbows any remnant of sentimentality to one side, and my tears dry instantly. I go over in my head again what must have happened and allow the anger to give me strength. It's burning in the heart of me – white hot like metal in a furnace. I'm calm. Ready.

When he gets back from the hospital, he'll find me waiting. I'll wait all night if I have to.

A little over four hours later, I hear a car and see headlight beams sweep the window. I have finished the wine and I'm sitting on the sofa in the dark. Leo comes in and flicks on the hall light. I can hear him kicking off his shoes and hanging up his coat. Then he goes into the kitchen and must have opened the fridge, because I hear bottles rattling and the top of one being popped off. He belches and comes into the living room, switches on the standard lamp. He's whistling, which must mean Derek's okay, thank God. Then he turns, sees me and nearly drops his beer bottle.

'Fuck! You scared the shit out of me!'

Impressive. He maintained his Irish accent, even in shock.

'Did I? Oh dear.'

'What are you doing sitting here in the dark? I thought you'd have gone home by now.'

'Clearly.'

Patrick... no, Leo shoves a hand through his hair and does the chin stroke. But then he would, wouldn't he? He always has. He's not pretending to be *like* Leo. He *is* Leo. 'Are you okay? You seem angry.'

'Angry? Yes. You could say that. In fact, I am fucking incandescent!' I yell, and then uncontrollable laughter erupts from me. I have no idea why. Hysteria, I expect.

He frowns and sits on the coffee table opposite me. Then he picks up the empty bottle. 'You drank all this yourself?'

'No. I asked a few of the neighbours in. They had a sip each and then went home.'

Then a look of realisation dawns on his face and he gives me a sad smile. 'God. I know what's wrong. You're upset about Derek, aren't you?' Leo puts the bottle down and leans forward, elbows on his knees. 'You've lost your fair share of loved ones this year. But don't worry, Kerensa. The doctors say Derek is very poorly, but there's a good chance he'll be okay. He's booked in for surgery tomorrow. Janice was in bits, but I cheered her up by being there, I think.'

His self-ingratiating smile makes me want to slap it from his mouth. 'Yes, you are such a thoughtful and caring person, aren't you?' I glare at him.

The frown's back and he leans away from me, folds his arms. 'I try to be, Kerensa.'

'Pity you weren't so thoughtful and caring when you broke their hearts into tiny little pieces ten months or so ago. It's a wonder Derek's still alive, the damage you did to him.'

I watch Patrick's Adam's apple bob and he shakes his head as if trying to make sense of my words and finding them incomprehensible... terrifying. 'I... I don't get what you're on about.'

I lean forward, mirror his pose from earlier. 'Really? Well, I'll tell you straight. You're not thoughtful and caring. You're a cruel, evil and heartless piece of shit who nearly destroyed everyone you loved. And why? For money. What do you have to say to that, Leo?'

Leo's mouth drops open and his eyes fill with tears. He shakes his head slowly. 'I... I... I didn't...'

I want to launch myself at him. Dig my nails into his lying fake green eyes, rip them out. 'You didn't what? You didn't FUCKING WHAT?' I stand up, grab the wine bottle and go to bring it down on his head but he ducks and covers it with his hands. *No. No, that would be too easy. I want his confession.* I yell and hurl it at the wall instead. It smashes and sprays the dregs of red wine along the white paint, like a blood spatter.

He looks up at the wall, then at me, still shielding his head. 'How...?'

I sit back down and drag the box out from under the sofa. Thrust it at him. 'This, for one. I had plenty to be going on with, of course. The latest being that I read a newspaper obituary, which said that Will was a fucking reconstructive surgeon! But you kindly gave me the biggest decider of all earlier. I was in the laundry room on the way to the garage looking for the box, when I heard you take the call from your parents' neighbour. You sat there...' My voice wavers and I have to take a moment. 'You sat there and prayed to God.' I jab a finger heavenward. 'To God! How the fuck you have the cheek, I will never know. But you prayed to Him to save your dad. And in your grief and despair, Patrick's voice became yours. Your voice, Leo.'

He puts the box down beside him on the coffee table, covers his face with his hands and his shoulders shake. He says through his tears, 'Oh, God... Oh Kerensa I am so, so sorry. When I think what I put you through. Put Mum and Dad through.'

It's surreal watching Patrick speak with Leo's voice. I sit back, fold my arms. 'Glad you're not going to try to deny it all then.'

'No. God, no. What would be the point? If you knew how many times I've wanted to come clean. To tell you all of it...' He takes his hands from his face and wipes his eyes on the back of his arm.

'Not enough, it seems.'

'How could I?'

'How could you not. In fact, how could you do it in the first place?'

Leo looks at the floor, says nothing.

'So many clues were staring me in the face. But *your* face is something else. How long did Will take to construct it?'

Leo shakes his head.

'Come on, Leo. Tell me everything. I'm all ears.' I lean forward and study his. 'Bloody neat work he made of those lobes too. If Will's dad hadn't said he wasn't an orthopaedic surgeon, you hadn't acted so guilty about it, and I hadn't seen the newspaper obituary, it might have taken me a little longer for my brain to process what my ears were telling me earlier in the laundry room. But in the end, there was no other explanation for it.'

Leo sits back and exhales. Then he scrubs his fists in his eyes. 'It was all Will's idea. I needed to disappear so Donaldson could never find me, and what better way than to be dead? Will said he could make me look completely different and eventually I could come back home and so I went along with it.' I get a sidelong glance and then he looks back at the floor.

'This is priceless. So what did he actually do? Nose, chin, ears... tell me the rest.'

'Cheek implants and jaw augmentation too. I was gobsmacked that it wouldn't take that long. When Will said it could all be done fairly fast, I actually researched it to see if he was correct. I guess I didn't trust him completely... It was a huge step to take. But I couldn't bear not being able to see you. The nose took the longest. Will had to straighten the bump on the bridge and shave some off the tip, to narrow it. It changed the structure completely. There was still a bit of bruising six months on. But the chin and cheek implants took hardly any time. The jaw took a while to settle, but it went well. I had a bit of lip filler too. A friend of Will's did my teeth. I had them crowned and whitened. Money was no object, of course.'

'Of course.'

'I lost weight, worked out. My hair and eyebrows are dyed,

obviously, and I had a weave to cover the thinning parts. The accent was easy, 'cos of Mum. I even had my birthmark covered up by a little lion.'

An image of the tattoo on his shoulder comes to me the day he rolled his wetsuit down. 'Bloody hell. I saw it that day on the beach. Leo the lion. How arrogant of you.'

'I don't know what to say.'

'That's a first,' I spit. 'The eyes you did yourself – I found the lenses while snooping in your en suite a while back.'

Leo frowns. 'What were you looking in there for?'

'I was looking for the missing document box. I started getting curious when Patrick's mannerisms became so like yours.' I throw up my hands. 'This is nuts talking about you as if you are two people, but that's what you are now, I suppose.' Then I correct my thinking. 'No, actually you *are* Leo – you just look like someone else.' I close my eyes and focus. 'Anyway, the first thing wasn't the mannerisms and sayings of Leo's, it was when you slipped up over your lies about your sibling back in the old country. The first time I met you, you said you had a sister. Then on the boat, you said you had a brother. You always were a shit liar.'

Leo opens his mouth to say something, but I hold up my finger.

'No. I talk. You listen. So the fact you were lying about your past put up a red flag straight away. Then the mannerisms, and at the barbecue the fact you knew about my brother's splitting up with Jason. I asked Will and he said he confirmed he'd mentioned it, but I knew he was covering for you. Next you almost burst into tears when Janice and Derek were at the barbecue. Then you served your signature dish and Negroni at your house that evening. One thing after another kept the flag fluttering.' I stop, watch him carefully.

'Right... I see. I must admit I thought if I was more like my old self... face and accent apart, you might be more friendly towards me.'

'Are you kidding? You freaked me out, Leo.'

He sighs. 'I see that now. And I went overboard with the paella. I just wanted you to remember Leo but went too far... But why did all that lead you to think Patrick had taken my document box from ours?'

'It didn't. I was suspicious because you were a liar, and I thought that you must have known Leo because of all the similarities. Maybe you were involved with him in taking Donaldson's money, or even had something to do with his death. Will too. But I didn't really know. The thing that really convinced me you did something to Leo, and were apparently in love with me, was an argument I overheard here between you and Will. The night you cooked the signature dish, I knew you were furious that Will and I were close on the beach earlier that day. So when you said you wanted him to help you get some beer and ice from the garage, I had a feeling that Will was going to get it in the neck. I pretended to go to the loo, but instead I followed you and hid in the laundry room.'

Leo sighs. 'Hell. You've known all this time that Patrick and Will had something to do with Leo's disappearance. You're a bloody good actress, my darling.'

'Don't you *dare* call me darling. You haven't the right!'

He holds his hands up. 'Okay, don't get angry.'

'Get angry? I think it's too late for that, you sick bastard.' My voice is cold, freezing. 'I wondered what to do next and I thought I'd look in Leo's important document box, see if there were any clues. Any mention in there of where the money was, or of Patrick and Will maybe? I needed some proof before I could do anything. But it had gone. I assumed that one of you must have taken it.'

'Look, as I said, it was all Will's idea–'

'Stop lying. I heard the argument, remember? He said he only did what he did – which I now know meant altered your face – to help you because of his friendship with you. You said you'd lie your head off to me about it all if he didn't leave me alone.'

'I had to say that because I was scared he'd tell you about everything. I knew you weren't ready to find out that I was still alive. I had to win you round first.'

'Ha! That would never have happened.'

'I had to try. Will tricked me. He said he'd help me to win you round, but all the time he was scheming to get you for himself!' Leo's fist comes down on the coffee table with a thump and I see the manic fury in his eyes. Then he exhales and gives me a sheepish smile. 'Sorry, it's just that I love you so much.'

I'm fascinated by the switch from monster to meek in a matter of seconds. For the first time I realise just what he could be capable of. My imagination has had him pushing Will downstairs, but until this moment, I wasn't totally convinced he'd do such a thing. Now I am. I say, 'If you love me you wouldn't have put me through that.'

'There was no other way. Leo had to die and Patrick took his place.'

'Interesting that you talk about Leo as if he's actually dead. You did when I overheard the argument too. And Will called you Patrick. Why? It's not as if he knew I was listening behind the door?'

Leo shrugs. 'It's so we never slipped up. Once I became Patrick, we agreed Leo was actually dead. Will never called me Leo, or even thought of me as Leo anymore, he said. It was harder for me, of course. But I was now Patrick. A totally different man, with a completely different life. A separate past, everything. It was the *only* way. *Everything* had to be airtight. Same as hiding the reconstructive surgery thing from you. It was done to be absolutely sure you'd never suspect he'd changed my face.'

I shake my head, bewildered. 'Why the hell would I even have considered that he'd done that? It was sheer madness!'

'You wouldn't, but as I said – we had to be a hundred per cent sure.'

This is surreal. 'And your great plan? When you'd made me fall in love with you, you'd just leap out, do jazz hands and say – actually, Kerensa, I'm Leo – your dead husband, back from the grave?'

'I don't know if I would have told you... I hadn't thought that far.' He looks at his hands, examines his nails.

Then a thought occurs. 'And how the hell did the funeral work? Did you pay off the funeral directors to pretend there was a body in your coffin?'

'No... there was a body. A homeless guy.' He stops when he sees my look of horror and has the good grace to look ashamed. 'Will knew people at the morgue through his work. He organised a private ambulance to take the body to the funeral directors. A few palms were greased. He paid them off and got the paperwork sorted that way too. It was all Will's idea. I gave him the money to do it, that's all.'

'My god, that's despicable.'

'I know. I'm sorry.'

There's an uncomfortable silence and then I point at the box. 'And who the hell is Howard Fisher?'

Leo heaves a big sigh and spreads his hands. 'The money I got from Donaldson is in Fisher's name. Just an extra precaution. And if he ever found me – yes, I know – impossible, I could skip the country quickly. He'd not be looking for a Howard Fisher.'

As I look at the man who used to be my lovely husband, a deep sadness washes over me. 'All this for money, Leo. Why?'

'Believe me, it wasn't done lightly. I stole the money so we could have the life we always wanted. Donaldson has more than he could ever spend. He didn't need it, Kerensa... I did the facial reconstruction so Donaldson wouldn't find me... and also to protect you.' Leo's got a feverish light in his eyes.

'I've heard it all now. You did it for me?' I point at myself and give a humourless laugh. 'How do you work that one out?'

'Because if I was dead, Donaldson would leave you alone.'

'But he didn't, did he? No, he showed up at the funeral and asked me where his fucking money was! I lost our baby because of what you did to protect me!' I stand up and pace. I want to slap him. Pummel him until he begs for mercy.

'I know... I know. It nearly broke me when I found out you were pregnant and had lost it.' He's standing up too, wiping tears from his fake cheeks.

'Nearly broke you? You have no idea what the pain of losing a child is, Leo. None!'

'Not as much as you, but it did hurt. Honestly it did.' He's crying more, looking pathetic.

I stick my neck out, yell in his face. 'You don't know the meaning of the word honest! You have lied, lie upon lie. And none of it is for me. It's all been for you. Everything you've done is for you! Have you any idea at all what your pretend death did to me? And losing the baby? Did you actually give a shit?'

'Of course I did. I told you it nearly broke me, you have to believe that!' He's crying in earnest now and wipes snot away from the end of his fake nose with the back of his sleeve.

'How can I believe anything you say? There's a stranger standing in front of me speaking with my late husband's voice. A voice. That's all that's left of the man I loved.'

'Not all.' He tips his head and puts his finger to his eyes.

When he looks back at me I'm staring into Leo's kind hazel

eyes and a rush of memories send a sucker punch to my heart – threaten to bring me to my knees. 'Leo...'

He reaches out his hand to me and then lets it fall. 'I'm begging you, Kerensa. Please let's try again. I can see in your face that you still love me, deep down. Of course it will take you some time to forgive me, that's understandable... but we're meant to be together. Always have been. We could have another baby too. Till death do us part... and we're still married, don't forget. I didn't die.'

He does a hopeful smile, and suddenly the rage I've had a rein on slips free and I fly at him. Slap his face, his head, punch his chest. Scream and scream and scream. He takes it, then falls back on the sofa, crying.

Once I've got my breath back, I say, 'I would rather kill myself than have you anywhere near me. Ever. Again.'

'No. No, you don't mean it. Give yourself time to think.'

'I don't need time.'

'I'll do anything. Anything at all...' He shuffles along the sofa, pats the cushion beside him.

I sneer and shake my head. 'You've shown you'd do anything. Will found that out.'

Leo's eyes speak volumes, then they slip from mine and he closes them, rests his head back on the sofa cushions and says, 'Now what are you on about?' His tone is bored. Unconcerned. Fake. I'm glad he took out the lenses, because I've just seen his thoughts. And the eyes-closing thing, the weary act. I've seen it in the past. Leo would do it if he was trying to hide something. And this time I know exactly what it is.

'You killed Will. You went to his house and pushed him down the stairs. You did it because you were jealous and thought he was going to take me from you one day.'

Leo's eyes flick open and he tries a laugh. 'That's ridiculous. Yes, I was jealous, but I would never hurt him.'

'You're a liar, Leo. A fucking liar and I hate you. The times I'd lay awake thinking of how happy you made me and how my heart ached for you.' I thump my chest. 'Physically ached in here. At one point I thought I'd be better off dead than without you, even though you'd buggered everything up with Donaldson. I'd have given anything to have had you back again with me. But now. Now I wish you'd really died.'

He covers his face with his hands and says through his fingers. 'No. No, love. You don't really mean that.'

'I do. You dead is better than this vile creature you've become.'

'Please. Kerensa, listen.'

'No, *you* listen. Look me in the eye and tell me you had nothing to do with Will's death. If you lie, I'll know. Go on. Tell me!'

Leo stands up, rubs his eyes. He's silent for the longest time, then he releases a slow breath. 'Okay yes. I did it. I went round that night and we argued over you. He admitted he loved you and I saw red. We were at the top of his stairs so... It all happened so fast.' He lifts his arms, lets them fall to his thighs with a slap.

Leo's not avoiding my gaze. He's looking right into my eyes with an intensity and honesty that shocks me. He's just confessed outright... What does that mean for me? He knows how I feel about him. What's to stop me going out right now and phoning the p... A chill runs the length of my spine and panic flutters against my ribs. I think about the manic fury behind his eyes earlier. He's capable of anything.

I cover my mouth and walk to the kitchen, run some water into a glass while I think what my best move is. He follows me. 'Say something, Kerensa. What are you going to do?'

I turn. 'I'm in shock, Leo. Not just about Will, but about

everything that's happened... I'm going home now to bed and in the morning we'll talk.'

Leo narrows his eyes. 'You promise you're not going to call the police?'

'I told you, I'm going home to bed. I'm traumatised and emotionally exhausted. It's a wonder I can keep standing.' I down the water and then go to the hall, grab my coat, bag, and shove my feet into my trainers.

Leo shakes his head. 'I don't believe you. I think you're going straight to the police.'

His voice is trembling and he's blinking rapidly. He's shoving his hands through his hair repeatedly, pacing in circles and shaking his head. I'm reminded of a malfunctioning robot. I need to calm him down before I end up like Will.

'I'm not going to call the police. I just need to sleep before I fall down. I'll call you in the morning.'

I flinch as he grabs my arm. 'Promise. Promise me, Kerensa!'

I swallow hard. 'I promise.' He relaxes his grip and I shake him off, grasp the handle of the front door, all the time thinking he's going to stop me, but he doesn't. The door's open and then I'm outside in the howling wind and driving rain. The storm's arrived early after all.

The light from Leo's windows guide me, but as I get further away, even with my little pocket torch, it's not easy to see the wiggly cliff path ahead of me.

I pull the toggles of my hood as tight as possible, and battling against the wind, I lean my weight into it and put one foot in front of the other as fast as I can. I need to get indoors and lock myself in. Call the police. Leo might be packing a bag right now.

Except he isn't...

He's behind me.

'Kerensa! We need to talk about this some more!' Leo catches up to me and grabs my shoulders. He's come out without a coat, his hair's plastered to his head and his feet are bare.

I shake him off and have to yell too to make myself heard in this wind. 'Not now, Leo! And not here at nearly midnight in a bloody storm!'

'No, of course not here. We need to go back to the house. Now! Come on!' He grabs my arm, digging his fingers in so hard it's excruciating.

'Ow, you're hurting me!' I try to pull my arm back, but I can't shake him.

'I'm holding onto you, that's all. This path is dangerous in the wet!'

It's then that I realise how close we are to the cliff edge and fear clamps my mouth shut. It would be so easy for him to push me to the side and that would be it. There are some vicious rocks down there and the tide is out. Is that why he's followed me? I dig in my heels. 'No!' I yell, and try to wriggle free.

'Yes! You *will* do as I say!'

I shine the torch at him. His face is inches from mine and the look in his eyes terrifies me. I can't give in. If I do, I'm dead. 'Get off me!' I summon all my strength and willpower and yank my arm free. At the same time with my other hand, I thump the torch into his chest.

Leo rocks back and yells as his feet slip on the wet mud at the edge of the cliff. He's down. 'Kerensa! Help!'

And then he's gone. Just like that... Leo's gone. Again.

29

There's someone knocking on my window and yelling my name. But how can they be? I'm under water... scuba diving. Aren't I? I feel myself drifting up through the water until my head breaks the surface. My eyes feel like they have glue under the lids, so I force them open and see my stripy blue and white pillow. Just dreaming. Then I hear the tap, tap, thump, thump again and 'Rens! Kerensa, are you there?'

It's Sally. I sit up in bed and the room spins. My head feels like it's stuffed full of cotton wool, and bits of last night's events try to form a picture, but the edges are muted and fuzzy. Every time my brain catches hold of a coherent sequence, it disappears – drifts off like smoke tendrils into my subconscious. The clock says 15.23. How did I sleep so long? I stand up and nausea rolls in my stomach. Booze. I stink of booze. Holding onto the furniture, I go over to the window and open it. Sally's anguished face is looking up at me from beneath the hood of a red anorak, the rain's drenching her through. 'Thank God! I was so worried!'

'Why?' I manage, my voice sounding like a squeaky hinge.

'Why? Because you didn't open the shop and I've phoned you at least ten times today. In the end I had to come. I saw your car was here so knew you were probably home. Anyway, let me in – I'm bloody soaked!'

'Okay... hang on.' I close the window and grab my dressing gown.

On the way downstairs, pictures of last night are at last clearly revealed to me and suddenly it's there in all its terrifying reality. Oh my god. Patrick, Leo, Will, the cliff path...

By the time I open the door, I'm crying hysterically and fall into Sally's arms.

'Rens, hey. Shh. It's okay, love.'

'It's not okay...' I say between sobs.

'What happened? You smell like a brewery... Come on.'

She supports me into the kitchen and then my stomach rolls and I rush for the downstairs bathroom, vomit my guts up.

Sal's voice comes from outside the door. 'You all right, sweetheart?'

I manage to grunt. 'Yeah. Be out in a minute.'

'I'll put the kettle on and make you an egg sandwich. Best cure for a hangover I've found.'

I run water in the sink and splash my face. So far, I've avoided my reflection, but as I clean my teeth, I see a dishevelled nest of auburn hair and in the middle of it, the white face of a wraith. Fear in her huge green eyes. A scene of me running in here last night panic-stricken flashes in my mind. Soaked through, I stripped my clothes off and sat in the shower for ages, hugging my knees, letting the water pound my head. Then I went downstairs and opened a bottle of wine. Drank it... must have been all of it, the way I'm feeling. The second one of the night. I had to numb my senses. Shut out the nightmare. The terror of what would happen to me now. The look on Leo's face in the torchlight as he slipped. As he fell.

Sally's in the kitchen frying eggs and my stomach twinges again at the smell of them cooking. A shiver runs the length of me and I shake. I pull my fluffy dressing gown tight around myself but it doesn't help. Sally notices and hurries to the living room, comes back with a blanket and tucks it round me. Her kindness starts my tears again. I don't deserve kindness. I murdered someone, I murdered my husband last night. Then the absurdity of that statement has a bubble of hysterical laughter rising, so I swallow it down. How can I have murdered my husband last night when he's apparently been dead nearly a year?

A mug of tea is set before me and Sally prattles on about how worried she's been all day and that she even thought about trying to contact my mum, but that she'd see if I was here first. Then she asks me why I got so drunk and I shake my head. I shake my head because I'm trying to focus. Trying to think of how much to tell her. Has Leo's... no, has Patrick's body been found? I'm assuming he's dead. He has to be... the tide was out, the rocks would have...

The image of what would have happened to Leo makes my stomach twist, and I concentrate on keeping a sip of tea down. Even if he hasn't been found yet – unlikely – it won't be long. Then the search will be on for people who knew him, and then they'll come and arrest me, put me in prison. I can't tell Sally about Leo. It sounds impossible – crazy. It was Patrick who I pushed... no... who slipped last night. Patrick. A story plays in my mind and I run with it, develop it, embellish it. I take deep breaths, hope it's feasible.

Sally puts the egg sandwich in front of me and sits opposite. I look at the sandwich and want to heave. Nodding at the plate, I say, 'I don't think I can, Sally.'

'You might not want to, but believe me it works. Come on – just a bite.'

She watches as I do her bidding, and after a few minutes unbelievably, I am starting to feel better. The sickness passes and I realise I'm hungry. Half a sandwich down, I have a sip of tea and say, 'Thanks, Sally. I do feel a little better.'

She smiles. 'Good.' Then she folds her arms, gives me her no-nonsense stare. 'Right. Now you can tell me what happened last night. Why you got so drunk you were incapable of opening your shop.'

'It's Sunday... no big deal.'

'Sunday in the tourist season? Try again.'

I heave a sigh and hope she swallows what I'm about to say. 'God, Sally. Last night was... It was terrible. I can hardly bring myself to say the words. Has... has anything happened? I mean have you heard anything upsetting on the news about here today?'

Sally frowns. 'If you mean the body of a man found washed up in Treyarnon Bay... yes. But how did you...?' A scan of my face stops her words. 'Oh Kerensa. Oh God, you know something?'

I start to cry and cover my face. This is too, too awful. I need to concentrate. Be strong. 'I know who it is... it's Patrick.'

Sally gasps and covers her mouth, says through her fingers, 'Oh my god!'

I tell her that I went round to work in the studio last night when he went out. He came back because he forgot his wallet and got a call about Derek being in hospital and went to visit. When he came back, I was still working. It was late, but I'd got engrossed in a piece and he insisted I had a drink with him because he was upset about Derek. I did, to be polite, and I wanted to find out about Derek. But then later Patrick tried to kiss me, became aggressive when I pushed him away. His hands were all over me. I slapped and kicked him and ran out onto the cliff path in the horrendous storm. He followed and we struggled. He slipped and that was it. I came home and drank myself into oblivion. Now I'm terrified that the police will say I killed him, and I'll get locked up.

There's a stunned silence for a few moments. I'm stunned too at the way I've come up with such terrible lies in such a short time. What am I becoming?

Then Sally dabs away tears with the back of her hand and says, 'There's no way you're getting the blame for anything. He was a bastard... and though I'm not glad he's dead – he was a human being after all – he was the one to blame. You said you think he killed Will... and maybe had something to do with your Leo. Who knows what he might have done to you if you'd not escaped.'

Again, the fact I'm not telling the whole story to my loving and trusted friend pricks my conscience... but needs must. Even if she believed me about Patrick being Leo, she'd assume I killed him out of revenge. She might not, but I need her onside. I need to stay out of prison. I cover my face for a few moments then let out a slow breath. 'It doesn't bear thinking about, Sal. I was terrified. He as good as admitted he'd been involved in Will's death too. When I pushed him off me the first time, he said, "Sorry I'm not Will. You wanted him, not me, didn't you?" Then he gave me a nasty sneer and said that he'd seen the back of him, or something like that. That's when I knew I had to get out straight away.'

'What a bastard.' Sally comes round the table and gives me a hug. 'Thank God it wasn't you who fell off the cliff.'

'It could have been me, easily.' At least that bit is true. I sniff and blot my tears with my dressing gown sleeve. 'But what am I going to do?' I wail. 'They won't know who he is... He had just his shirt and trousers on – so no ID. But he's made lots of friends round here. Leo's parents are particularly close to him. They'll expect him to go and see Derek again in hospital. One of these friends will report him missing soon, and then it will look weird that I haven't reported him... or that you haven't for that matter.'

Sally nods and stares into space for so long that I can hardly stand it. Then she says, 'We'll wait a few days and I'll report him missing. I'll say I called him – you and I should do that tomorrow, or the next day – and then I'll say I went to his house. I found the door unlocked and he wasn't around. His car was there, so I began to worry and phoned anyone I had the number for that knew him. You being one of them, obviously. We were particularly worried, because we heard a body was washed up in the bay just along from his house.'

I think this sounds promising but I'm still worried. 'Won't they want to question us though?'

'They might. But we have nothing to hide. Just stick to the story. You were at home on Saturday, so was I.'

'But you have your kids to corroborate. I have no alibi.' The fact that I'm beginning to panic is evident in my voice.

'Hey, don't worry.' Sally leans across and grasps my hand. 'They won't suspect that you had anything to do with it. Why would they? It's not as if you could have gone into Patrick's and dragged him out of the house and chucked him off a cliff, is it? They might suspect suicide. If they know he was a friend of Will's, they might put two and two together and imagine he killed Will and couldn't live with the guilt. Or that he couldn't cope with his best friend's death. Who knows? What we *do* know is they won't be able to prove anything.'

This makes me feel calmer but then another thought occurs. 'What if someone saw us from a neighbouring house?'

'Is that likely? At midnight, in a storm?'

'They might have seen my torchlight if they looked out of the window.'

Sally sighs. 'They might, but they probably didn't. And if they did, they wouldn't have actually seen *you*, would they?'

'No... but if the police question the neighbours and they said they saw a torchlight by the cliff edge, the police would be suspicious.'

'Yes. They might, but like I said, there's nothing to tie any of it to you.'

I go over it all again while we finish our tea in silence. Then I nearly choke on the last mouthful. 'Shit, Sally. What if the police have already been along that row of houses asking questions? The body was found a spit away. What if they've knocked on Patrick's door and wonder why he doesn't answer? His car's there, as you said. What if they didn't have to knock, because he left it wide open when he ran after me?'

Sally starts to answer with her best calming voice, but I switch off after a few seconds because a new realisation thumps into my chest like a sledgehammer. The box. The box with everything in it is still on the sofa. The different passports, the bank accounts... everything.

30

After Sally's gone, I shower and get dressed. I can't believe how calm I am, but I know what I have to do. I'm going to get a shopping bag and walk over to Patrick's. I'm going to pray the door wasn't left open and I'm going in and getting the box. If it was left open, the police will probably have been in and taken the box. If that's happened, I'm going to call them and tell them everything. I'll have no choice. I'll have to take my chances. Let's hope my chances are good for once. It's time things went my way, isn't it? The universe owes me one, as the saying goes.

It's ridiculous how important that box is to me. Right from the off, I've hidden from Sally the fact I was looking for it. Sally, who's done more to help me than I could ever have expected or ever hope to repay. And why? Because I want the money. The filthy money that Leo stole from Donaldson, the money he changed his identity for, his whole life for, killed for... and ironically died for – twice.

Why do I want the money? Because I deserve it. I've suffered for it, my baby died because of it. I don't want it for myself. Though I'll take some, to make sure I'll never have to worry. But I'll do so much good with the majority of it. There are so many different charities involving the death of infants who will benefit, so will those organisations who are trying to promote recycling, clean beaches, and raising awareness about climate change and what to do about it. Animal charities. The list is endless.

After more tea and some biscuits to give me a bit of energy, I take a heart-pounding walk along the cliff path up to Patrick's... or Leo's. It's still so hard to get my head around the fact that Leo was Patrick and vice versa. It's so unreal. Huge puddles from last night's rain mean the journey takes longer, as I have to climb round them, but at last I'm there at the top and away across the green. I can see Leo's house and the door is shut. I hurry towards it, wondering if the box will still be there or if the door was open, and the police have been in. The door's unlocked still and I take a deep breath and am about to go in, but then remember to knock, just in case someone is watching. I knock a few times and then go round the side for good measure to look at the car. Then I go back round, knock once more and go inside.

I shut the door behind me, take off my muddy boots and shout Patrick's name on the off-chance the police are inside. Then I realise that's stupid because they would have answered the door wouldn't they? But then is there any wonder I'm a nervous wreck? I kick Leo's... no, Patrick's shoes along the hall floor, and hurry down the hallway and into the living room. Thank God. The box is still on the sofa. I flip open the lid and check everything, then close it again and shove it in my shopping bag. I need to get out, pronto. Glancing round the living room to make sure I've left nothing behind, I nearly go into meltdown when I see the wine "blood" spatter. I have to clean it off and take the bottle with me. It will have my fingerprints all over it.

My hands shake so much I can hardly get a grip on the bucket of hot soapy water and the scrubbing brush. Ten minutes later it's almost gone, except for a pinkish blush on the white paint. Nobody would notice if they weren't looking for it. Back at the sink, I empty the bucket and wipe round. Then I go back and check everything is as it should be. I think it is. My fingerprints will be all over the place, but that's okay, because I'm his friend, here often and using the studio. But the smashed wine bottle would have been damning. Thinking of wine jogs my memory. The glass I had in the laundry room when I was hiding from Patrick must still be there. The police would think it was an odd place to leave one. I hurry along, grab it from behind the washing machine and pop it in the shopping bag too.

On the way back home, I count to ten, take a deep breath and phone the local police station. I explain who I am and that I've heard about the body on the news. I say I've just been to my friend Patrick's house who lives near where the body was found and the door was unlocked, his car was outside, but he wasn't there. He's not answering his phone. His shoes were tossed in the middle of the hallway too. Patrick is a very neat person and would never do that. Most odd. They ask me to describe Patrick's appearance. I do. Then they say they're sending someone round to my house in the next half an hour. Shit. Okay, I need to stay calm and I need to phone Sally soon too and tell her what's happened.

Two hours later I stagger into my living room and collapse, exhausted on the sofa. I've made a statement, been questioned, and shown them photos of Patrick on my phone. They are investigating further – searching his house, hoping to speak to friends and relatives before they can confirm anything. I could tell by the look on the DI's face when he flicked through the photos that it's obvious that Patrick is the man washed up. But I suppose they have to dot the i's and cross the t's. They will get back to me if they need to speak to me again.

I make tea, sit out on the balcony to watch the sunset, and my mind drifts over the past few months yet again. Little things Leo did keep coming back to me, such as the fact that he printed the card he left for me in the studio with the chocolates that day, because he knew that if he didn't, I'd recognise his handwriting. Such meticulous planning. And if I'd not overheard him begging for his father's life that day, I might never have known who he really was. Not a hundred per cent.

I shake my mind clear and call Sally to explain what's happened with the police. She wants to know why I didn't leave it to her to contact them like we agreed. I wish I could tell her it was because I'd forgotten to get the box. I just say it felt the right thing to do. I didn't want to have to involve her.

'They will contact me anyway, but I honestly wouldn't have minded helping out. How are you feeling now?'

I look out at a boat sailing past and wish I was on it. 'Pretty down. But then I would be, wouldn't I?' *Having my husband die a second time. Knowing he was a murderer and being not entirely sure that I didn't push him over on purpose. My conscience keeps whispering doubts in my ear and I keep blocking it out.*

'Of course, you're down. It's been such a huge shock too. And now you'll never know how Will and Patrick were involved with Leo. It must be so frustrating.'

Once more I have to lie and I hate it. 'It is, Sal. But I'll have to try to put it behind me.'

'That's my girl. I can come round and see you tomorrow if you like, before work. I expect you're staying home?'

Am I? I haven't even thought about it. But now I do, I know I can't be here alone with my thoughts and a nagging conscience. 'No, I'll be opening up. It'll take my mind off everything and help to get things as back to normal as they can be.'

'That's good. Best thing all round. I'll bring some cake at lunchtime and we can have a chat.'

'That sounds like a plan. See you later, Sal.'

Once there's a little shape to my day, I feel better. Thank God for Sally.

Three weeks later the police are baffled, as I knew they would be. They spoke to Sally and to me again. They confirmed it was Patrick from the photo, but they were a bit puzzled about his eye colour. I explained he often liked to wear contact lenses to have a change, which satisfied them. They were baffled because they'd not been able to contact any friends or relatives in Ireland or in Australia. There had been no record of a Patrick O'Brien coming in to any major airport from Australia either. Well, there had been, but none fitting Patrick's ID.

They had contacted Will's friends and family, as Sally and I had told them Patrick and he were good friends. And while some remembered meeting Patrick at one place or another, they didn't have any pertinent information about his background or family. Derek is back home, thank goodness, and doing okay. He was so upset to learn about Patrick. Janice too. Little did they know that it was their own son that had died a second time. I hate Leo so much each time I think of what he did to his parents.

The rent on Patrick's house in Treyarnon Bay had been paid for with cash and the car bought outright in cash too. So there were no leads to a bank account or further information on Mr O'Brien. I asked the police if they thought it was suicide. As usual they were non-committal and said they were still working on it, but if I think of anything at all, no matter how small, I must get in touch straight away. In other words, they have no clue what to make of it.

I'm doing much better than I expected. Maybe it's because I actually lost Leo a year ago. The dark deception over Patrick just added a few more layers to the depth of pain I've already suffered. And as my conscience keeps trying to tell me – I got my revenge. I'm still not listening properly though. Did I intend to push him, or was it an accident? It's a moot point. If I hadn't acted as I did, chances are, it would have been my body broken on the rocks and washed up in the next bay. Will's passing wounded me too. I know I never got the whole truth from Leo because of his incessant lies, but I'll have to accept that and move on.

I've already drawn some of the money out of the offshore account. When I first saw the balance online, I just stared at the screen, unable to comprehend the number of zeros. There was nearly two million pounds in there. To begin with, Leo must have had closer to three, when the surgery, the car, boat, and the rent on the house are taken into account. I transferred some money to my regular account this morning because I want to treat Sally and the children to a lovely holiday somewhere soon. It's the least I can do to repay her for everything she's done. I'm careful not to transfer too much at once though, because I don't want to raise anyone's suspicion.

I close the fridge and am about to leave for work again after popping home for my sandwiches, which I made and promptly forgot this morning because I'd been faffing with the transfer, when a delivery guy arrives. He's got a small padded envelope in his hand and asks me my name. Satisfied, he says, 'Can you sign here please?'

I sign and take it back to the kitchen. At this rate I'll never get my lunch. I'm about to toss it on the side for later, when I notice it has an Australian postmark. I open it and find a letter and a second envelope inside with my name on it. The letter is from Valerie, Will's mum.

Dear Kerensa,

We brought Will's very personal effects back home with us as we needed time to prepare ourselves before we sorted through. We came across this envelope with your name on it. There's something very little inside. We haven't opened it, of course. I hope whatever it is brings you some comfort. Our son thought so much of you. I often think how different our futures would have been if you and he had got together... and if he...

Anyway, all the very best for the future, Kerensa.

Love from Val & Andrew x

I swallow down my emotions and undo the envelope. Inside is a USB stick. I look at it and decide I can't wait until later to see what's on it. I hurry to the living room and grab my laptop from the sofa. I minimise the screen with all the zeros I'd been looking at earlier and insert the USB.

After a few moments, my breath catches in my throat. It's a video clip of Will. He's sitting at his kitchen table, looking so alive. So fit and handsome in a green shirt with the sleeves rolled up. And while not exactly happy, he's smiling at the camera. A sob escapes, and I have to pause it, while I get some tissues. All the old feelings I had for him are back and they've brought a barrowload of sorrow with them.

Back at the laptop with a glass of water, I press play.

'Hello, Kerensa. I expect you've had a visit from the police and are watching this with them? I hope so, because I'm going to instruct my solicitor to pass this recording to them in the event of my death. If something happens to me before I get the chance to instruct my solicitor, then maybe it's been left in my personal effects? But I'm waffling, because I don't want to tell you what I know I must. It's taken me some courage to make this for you, but if you're watching this... I'm dead... either in some freak accident...' He raises his eyebrows and gives a wry smile. 'Unlikely... or Patrick will have done what I have come to realise he is capable of. This will come as a shock, Kerensa, but Patrick...'

Will takes a sip of water and heaves a sigh.

'Patrick is actually Leo. Please believe me, I didn't want to go ahead with his fake death because I knew you'd be devastated. I never forgot the despair on your face that day in Plymouth when I told you Leo had had a fatal accident. Then when you told me you were pregnant...' Again he stops for a drink and draws a tissue from a box. I'm struck by the similarity between us. I pull another tissue out too and blow my nose. I watch Will get himself together then he continues.

'As you know, Leo came to me for help. He was all over the place, so I came up with a plan for him. I said that Leo should go away – go abroad until Donaldson had given up. I promised that I'd keep my eye on you – tell you what was happening. And once a few years had passed, Leo could send for you. But Leo said that would never happen, Donaldson would never give up and only Leo's death would convince him.

'Also, I'm a cosmetic and reconstructive surgeon, not orthopaedic. I kept it secret as a precaution.' Will shakes his head. 'Don't worry, it will all make sense when I've finished. Anyway, Leo latched onto my job, begged for surgery. He said he wouldn't come back to you ever. Said you deserved better. And I couldn't argue with him there. He promised once I'd done the surgery, changed his appearance completely, he'd go away and never come back. I agreed I'd make sure I was in touch with you, look out for you... make a friend of you. Trouble is, you became much more than that to me...'

My heart lurches at his sad smile and I want to reach out,

comfort him, but I know that's impossible. I trace my fingers along his face and bite back a sob.

'But later he tricked me. Once the surgery and everything had been done to turn Leo into a new man, into Patrick, he made me introduce him to you. I said no way, but in the end I had no choice. You see, Leo was prepared to tell you everything and say it was all my idea. He would say I was in it from the outset, on the swindling of Donaldson. He'd ruin my life, my career, go to the police.' Will shoves his hand through his hair. Is silent for a few moments.

'It all sounds so crazy now I'm saying it out loud to you. But he said he'd tell the police I forced him into it, blackmailed him. Leo would say that he'd told me he'd embezzled a few thousand two years ago from his boss. I latched onto this and I said if he didn't get more, I'd tell Donaldson about it. All lies of course. But what wasn't lies is the fact that I agreed to go along with his madcap scheme of cremating a homeless man, arranging a private ambulance to transport the body here, and bribing officials with Leo's money to get fake authorisation forms. That alone would be enough to land me in prison and have me struck off.'

Will sighs. 'I expect you're thinking what a weak and pathetic creature I am. Maybe you're right. But he's a good liar and I did the surgery, didn't I? Nobody forced me. There was so much against me. I stood to lose far more than he did. Poor misunderstood Leo, who'd been cruelly used by Dr Frankenstein. I think they'd believe him over me. The only thing he cared about was getting back into your life. How he thought he'd win you over as Patrick, I will never know. But by then I realised he wasn't the old friend I remembered. The old friend I took pity on, who was running for his life from a ruthless businessman. He was a monster. He'd tricked me and there was nothing I could do about it.'

Will takes more water and looks out at me, his sapphire eyes full of pain. 'I was scared he'd tell the police. But what hurt me more was you knowing about it. I was scared you'd believe him, and then any hope for me and you would be gone forever. Turns out that it looks that way anyway after this evening, when you said you didn't want to even be friends anymore. I wish I knew why.' His eyes fill. 'I had hoped we'd go to Australia and make a new life... but I was kidding myself. Patrick... Leo would have found us. But there's no way he's getting away scot-free. I've filmed this so he can be made to pay. Made to pay for what he did to you, to me and to his parents.'

I have to pause it because I'm crying too much. Poor Will. He must have gone straight home and recorded this the night I told him to leave and that I didn't want to see him again. I wish he knew that Leo is dead. Maybe he does... But then if there is a heaven, Leo won't be there. There's only a few seconds left and I press play again.

'Once more, Kerensa... I am so, so sorry. If I could change it all, turn back the clock, I would. But I can't.' His eyes hold mine in an intense stare and it's like he's in the room. 'There is one thing I wouldn't change though. Meeting you and falling in love. Know this, Kerensa. I love you with all my heart and always will.' His voice breaks on the last word and he leans forward, ends the recording.

My heart breaking, I collapse in floods of tears on the sofa, ask futile questions to the air about why it all happened and how will I be able to carry on with my life. Because I realise far too late that I love him too. Even though he was foolish, or just too kind a person to say no to Leo. Whatever. I love him. I love him, but there's nothing I can do to bring him back.

31

How I went to work this afternoon after watching Will's recording, I don't know. But an inner strength had me up splashing water on my face, make-up on, and in the shop. In the shop I can almost pretend I'm someone else. A successful artist who has no cares beyond trying to promote green ideas and a love of her environment. Sally came round as promised, and we ate cake, and talked about nothing of any consequence. I made her tell me her favourite holiday destinations. Little does she know that a few weeks in Corfu will be coming her way soon. I'll tell her I took the money out of the life insurance pot from Leo's death. It's not exactly a lie.

My heart yearned to tell her about the video, but that's impossible. When I get home I'll take the USB out of the laptop and hide it in a safe place. Maybe I'll even destroy it. It's not going to be shown to anyone else. But the more I think of destroying Will's lovely message to me at the end, the more I think I'll keep it. It's all I have left of him.

I get out of the car and heave the shopping bags out of the boot. I needed some groceries, but might have overdone it a bit. I set the bags down on the doorstep and root in my pocket for my keys. When I insert it into the keyhole, I realise it's unlocked. Odd, must have forgotten to lock it after being upset about the video. I open the door and drag the shopping into the kitchen. Then I stop. My heart rate's thumping up the scale. What if someone's been in? Picked the lock? What if they're still here? I tiptoe into the living room and see the laptop's still where I left it. If someone had been in, they would have nicked that. Then I search the house. There's nothing out of place. Not one thing.

I come back downstairs and put the shopping away. It's no wonder I'm anxious and jumping at shadows after everything that's happened lately. I need to chill out and have a night eating rubbish and watching TV. If I don't get a grip on things, I'll go downhill fast. Become ill. The past is behind me and I need to plan for the future. It's up to me if it will be good or bad. And my god, I'm determined to make it a good one. I smile as I chop a few carrots. From somewhere deep inside, I seem to have acquired a new dollop of confidence and a helping of optimism. Long may it continue.

Paul Donaldson steeples his fingers, rocks in his comfy leather chair, and gazes out through his office window across the London skyline. The Gherkin's glass reflects the pink and indigo sunset, and on The Shard, its taller neighbour, winks a red aviation light warning to passing aircraft. Paul releases a deep sigh. A satisfied sigh. All these months of surveilling Kerensa Pethick and her chums has paid off. He knew he'd get his reward, with a little patience. Though Paul never expected anything quite so fantastic as the latest information coming from Frank Delaney this evening.

Frank had become suspicious when William Gray, the good surgeon and big friend to Leo and Kerensa, took a tumble a while back. Paul's loyal bodyguard had convinced Paul that he needed to stay down in Cornwall a bit longer to see what happened next. Paul was suspicious that Frank had fallen in love with the place after six months of being there, but that didn't matter, because Delaney's hunch had paid off.

A few weeks ago, William's good friend Patrick O'Brien had been found washed up on a beach, not far away from where Kerensa lived. Now that *was* odd. Two young men in their thirties, who had been friends with each other *and* Kerensa, suddenly end up dead? Paul had given the green light to Frank to up his surveillance and today he'd gone into Kerensa's to have a look round. What Frank had told Paul he'd found earlier had shocked Paul to the core.

Paul takes sip of wine and thinks again about what Frank told him was on the video on Kerensa's laptop. Bloody ingenious. And the guts it must have taken. What a shame Leo had turned out to be so disloyal; with brains like that, the world would have been their oyster. And Paul had been overjoyed to find his money, or most of it, was still sitting in an offshore account. Frank had said it was all there on the screen. Now Paul just needs to access it.

As the remaining streaks of sunset meld into night, Paul's phone vibrates on his desk. 'Frank, how's it going?'

'All set, boss. I'm watching the spy cameras I hid around the place earlier. She's had dinner and now she's watching TV. Her eyes keep dropping closed, so I don't think it will be long before she goes up the wooden hill to Bedfordshire.'

Paul smiles. 'Excellent. Now don't get carried away. Make her tell you the passwords and give you all the information relating to the account and then get out straight away after the deed is done. Try not to make a mess either. She's had a rough time, poor love. Make it quick and clean. I don't want her to suffer, okay?'

'Yes, boss. You can rely on me.'

'I know I can, Frank. You'll be getting a big bonus for this one.'

Paul ends the call and pours another drop of wine. He raises the glass to the night sky and says, 'Cheers, Leo. Nobody ever gets the better of Paul Donaldson. No matter how long it takes, and no matter how clever they think they are.'

I slip under the covers and stretch. God, I'm tired. Is there any wonder? It's been a traumatic day. I still can't sleep though, and nearly an hour later, I hear a creak on the stairs... and another. Here we go again. I take a deep breath and punch my pillow. It's just the house settling. There's nobody here apart from me. Me and my overactive imagination and it's time I switched it off. Tomorrow is another day and I'm going to make it a good one. I say a mental goodnight to Will and hope he knows how I feel about him. One day I'll find someone else, but I'm not rushing. In the meantime, I'll cure my loneliness by getting that pet I was thinking about a while ago. A cat, I think. It will keep me company by my side on the bed. With that comforting thought in my head, at last I feel myself sinking into sleep.

THE END

ACKNOWLEDGEMENTS

Firstly, a huge thanks to Betsy and Fred and the entire Bloodhound team for all your hard work on every book. You are always there for advice and are thoroughly nice people too!

To all my writer friends, readers and bloggers - your support is invaluable. Though you are too many to mention individually here, a particular mention must go to the lovely Patricia (Trish) Dixon who read this book first and gave me the thumbs up.

To my wonderful ARC group too. Your early feedback was crucial and very much appreciated.

And finally, a heartfelt thank you to my family who are always there cheering me on and encouraging my every endeavour. I couldn't do any of this without you.

Printed in Great Britain
by Amazon